KEEPER OF
CROWS

CASEY L. BOND

Bestselling author
of The Frenzy Series

Olivia!
Welcome to
Purgatory!
Casey B

ALSO BY CASEY L. BOND

GLOSSARY

Crosser – One of the original souls to escape Purgatory and walk the Earth after Christ's crucifixion when the veil was torn in two. Once a soul escapes Purgatory, it can freely cross the barrier between the two realms.

Fissure – A tear in the veil that opens for a short time.

Floaters – Souls smuggled into Purgatory by Merchants. Only those souls undergoing a near-death experience can be pulled across the barrier.

Keeper of Crows – Guardian of Purgatory, who leads a murder of crows. The crows carry souls to Purgatory (that are meant to be there) and follow the instructions of the Keeper.

Lesson – Soul brought to Purgatory by a demon to be taught a lesson before entering Hell. Either their eyes, ears, or mouth are blocked, depending on the lesson they need to learn. See no evil. Hear no evil. Speak no evil.

Manna – Food that rains down from the sky to feed the souls in Purgatory.

Marum – Secret, bottom-level of Heaven itself, where punishment is decided and meted out by one of the seven angels banished there. It is a desolate and frightening place.

Meat Market — Where souls are sold into slavery; sexual or simple servitude.

Merchants — Granted power by crossers to kidnap souls. They have no power of their own and have to be granted power each time they are told to cross the barrier.

Reddies — Female souls smuggled into Purgatory and sold in the Meat Market for sexual purposes.

Soul — A human who has crossed the barrier. They develop a body in Purgatory that reflects the state of their human body back on Earth.

The Cleansing — Daily rain shower in which souls can bathe.

The Killing Fields — Grassy area between two solid stone walls and their gates.

Triple — A Lesson whose eyes, ears, and mouth are bound.

Veil — A thin fabric that stretches between the earthen realm and Purgatory. It was torn in two when Christ was crucified, and was weakened when mended.

PART
ONE

CHAPTER ONE

My father was the antichrist for sending me to this place. Rehab, it turned out, smelled like lemon-scented disinfectant, and apparently, 'rock bottom' was comfortably padded with heaping piles of Benjamins. Father spent enough on this place to justify the brocade upholstered couch beneath me a thousand times over, but no amount was too large to show how much Warren Kennedy loved his only child. Just pick up a tabloid; my face would be plastered there, along with bold-printed words like rebellious, addict, and promiscuous. The sad part? The tabloids were right for once.

Sunny Bridge was just as perky as the name implied, from its glistening, polished tile to the overflowing motivational posters that dripped from its walls. Even the staff seemed happy as they went about their daily tasks.

The most annoying of the smiling faces here belonged to my shrink, Doctor Coleman. When he greeted me, and the orderly who escorted me to him, in the hallway with a broad smile and pink cheeks and asked me to go in to his office and have a seat, I decided to call him Doc.

"I'll join you in just a few minutes," he said, returning his attention to a small stack of papers at the nurse's station that he thumbed through and scrawled his signature on at precise intervals.

He reminded me of a professionally dressed version of one of Snow White's dwarves. As I waited for him to finish his paperwork in the hallway, I looked around his basic-looking office. File cabinets lined the longest wall, overflowing with files stuffed with paper and unfortunate circumstances. Inkblot pictures were Doc's preferred décor. How they used them was beyond me, and I hoped Doc wouldn't ask me to find the hidden meanings and shapes in the paintings hanging all around his office. If he ever tested me, he might recommend I be transferred to a mental institution. The blending colors and shapes looked like Kindergarten art, globs of paint on a page that had been folded. The fact that I couldn't tell a pelvis from a bat was disturbing.

Doc strolled into the room and assumed his position behind the large mahogany desk situated between us, shuffling more papers and shifting stacks of files until he had a clean space. Doc wasn't the most organized person. I looked around at more inkblot pictures, trying my hardest to decipher them. He started asking questions. I didn't feel like answering them, so I ignored him. He folded his hands over his stomach and stared at me.

I let him. It didn't bother me if he stared.

He sat across from me with a resolute expression, tapping the end of his pen against the clipboard of paper he thought summed up my life. The court told him all he needed to know, so I didn't know why he wanted to delve deeper. I was a junkie, a rich girl, a girl with a chip on her shoulder. A nineteen-year old getting ready to start her senior year of high school. He would assume I'd failed a grade, but I didn't. I'd gotten sick as a child and couldn't start school when I was supposed to, so my parents kept me home an extra year.

Doc wouldn't care about any of that. He just cared about my apparent drug problem. The facts were all there, what he wanted to see, what he thought I wanted to hide, but Doctor Coleman wanted more for some reason. He needed me to believe he wanted to help me come to grips with my drug use and how it impacted my loved ones.

But did he really care?

My opinion? He was paid hourly by this lovely, expensive place to ask questions. Time was important to Doc. I could tell by the way his eyes kept shifting to the clock hanging on the wall just above my head. Only one hour. In one hour a day, three to five days per week, he was supposed to fix what was broken inside me, or fill sixty minutes appearing to do so. Then, he could move on to the next person, and so on until his day was over, his week was finished, and he could pick up his paycheck. I wondered what he did on the weekends to fill his time.

"You can lie back if you want," Doc said, his eyes flicking to the minute hand.

I smirked at him, crossing and uncrossing my legs and leaning forward. Hospital scrubs weren't sexy, but I did have a V-neck working for me. My ample cleavage caught his eye. "Would you like me to lie down?" I asked seductively.

Doc swallowed, staring down at the clipboard again. The tapping of the tip of his pen quickened.

"You can do whatever makes you comfortable, Miss Kennedy."

"Carmen," I corrected, hating the family name and the sound of it coming out of his pudgy lips.

"Alright. You can do whatever makes you comfortable, Carmen. It makes no difference to me whether you sit or lay. What does matter to me is making progress, so I'd like to start with you. Describe yourself in a few sentences or words."

The truth? I wasn't sure Doc really wanted the truth. Maybe he just wanted me to vomit the same crap that was on the documents he read. He wanted me to tell him I was a spoiled rich girl and an addict who wanted to do more with her life, but that would be a lie. I was spoiled. My father was rich. My mother was dead. I had no siblings. Did I enjoy blow? Absolutely. I wished I had some now. But could I stop using it? It would suck and life would be boring, but yes. I could. But back to Doc… He wanted three words, all about little ole' me.

"Sexual, sarcastic, and intelligent." Those three were accurate.

Doc raked a free hand through his gray hair. He was in desperate need of a haircut. Thick tufts of it hung over his ears and thick strands crawled up the back of his neck. I bet he was hairy all over.

"Those are interesting terms, especially in that order. If you open up a little, I can better judge their accuracy."

He tried to smile and then glanced over my head at the clock again.

"If you really want me to open up…" I trailed my fingers over my thighs and spread my legs wider.

He quickly removed his eyes from my skin and stared at the documents in front of him. Clearing his throat, he remained professional. "I'm not going down this road with you, Carmen, so let's discuss something else so our time is not wasted."

Would I really spread my legs for an old man? No, but seeing Doc squirm a little was priceless.

"Tell me about your relationship with your father."

"Why do you want to know?"

"He's an influential man, powerful. I'm sure his choice to run for office made your life different; more difficult, maybe." Doc cleared his throat. "When he brought you here, he mentioned an incident with the paparazzi right before your accident."

Well, wasn't Father just the proponent of airing dirty laundry—as long as it wasn't his. "There isn't much to tell, really."

"Try." He began tapping his pen. My teeth raked together.

Hell, why not? Maybe if I talk a little, he'll let me out of here early.

"I was never beaten or abused. Father worked long hours when he was CEO of Lyta Pharmaceuticals, and now he's running for President. He thinks his connections and money can buy him a one-way ticket into the White House, and according to the latest poll numbers, he might be right."

"What about your mother? How did you feel about her?"

"Do," I corrected.

"Pardon?" he asked, sitting up straight.

"How do I feel about my mother, is the question you should have asked. She might be dead, but she's still a part of me. I love her. She had problems, but who doesn't? She dealt with a lot of bullshit from my father, and in the end, she was too weak to endure it all. End of story."

Doc shifted in his seat, glancing at his papers again. Maybe he had copies of Psychiatry for Dummies under there. A checklist for crazies.

"Tell me about their marriage."

"It wasn't bad in the beginning. At least, she said it wasn't. But over time, Father changed. She wasn't enough for him, apparently, because he began sleeping with other women. She always managed to forgive him for all the bad things he did, even though he never apologized for hurting her. He didn't care. Father only cares about one person in this world. It wasn't my mother, and it sure as hell isn't me."

"He brought you here to help you. That sounds like he does care."

"Oh," I smiled, "he cares—about his public image."

He dug his heels in. "Tell me about your mother's addiction and how it affected you," he said sternly. "Addiction can be hereditary. There are studies to suggest it."

Doc stared at me intently. I wondered how badly he wanted to glance up at the wall to see if the session time was up. Why he didn't ask more questions about my father blew my mind. Everyone always wanted to know about the private life of the great Warren Kennedy; his habits, secrets, and scandals, but Mother and I were usually just background noise to all of his indiscretions. But, since he asked about her, I'd answer. She deserved that much.

"First of all, I make my own decisions and Mom made hers. I can empathize with her, though. Mom loved to look at the bottom of liquor bottles. It was her repeated goal in life to find them. She stared at them like she was looking through a kaleidoscope, but she never found any pretty rainbows at the end. She would chuck the empty bottle into the trash and start searching again."

"How'd she die?" He already knew, but he wanted me to use my words.

"She took too many sleeping pills with her vodka."

My mother liked to drown her sorrows. I liked to snort mine. The difference between me and my mom? She knew what she was doing when she ended it. She knew what to take and how quickly it would kill her. She died with a suicide note addressed to me curled in her cold, stiff fingers.

"Were you the one to find her?"

"No," I answered simply.

Thank God. I couldn't have handled seeing her like that. My father was busy fucking his girlfriend across town, and I was out partying when she died. The staff didn't find her until the next morning. When they called him to come home, he told them, 'Why bother? She's already dead, and I need to eat breakfast.' At least, that was what our maid told me. I believed her.

"Were you home the night she passed away?"

"No." I shifted in my seat.

"Where were you?"

"With a friend."

"Who told you what had happened to her?" he asked, brows raised in expectation. This was probably better than reality TV for him.

"My father told me when I got home." My cell phone had died sometime during the night. I'd found a guy at the bar to go home with, so when I finally rolled in the next afternoon, Father told me very bluntly, 'Your mother is dead. She killed herself and left you this. I suggest you take her advice unless you want to end up just like her.'

He'd read my fucking note. He didn't ask whether I wanted to be in her shoes. I'd trade places with her in a heartbeat. But guilt ate at me all the same. Mom was dead, I was alone, and it could have been prevented. If I cared enough to stay home, if I stopped partying and sleeping my way through the worthless guys in Beverly Hills, I'd have been there and might have been able to save her. I could have called 9-1-1.

What killed me the most was that all she needed was a reason to live, and I didn't give her one. I wasn't enough for her to want to stay.

"It says she left a suicide note behind. What did it say?" Doc sat, poised with his pen, ready to scribble psychobabble. Fuck that.

"I'm not gonna tell you that. The note was for me." Only me. It didn't say much, not nearly enough to justify taking her own life. It just said she was sorry, she felt like a failure, she would miss me, and that I should stop partying and go to school, to do something with my life.

Quite a lecture from a woman who felt life wasn't worth living.

"You need to open up to me, Carmen. It's the only way I can help you."

I snorted. "Maybe I don't want your help, Doc."

He sighed and sat back in his desk chair, testing the weight limit with his ample stomach.

"Will you tell me about the incident with the paparazzi?"

I smiled. "Since you asked so nicely… That jerk deserved what he got. I want to state that first. When my father was actually around, he always lectured me about being proper. He would say that cameras were everywhere, and they could capture us at our weakest moments. We couldn't afford to be seen as weak. He needed the White House. 'Imagine another Kennedy in the Oval office,' he would boast."

The photographer clicked as fast as his finger would move. 'Ms. Kennedy, would you like to make a comment about your father's latest affair? Is it true that she took you to Cancun for the weekend? You look awfully pale. Is she really only twenty years old?'

Flash.

'Did your Father give your mother the sleeping pills that killed her? Were they manufactured by Lyta Pharmaceuticals? Are the police investigating the matter?'

I ran around my car, pushing the lock button on the key fob.

Flash.

'Get out of my way!' I shouted, shoving him out of my personal space. If I shattered his lens, he would think twice about coming near me again.

My key fob remote that unlocked and locked the gate surrounding our house had broken earlier that week and I hadn't gotten around to asking for a new one. The guy had popped up out of our bushes when I left my car to punch the security code into the pad to close the gate behind my car. If I'd left it open, my head would have rolled. Not that the whole shit show was my fault. Who could have predicted Hurricane Kennedy would tear a path through the networks? The news of Father's latest affair had been made public and my life fell apart in a blink. Father was on a rampage, his cronies trying to squash the news with pictures of our fake, happy family.

But the press saw through the façade and they wanted blood. Vultures like this guy made it that much worse, because he didn't care who he wounded to get it. Day one was a swarm of the camera-toting bastards. Day two, three-quarters had given up or went to bother someone else. Day three and there was only one left. I gave him props for tenacity and patience.

Flash. Flash. Flash.

'Would you like to make a comment? This isn't your father's first indiscretion. How do you feel about his unfaithfulness?'

I shouldered around him.

'How do you think I feel?' I answered briskly.

Spitting at his lens, I wrenched my car door open and peeled out through the iron gate that was parting like the red sea. Let him tell his friends about how the Kennedy diva handled pigs like him.

"The guy ambushed me and I wasn't in the mood for it. I spat on his camera and shoved him out of my way. He called the police and said I assaulted him—which I was cleared of." I held my finger up to stop the questions I knew were about to tumble out of his open mouth.

"Father was livid because he automatically believed the reports and said I'd done nothing but cause him more problems. Mom was six feet under fresh earth and Father was already on the phone, pacing across his office and much too busy to notice when I left. I couldn't listen to his voice for one more second."

Steepling his fingers, Doc leaned forward expectantly. "Where did you go?"

"The Castle."

Bass pulsated through my body, reverberating through my bones. The vibrations were the only reason the backs of my thighs weren't sticking to the leather seat. Father forbade me from leaving the house, but the joke was on him. He couldn't keep me locked away. As soon as he left for his girlfriend's house, I slipped out the back door. With the top down on my convertible, I sped through the warm Cali air. My tight black dress barely covered my ass. With my unfortunate flat chest, I wasn't in danger of a wardrobe malfunction from the top, but the bottom was another situation entirely. I had wide hips and a booty to match.

Gripping the steering wheel tightly with my left hand, I shifted with the right. My thighs trembled with need and I knew exactly where to get what I craved. From the front door, The Castle looked like a nightclub, like one of dozens of others that peppered the city of Angels; but in the back, the magic waited. Blow—so finely cut, it would fill the ache in my stomach for a little while. It was euphoria in powder form, and I couldn't wait to fly.

I parked in the alley, put the convertible top up, and locked my little white Mercedes up tight. The spikes of my heels clicked across the gritty pavement, littered with shards of glass and puddles of oil and piss. The overflowing dumpster hadn't been emptied in weeks, maybe longer judging by the stench. Holding my wrist beneath my nose, I inhaled Chanel No. 5.

Doc flipped the front paper up and curled it behind the clipboard. "Was it your first time at 'The Castle?'"

"No. I went there almost every weekend."

The sun was just setting, painting the piss puddles in shades of shadow, purple and orange. Two steps led to the back door. I knocked twice, jarring the metal. Jones answered, a tall bouncer three feet taller than me and four times as broad. "Carmen," he greeted warmly, holding the door open so I could squeeze past him.

"Hey Jones."

"Dimitri's upstairs."

I gave him a smile and left him in the hallway, winding through the dimly lit corridors to the staircase that only a few select patrons knew about. My wristlet flopped against my thigh. I couldn't stop the tremors that started in my gut and rippled to my fingertips, down to my toes. It had been two days. Two long days. At the top of the staircase, I stepped onto a landing and knocked gently at Dimitri's door.

"Who is it?" Dimitri asked from inside, his Russian accent thick and commanding.

I cleared my throat, mentally preparing to walk into the lion's den. "It's Carmen."

"Come in."

"Did you meet friends at the club? Why did you go every weekend?" Doc asked, his bushy eyebrows raised slightly.

"I don't have friends, Doc. I bet that's a real shocker."

As the door lock disengaged with a click, I twisted the cool metal and pushed. Dimitri's apartment was sleek and modern, clean but uninviting. Everything was black, white, gray, or silver. The furniture was masculine; powerful and angular—just like Dimitri. He was sitting on the couch in the living room, counting his way through a large stack of hundred-dollar bills. Seeing me enter his space, his hands stilled. His frigid blue eyes, sharp as diamonds, tracked my movements. He wasn't muscled in the way his bouncers were, but he was fit. His silk suit was custom-made and his blond hair was naturally wavy.

"Come."

Easing out of my heels, I padded across the hardwood floor, stopping on the stark white, plush rug that anchored the living room furniture.

He turned to face me, laying the stack of bills down on the coffee table. "You have needs?"

I nodded, sniffing and wiping the underside of my nose discreetly.

"I, too, have needs," he replied, standing up and looking out the wall of windows toward the sliver of sun that was losing its battle with the night. This wasn't the first time he'd propositioned me. It wouldn't be the last. I gripped my wristlet tightly in my palm.

"I have money."

Dimitri snorted, his eyes raking over my tiny dress as he stepped closer. He didn't care about money. Both of us knew that. He already had enough to fill an Olympic size swimming pool. He prowled toward me until the tips of his shoes hit my big toes. "I have a new supplier. Better quality means more money. You understand, of course." His Russian accent seemed thicker today. He'd lived here for fifteen years, but it hadn't melted away. Most people felt the need to protect their heritage, whereas I wanted to forget mine entirely. However, I could never seem to escape the family name, the expectations—not without chemical assistance. It was the only way to feel like another person, even if only for a short while.

Dimitri stood up, fastening the second button on his jacket. "I give you a taste, but it will cost you. Next time, it will cost you more. I have clients coming in from Canada. You help show them how hospitable California girls can be, no?"

My brows knitted together in confusion, but when his knuckles raked across my breast, I batted his hand away. "I'm no whore, Dimitri. If you don't want to sell me the flake, I'll go somewhere else. I'm not entertaining your friends. Hire some fake tits for that."

His blue eyes cut into me like diamonds raking across my flesh, drawing blood. For a split second, I could have sworn the coppery scent wafted into my nose. "Leave the money on the table," he barked out finally. "Five."

He walked to the back of his apartment while I fumbled for the cash. Five grand. Father wouldn't even notice it was gone. The stack of greenbacks stared at me. The sound of Dimitri's wing-tips retreating farther into the apartment was music to my ears. I could breathe again.

When he approached me again I snatched the bag of euphoria from his hand and ran toward the door, grabbing my shoes. Downstairs, the club had opened. The bass was thumping. The ladies room was empty. Black and white tile, cool against my bare feet, looked like a chess board, the pieces of good and evil alternating in a pattern that bled onto the walls. In my wristlet was a small, circular compact. Silver filigree crawled around the outer edges and the center held an engraved, "C." I flipped it open and wasted no time pouring some powder onto my reflection, using my credit card to line it up. The empty shaft of an ink pen delivered the drug into my nose with a long sniff.

I blinked as it entered my system. The weightlessness hadn't hit yet but I already felt better, more energetic and less tired. I felt calm, free.

Doc looked genuinely concerned. "Was this where you bought the cocaine?"

I ignored his question. He was fishing and I hated being used as bait.

Jones was waiting outside the bathroom door when I finally emerged, holding my shoes out for me. I took them and slid them on one at a time. "Thank you."

He nodded. "Be careful, Carmen. You're one of the good ones."

I snorted. "If that were true, I wouldn't be here."

"There's something in everyone worth redeeming."

Jones. What a good guy. What an optimist.

"We all do things we aren't proud of. Take you, for example. You're telling me I'm redeemable, yet you work for a viper." He tugged on his collar. "We all do what we have to do to survive, Jones. Club's getting busy. I'll see you later."

"With all due respect, ma'am, I hope not."

CHAPTER TWO

"There were drugs found in your system that night. I have the record right here if you'd like to see it," Doc offered, unclipping a paper from the small stack.

"That's okay. I'm well aware that I snorted flake, but there's no way I'm ratting anyone out."

Doc shifted in his seat. "Why did you make the choice to use drugs, Carmen?"

Crossing my arms over my chest, I told him what everyone in this place had probably told him before. "To escape."

I swallowed, leaving Jones behind. Why did he show up everywhere I was tonight? Did Dimitri tell him to follow me?

The evening was a blur of hands and touches, of bodies grinding against my own. Sweat and flashing lights. Alcohol and hits in the bathroom. My head was spinning in the best way when I took one last hit in the ladies' room and stumbled out the back door to the alley. Jones followed me, crossing his arms and watching me wade through the piss, glass, and strewn trash. He watched me fumble with my keys, finally managing to click the unlock button. My parking lights flashed happily while my car chirped to see me.

"I can call a cab," Jones called out to me. "I don't think you should be driving, Carmen." Jones was too stiff. He needed to loosen up a little.

"I've got this," I muttered. I fell into the seat and slid the key into the ignition. She purred to life.

Where were the headlights? I fumbled with the levers and switches until the lights blinked on. There they are!

Clutch. Accelerator. I could do this.

I eased out of the alley and onto the street. The streetlights had auras around them. They looked heavenly. And the freeway was so busy. It glittered in white and red streaks of light. Blinking, I tried to focus on the red taillights in front of my car. The music wasn't loud enough, so I reached for the dial.

Everything slowed down.

Crunching metal.

Screeching brakes.

Shattering glass.

Blaring horns.

My car skidded across the road, metal against pavement.

My head slammed against its rest.

I should have worn my seatbelt.

More crashing sounds.

Deafeningly loud. Ringing. My ears were ringing.

My car hit a bump.

Airborne. Hanging upside down.

I did wear my seatbelt.

The tips of my dyed blonde hair dangled onto the asphalt, soaking up my blood. It trickled steadily from my head with an unfaltering splat, splat, splat, splat. Lights fixated on me. Words were shouted at me.

"Hang in there. Help is on the way."

They can't help me now.

Sirens.

Screams.

Crying.

Peaceful.

This was what I was looking for.

Peace.

Doc nodded knowingly. "Do you remember the wreck itself?" he asked.

I'd dreamed about it every night since, waking with my clothes damp with sweat and my heart thundering, feeling like it had just happened. I could still hear the twisting of the metal frame.

My chest hurt. Something was... I was choking. I gagged. "Easy, honey. There's a tube down your throat."

I gagged again. My eyes watered as I fought against the intrusion.

"It's okay. It had to breathe for you for a while. I'll check with the doctor and see if he wants to remove the tube, but for now..." She bent over and scanned a syringe with her machine, waiting until it beeped. Staring at the computer, she smiled. "This should help you relax. You'll feel better soon. You're very lucky to have survived such a crash." The nurse, a heavy-set woman with dark hair cut into a cute pixie, squeezed my hand sympathetically. "Be right back."

I blinked, staring at the speckled tiles of the drop ceiling. I could feel the medicine working. It relaxed my muscles and I stopped struggling against the tube. The window blinds were pulled, but I could see the sunshine peeking in between every vertical piece of plastic. Two chairs next to my bed sat empty.

My muscles were sore and everything hurt. I tried to reposition myself, to find a comfortable way to lay, but couldn't move. The nurse strolled back into the room with a smile.

"Doctor Bragg is on his way. He's going to evaluate you and see if we might be able to get rid of that tube."

I nodded, tears welling in my eyes, blurring her for a moment.

"We called your father, but he isn't here yet. I'm sure he'll come as soon as he can. Is there anyone else I can call for you?"

I shook my head no. There was no one.

The clock on the wall opposite my bed read three forty-five. I'd been in a wreck. I remembered leaving the house and Father behind, and I remembered Dimitri and going to him in a moment of weakness. The club was busy. The lights, the alcohol, the drugs, the blood. I remembered the wreck. It happened last night, but my father still hadn't come? Of course, he hadn't. Father must be with Bianca. Home wrecking bitch.

It was easy to be angry with her. I'd learned from Mom to hate her. Mom poured all of her energy into hating Bianca, but she never once faulted Father for being so willing to throw the years of their marriage away for each younger, more plastic piece of ass who looked his way.

The doctor, a middle-aged man wearing royal blue scrubs, a stethoscope, and a frown stepped into the room. He pumped the hand sanitizer and rubbed it in, staring at me as if I were a waste of his time. He was none too gentle about poking and prodding me.

"We can remove your tube, but you'll be here for another day or so. Have the police been in to talk with you yet?"

I shook my head, tears welling up again.

"You'll be remanded to their custody because of the circumstances surrounding the accident you caused. You aren't a *juvenile anymore, so you need to stop acting like the world and everyone in it owes you a favor. I don't care who your father is. Your car was the only one involved, but you easily could have killed someone. You have a drug problem. The level of cocaine in your system should have killed you. If you were looking for a wake-up call, this is it. If you were crying out for help, you've got it."*

He typed a few things into the rolling computer and then motioned for the nurse to help him. As the intubation was removed, I gagged on plastic and bitter truth.

It was easier to lie to Doc. "I don't remember much about that night."

He nodded and made a note on the white paper; black ink marring the pristine.

"You could have gone to jail. You're lucky your father has connections, money, and an impressive team of attorneys that got you into this rehab facility instead."

Yeah. I was lucky. That's exactly the adjective I'd use to describe myself.

Doc used his pinky to itch the inside of his ear, bringing me back to dismal reality. I looked at Doc Coleman. His cheeks were ruddy and his glasses sat askew on his nose, crooked but somehow fitting him, their silver wire frames ten years too old for today's styles. Even his beard was salt and pepper. His eyes flicked to the clock and I finally told him, "I need a cigarette, Doc."

"Will a cigarette help calm you down?" He looked to my bouncing foot. I stopped moving it.

"Couldn't hurt."

"No." He sat his clipboard and pen down.

"Why the hell not? I can smell smoke on your clothes. Just give me one."

He shook his head. "I'm not here to replace one bad habit with another, or to foster any of yours. And I won't discuss my own habits with you."

I stared him down, but he didn't give in. "You aren't leaving this afternoon until you talk to me. We've been going around and around and getting nowhere fast."

I smiled, thinking of hamsters. They were fat, happy little rats, just running on the wheel all day long. Dig. Spin. Eat. Spin. Around and around and around.

"What made you smile just then?"

"Hamsters."

His wiry eyebrows threaded together. "Care to explain?" He brought his pen and clipboard back to his lap and proceeded to tap the end of it repetitively. Tap. Tap. Tap.

"Would you care to stop tapping that pen like you'd rather be anywhere but here? And for the love of all things holy, stop looking at the fucking clock. I don't want to be here either." It would have stung anyone else. Unfortunately, it seemed that the good doctor had heard all kinds of bullshit before. Mine didn't faze him at all. He did stop tapping the pen, though. I grabbed the small victory and held tight.

"I think you're depressed, Carmen."

"You're brilliant. How many years did it take you to earn your degree?"

He ignored the insult and barreled forward. "I'm prescribing an antidepressant for you that's just been approved by the FDA. While there are some side effects, I think the reward outweighs the risk in your case. Do you know if your mother was on any similar medication?"

What was this bullshit? "I am not my mother, Doctor Coleman."

"Are you angry at her?" he asked. "Or me?"

"Yes."

Doc put the pen down. "Because she took the pills, or because of her alcohol addiction?"

"Both. I should have been reason enough for her to want to live. She should have been a mother. She should have flipped the middle finger to my father the second she heard of his first affair and walked out the door. She should have lived the way she fucking wanted to, but instead, she just existed. My mom gave up, and that's what makes me madder than anything in the world."

Doc smiled slightly. "There's still some fight in you."

"There isn't; I just feel gray. All the time, Doc. Like there's nothing in me here." I tapped my chest. "Like my soul's gone." Maybe Mom felt the same way. Maybe that was why she gave up. She never took sleeping pills before, which meant she knew what she was doing. Mom wanted to end it.

Swallowing thickly, Doc eased his chair back. "Were you raised to be religious?"

"No."

"But you believe in souls?"

My foot began to bounce my leg up and down. "I believe there's something missing in me. That's all I know. You can call it whatever you want."

"You called it a *soul*, Carmen. I don't think that was a slip. You believe in something. But do you know what I believe?"

I snorted. "I'm sure you're about to enlighten me."

Doc smiled. "I believe there's a soul inside all of us, inside of you. We just have to find it again."

I tensed, ready to be released from this inkblot hellhole. Easier said than done, Doc. Like Mom, my soul was a coward, and it was going to take more than ink blots, psycho-babble, and stilted conversation in a boring office to rehabilitate it. I doubted rehab could handle such a chore.

———

The orderlies here wore white scrubs. Everything sterile, blank—everything, except for the walls. Those were littered with inspirational quote posters, everything from the cliché, 'If you believe it, you can achieve it,' to, 'Every journey begins with one step." Last night, a nurse brought in the new miracle medicine and proceeded to tell me about all the warning signs to watch for, and that they would be watching out for: suicidal thoughts, worsening mood, hopeless feeling, and blah, blah, blah. Today, it was time for my two o'clock appointment with Doc for all things touchy-feely.

A male orderly was escorting me through the maze of hallways. I smiled at him and his eyes opened a little wider. When my arm brushed his, his nostrils flared ever so slightly. He knew it was no accident. I wasn't exactly subtle about it. I wondered just how far he was willing to bend the rules…

"Are the cameras always on in this place?" I asked.

He swallowed, staring at the black orb on the ceiling ahead of us.

"Yes."

"Do you have any friends in security?"

He paused outside of Doc's office. "Maybe," he smirked.

"Maybe…they would turn one off for you for a little while."

The guy wasn't smoking hot, but he was good looking enough. I needed a release and he might just be the one to give it to me.

"I can make that happen," he said, standing straighter.

"Tonight?"

He smiled. "Will you make it worth my while?"

I raked my nails down his obvious erection. "Absolutely, if you bring me what I need…"

The door to Doc's office swung open suddenly, interrupting us. I rolled my eyes and strolled into the office as Doc stared at my new friend threateningly. When he finally slammed the door, the blinds on the window rattled. Doc walked quickly to the desk chair and it sighed as his considerable weight sank into it. I was still standing. He gave me a smile, trying to hide his irritation and failing miserably at it.

"Have a seat, Carmen. Make yourself comfortable."

"Not possible."

He smiled, folding his arms across his middle and leaning back in the chair. "Why is that?"

"I'm not comfortable in this place, and no shrink couch is going to give me the warm fuzzies."

He exhaled loudly. "How do you feel?"

"Cold."

Doc tilted his head. "Mentally, how do you feel?"

"Numb."

"You're awfully chatty today," he smarted.

"I'm a bursting ray of sunshine every single day, Doc. What did you expect?" I deadpanned. He chuckled and reached for his pen. He started to tap it, but caught himself and cleared his throat. Smart man.

"Do you feel more or less tired today?"

"The same."

"Did you have vivid dreams last night?"

I perked up. "I did have a strange dream. I dreamed of burning unicorns."

He looked up and pinched the bridge of his nose. "If you aren't going to take this seriously, I'll have to report back to your parole officer."

I was serious. The damn unicorns were burning as they flew through the air, trying to skewer me with their fire-poker horns as I ran away. But apparently, he didn't want to hear it.

"Fine. I'll try to do better. If you give me a smoke, I'll play nice."

He didn't take the bait, and the daily inquisition began. "Have you had any thoughts of harming yourself or others?"

Doc was a good guy. He was earning his money. He probably had a happy wife at home. She cooked well, by the looks of it. Maybe his kids were grown and he liked to play with his grandkids on the weekends. He thought he was doing a service by helping druggies like me, and in his perfect, average life, he didn't give a shit if I had those thoughts or not. I knew that telling him I'd thought about stabbing a female orderly with an ink pen wasn't in my best interest. She'd been a dick about bringing my food, slopping it all together. I hated it when food touched, let alone got mixed together. Telling him I thought about slitting my own wrists after I stabbed her? Definitely not something I felt like revealing.

"No, I'm not having any of those thoughts," I lied.

My scalp itched, but it was tender to the touch so I tried not to scratch it. During the wreck, something lacerated my head. The ER had to shave a section of my hair off to evaluate me, and ultimately used nine staples to hold my skin together. When I got home, I shaved the rest. It looked stupid to have long hair and a streak of skin in between. The staples had been out for a few days, but the itch was constant. I would have a nasty scar. Eventually, my hair would grow back out and cover it, but I doubted the itch would ever leave.

His eyes followed the motion of my fingers. "How do you feel about your hair?"

"I look like shit. How do you think I feel?"

"Don't answer a question with a question, Carmen."

The fucking rules. I hated them.

"Fine. I hate that they cut my hair."

He stared at me. "Why is that?"

"They say a woman's hair is her glory, right?"

Doc smiled. "I've heard that, but there are more important attributes than beauty."

I snorted, rolling my eyes at his bullshit. "Name one."

"Kindness."

"That's *inner* beauty, Doc."

He chuckled. "Charity."

"Also inner beauty." I raised an eyebrow.

"Fine," he answered. "The most important attributes are not outer or physical beauty."

"If you say so." I learned very early on that if you were pretty, you got things. Your way, gifts, compliments, the attention of boys, drugs—the list went on and on. But that only got you so far. Shaved head or not, I wasn't hard on the eyes. The staples weren't going to define me. They were just a reminder of a royal fuck-up.

"Do you think some people are just bad, like bad seeds, Doc?" *If so, I'm one of them.*

Doc steepled his fingers. "That's an interesting question. I do believe there are people who are inherently bad, but I think those are few and far between. I think most people are good, even if they make bad decisions."

"You know, Doc, I think you're wrong." I stood up. "Can I go back to my room now?"

"Our session just began."

"Well, I can just sit here in silence if you'd prefer. I'm not in the mood for your brand of bullshit today." I didn't know if it was my tone, the way I defiantly crossed my arms and legs, or how I closed him out for five full minutes, but he finally called for someone to escort me back to my room. Luckily, it was the same guy from the hallway earlier.

When we were out of Doc's sight, he tapped the keys on his cell phone.

"My friend's working now. No cameras."

"Do you have smokes?"

He grinned, easing a pack from his pocket and placing the soft plastic in my hand. Full flavors, baby. "Lighter?"

He eased a light green lighter from his other pocket, giving it to me. I grinned. "Now, I wonder what I can do to repay you," I teased. I knew what I was going to do for him.

When we got to my room, I pulled him inside. The hallway was empty, luckily. I shoved him against the wall, and as I reached into his waistband, he shoved me to my knees. The asshole thought he was in control. I proved him wrong with one lick.

I milked him; every moan, every grunt, and every drop. And then I told him to get the fuck out so I could smoke. A girl needed her privacy.

He opened his mouth to say something, but I held my hand up. "Save it." I didn't need his thanks.

"I really like you."

The hell he did. He liked blow jobs. Every man did.

I winked at him. "Bring me something nicer next time, and we'll see what happens." Then, I shut the door in his face.

I flopped down on my bed, opened the pack, and flicked the wheel on the lighter, inhaling the glorious toxins. They erased the taste of him from my mouth.

CHAPTER THREE

The anti-depressants didn't work, FDA be damned. These things didn't make me any less depressed than I was when I walked into this place two months ago, other than the fact that I now felt that my life was a pointless and unfixable mess.

I didn't have any 'side effect' other than dry mouth, but Doc noted that I was irritable. He was right. I was irritable, as well as a slew of other colorful adjectives. I was also smart, and for the last sixty days, I told them what they wanted to hear with a smile. The good doctor was going to sign off on my rehabilitation, telling the judge I was healed. I pictured him as a televangelist, palms up, twitching around. Would Doc pray for me if I gave him a grand? *Probably. He'd use it to take his grandkids on vacation.*

My hair was now an inch long. I wouldn't look completely hideous when I left later this week. Although, getting home would be an issue. My car was totaled. Mom was dead. Father probably wouldn't bother to come and get me.

"Your release is scheduled for this Friday morning at nine A.M," Doc informed me.

"Friday is my favorite day of the week," I told him.

"You have no cravings at all for cocaine?"

The mere mention of the word made me yearn for it. It made my toes bounce, but I couldn't let him see how it affected me. "Nope. You've done a bang-up job, Doc."

"You had a visitor yesterday, but he wasn't on the approved list. I declined his visit."

I ticked my head back. "He?"

"Dimitri Astrov."

My skin began to crawl and my face felt hot. I dug my fingernails into the armrest. "I don't want to see him."

Doc perked up. "Why?"

"He's my dealer." I didn't want to snitch, but maybe Doc could do something, protect me from him. He may have denied his visit, but when I walked out those doors, I wouldn't be in Sunny Bridge anymore.

A groan from across the desk drew my attention. Doc dragged his hands down his face. "Listen, Carmen. If you have any contact with him and fall back into your old habits, party with old friends, anything at all, you will fail. Do you understand? This will all have been for naught."

I nodded my head. I knew that. I wasn't as worried about the coke as I was that Dimitri had come here himself. What in the fresh hell was that about?

"I can keep him away from you while you're here, but once you step foot off Sunny Bridge's property, my hands are tied."

"I know. Thank you," I said. I wasn't planning on staying around here anyway. Father wouldn't be home, but I needed a ride to get my things. Then I could 'borrow' one of his cars and skip town. "How will I get home?"

"Sunny Bridge will pay for a cab fare."

That was generous, considering the hundreds of thousands my father paid for this private facility. It was located in the middle of nowhere; ensuring his privacy and that the paparazzi wouldn't be able to get a picture of his wayward daughter, despite their tenacity.

"Sounds good."

"Carmen—"

"Save it. Can I go now?"

Doc stood up and adjusted his tie. "I'll call for an orderly to escort you back to your room." His eyes narrowed. "A *female* orderly."

───

It was finally Friday. Release day. Legally, I was being remanded into my father's custody and had to check in with my parole officer on Monday morning. Part of the deal my father's lawyers negotiated was that I would serve a minimum of sixty days in rehab, followed by a year of probation. Fun times.

A male nurse watched as I gathered my things. My belongings included my discharge instructions, a written prescription for the antidepressant Doc thought was giving me a personality, and Doc's business card—as if I would actually call him up to chat after I got out of this hell hole. I came here with nothing else. The police found cocaine in my wristlet and confiscated it; not that the blood hadn't ruined the leather anyway. My clothes were cut off by the paramedics on the way to the hospital. My life, or what was left of my life, consisted of only a few sheets of paper.

"Did you get everything?" the orderly's voice boomed in the small space.

I didn't have anything else and didn't want it anyway.

"Yep." I held out my arms. "This is everything."

He rolled his wrinkly blue eyes at me and waved me out of the room. It was more like a cell. I think Father tried to scare me straight with this place. It was kept so sparkling clean, one could eat off the floor, but everything else was exactly what I imagined jail to be like. No freedom, no privacy. Nothing but you and your thoughts. It was hell on Earth.

Doc waited outside. I guess he did leave his office chair once in a while. "Take care of yourself, Carmen. My cell phone number is written on the bottom of your discharge papers. If you need to talk, or if you need anything at all, please call me."

People said that all the time, right? *If you need anything, call.* But if you did call, they seemed to be put out by your needs. It was just a pleasantry, nothing more. Either that, or he wanted to continue to charge me by the minute for his shitty advice.

"Don't count on it," I replied breezily.

Doc frowned, but stepped away from me with a sigh.

I didn't bother to wave or say goodbye.

A yellow cab streaked with black and white checkered stripes idled past the security gate that surrounded the center. The upholstered back seat was warm. I sank into it and gave the cabby my address, watching in the side view mirror as rehab quickly became a part of my past.

The drive took an hour and fifteen minutes. The cabbie, a guy named Mike who slapped his gum when he chewed it and liked to sing lyrics to the terrible seventies music he insisted on blasting, whistled as he pulled up in front of the drive.

"They already paid you?" I asked before I opened my door.

"Yeah. All taken care of." At least Mike was honest. He could have said no and asked for more money. I'd expected as much.

"Good." Stepping out of the car, I listened as he cranked the music again and eased away from the curb. The sun was setting, something I was beginning to realize was a harbinger of bad things to come. Before I could even punch the security code into the keypad, another car pulled alongside me. The engine purred as it idled.

The black Mercedes was non-descript. I didn't recognize the driver, but as the tinted rear passenger window slid down, I knew I was in trouble.

In his thick accent, he ordered, "Get in the car, Carmen."

"Dimitri, why are you here?" It felt like a thousand needles were poking beneath my skin. Everything in me wanted to run, but there was no running when Dimitri told you to do something.

"I come to speak to you. They would not let me see you at that place, so I'll see you now. Get in."

I hesitated, looking back at the keypad.

"Do not test my patience, Ms. Kennedy."

If I made a run for it, I'd be caught. Best to go with him and figure out what he wanted. Maybe he just wanted me to entertain his friends, like he mentioned before.

The thought made me sick. I wasn't a prostitute, but maybe I could do it. Just this once.

The driver of the car walked around to hold the back door open for me. Dimitri slid across the seat to make room. The leather's cool temperature seeped into the backs of my thighs. There was a space between me and Dimitri—enough for someone else to occupy, but his presence made me feel like my face was pressed against the glass.

I half expected privacy glass to creep from the bottom up, like the cars my father frequently traveled in. The one difference between Dimitri and Father? My father guarded his secrets in varying ways, but Dimitri spoke openly. His men knew not to betray his trust.

"Where are we going?" I asked as the driver pulled the car away from my house. Each passing yard, fence, and gate taunted me that I might never make it home again.

"You tell them about me." It wasn't a question.

I shook my head rapidly. "No, I wouldn't tell anyone anything."

"No. I get visit from police yesterday. They say you tell them that I sell you the cocaine. I denied it, of course, but you have caused me a great problem."

"Dimitri, I never said anything. I was in that place just biding my time. They got angry that I wouldn't speak."

Suddenly, the conversation with Doc replayed in my mind. He asked who Dimitri was, and I told him, *My dealer.* He could have waited a few days. Jesus. Still, lying was the best solution here.

Dimitri instructed the driver to take us to an address I didn't recognize.

"Where are we going?" I asked again.

Dimitri didn't answer me. He didn't have to. My scalp itched where the stitches crawled over it, a centipede of thread. The silence in the car crept into my bones. "I swear I didn't tell anyone about you, Dimitri."

Still no answer. The car took lefts and rights, too many to remember in order. If they were trying to confuse me—and they probably were—it was working. Easing into an alley, the driver stopped the car. A man made of solid muscle stepped toward the car and opened the door for Dimitri, who barked two words. "Bring her."

As Dimitri walked away without a backwards glance, Muscle walked around, opened my door, and motioned for me to exit. My feet hit the ground, one at a time, almost as if life were moving in slow motion. The concrete was broken, cracks splintering from one tagged building to another across the alley. Garbage in a nearby dumpster made me cover my nose as I stepped out of the car, avoiding a questionable puddle. Was that blood?

Breathe.

Step.

Breathe.

Step again.

I had to remind myself to do both.

Climbing a small flight of stairs to a loading dock, the lackey led me inside a large, dilapidated warehouse. It was empty of everything but a few makeshift beds huddled in a corner. Dimitri waited in the center of the large space. Maybe the beds belonged to homeless squatters. My eyes searched for them. Maybe one would get help.

Empty. The building. The beds. Dimitri's eyes.

The guard shoved me toward the middle of the room, straight toward him. I stumbled and Dimitri caught me. "You caused me problems. Now I cause you pain," he said, before punching me in the ribs. Fire bloomed and spread through my abdomen and chest. I gasped for air he had no intention of allowing me to have. I was going to die in this piss-scented warehouse. "You know what to do," he ordered to the guard, walking away. "I'll call the others."

What others?

When the giant came at me, I blocked his arms, scratched out toward his face, and kicked toward his knees, his groin. It wasn't enough. He was much better at fighting than I was. In all honesty, it was only seconds before the fight in me was gone. I just wanted it to end.

I wanted it all to end.

The giant's fist crashed against my jaw with a sickening crack. I laid on the floor, staring at the air conditioning shafts and pipes that ran across it in predictable patterns. When he lifted me by the shirt to hit me again and saw I couldn't stand upright on my own, he let go of me. I flopped to the floor, trying to push myself up. Blood poured from my nose and mouth, pooling beneath me.

"Get up!" he roared.

I tried, not because he told me to, but because I wanted away from him and the pain. Pushing away with my toes, I made it a few feet before the kicking began. He laughed at me as my fingernails dug into the cracked concrete. He was going to kill me. This was it.

When one of his polished shoes connected with my temple, everything went black.

CHAPTER

FOUR

The rhythmic sound of air being sucked in and expelled from a tube woke me. I blinked, unsure of what I was seeing. How did I get here? The scent of antiseptic weighed heavily in the air. A man with dark, slicked-back hair pushed a bucket out of the curtained area, using the handle of his submerged mop to steer. He whistled sweetly. The floor shone, still wet with bleach and water. A woman lay in a hospital bed, wires and tubes streaming out of her like rays of sunshine. Her eyelids were taped shut. A stream of staples flowed down her scalp. Every inch of her face was bruised, swollen, or cut. One of her calves was raised in the air by a sling hanging from a metal contraption. The machines beside her, whose music had been steady, suddenly became erratic. An alarm sounded, its frantic beeps summoning a nearby nurse who slipped on the wet tiles on her way to the machines, righting herself at the last minute. She quickly checked the patient's pulse at her wrist. Two more nurses ran into the room, and then there were four. It was a flurry of activity.

"Her blood pressure's crashing," the first nurse who arrived announced. She was precise and sharp with each movement. "Ephedrine ready," she ordered the others.

One flew into action. It must not have been the first time the woman had needed the medicine, because they had it readily available on an end table near the bed. A nurse used a syringe to ease medicine directly into the IV. Within a minute, the alarm's shrill sound quieted and the beeping became rhythmic.

"I'll watch her for a few minutes," the first nurse said, punching words into the electronic medical record.

The other three nurses gingerly stepped over the drying puddles of water on their way out of the room.

I hovered near the ceiling above the scene, watching the machine breathe for the woman, watching as the nurse looked her over, checking the pulse at the ankle resting on the bed. She shook her head. "Keep fighting, Carmen. I hope they find the bastards who did this to you."

The woman was me.

It should have panicked me, but I didn't feel anything but tired. I saw that they had busted my head open again and beat my entire body, but it was hard to tell what else they did. A chill ran up my spine, causing me to shudder. Why did Dimitri leave me alive?

Was I alive?

If I were dying, why in the hell did I have to die wearing a hospital gown? Under all of the sheets and blanket, I knew my ass was hanging out. I hated those gowns worse than scrubs.

I covered my ears against the noise coming from above; a high-pitched scream so loud, it could shatter glass and bone. I was floating over my body again, over the room, but still felt the hair on my arms stand on end. Looking over my shoulder, there was a black, glittering film that stretched across the room in a slight arc. Though it was as black as coal, it was thin and swirling, molten. I reached my hand out, knowing somehow that the ebbing fabric wouldn't hurt me. Dipping my finger into it, I expected it to be drenched with goo when I pulled it out, but my finger came away clean. I couldn't see what lay beyond the fabric, only that there were shadows moving; like a light was cast from behind it, and their shadows were the only evidence that it was real.

From my right, I heard the sound of smacks on bare skin and shrill screaming. I eased through the building, through wall and ceiling, and peered into the hospital room next to mine.

A disoriented woman, also in a hospital gown, floated over her body. Two men grabbed her wrists and were pulling her toward the molten black dome hovering overhead. It looked like the fabric of the dome had torn in two, and a fissure sat directly over her head.

"Leave her alone, assholes!" I screamed. All eyes snapped to me.

One man looked at the other, grinning lecherously. "Two for the price of one. Our lucky day."

Before I knew what had happened, a noose of crackling blue lightning whipped around my neck. I was reeled further into the room by the man who'd struck me with the bolt. He was gray; his skin, clothes, hair—even the whites of his eyes—gray. He was taller and thinner than his friend, but his friend was gray, too. Soon, the woman I tried to save had a lightning collar of her own. It flickered and pulsed in a leaping, jagged circle around her neck, ever changing, but never loosening its grip. The shorter, broader gray man disappeared into the fissure, pulling the woman through the hole behind him. She cried out, but allowed him to pull her anyway. My captor followed suit, and then I was being tugged toward the tear myself.

Hell, no.

Reaching toward the ceiling, I tried to grab anything that I could anchor myself to, but there was nothing. My fingers slipped right through everything. He jerked me hard, and I resisted harder, leaning back against his tugs. When I came to within a foot of the hole, I looked at the fabric as it flapped along the tear; a torn, dark flag battling the wind. I was able to touch it earlier; maybe I could grab hold of it, keep myself rooted in this reality. Instinctively I knew that whatever lay beyond was bad. I could taste the bitter flavor of despair and desperation as it leaked through the fissure.

I grabbed hold of either side with both hands and held tight, gathering the fabric and twisting it around my palms. When the man tugged, he met resistance. When he tugged harder, I gritted my teeth and held tighter. The flesh of my neck sizzled as the lightning leash dug into my skin. The smell of burnt hair and flesh made my stomach turn. I screamed in agony, but still held on as tenaciously as I could. The more he jerked and pulled, the more the lightning burned me, but I didn't want to go inside the hole any farther.

My body was too weak to keep this up much longer.

Soon, my feet were inside. Then my knees and hips. Soon my stomach, chest, and head was inside. The only things keeping me near my own body, near my hospital bed, were my hands as they held onto two tiny swaths of fabric that gave way with each jerk the tall gray man gave.

My left hand slipped, leaving me holding on by only one hand. The torn pieces flapped angrily overhead, loud as a freight train. From below, my captor sneered, standing in a meadow that should have been a vibrant green, but was the same dull shade that he was. Gravity didn't matter here. I was either going to crash or float, and neither seemed to be a good option. I chose option number three—to fight. Fighting was all I had left. But I was so tired.

I tried to swing my other arm up to get a firmer grip, but it was too late. The fabric tore off in my hand. I held onto it stubbornly, expecting to crash to the ground, but it was as if gravity didn't realize I was here yet. My captor reeled me in. As soon as my feet hit the ground, gravity behaved itself, allowing me to stand on my own two feet.

"Stupid girl! Do you know what you could have done?" The man looked up at the hole. "You ripped it," he said in a voice that hinted at both fright and awe. "It ain't sealing! You...you tore it."

I opened my palm where a piece of the fabric still shimmered in my hand. I watched as it began to move, and as my skin slowly absorbed it.

The man's mouth opened wider than seemed possible. "What have you done?"

"I tried to get away from YOU!"

A loud buzz came from overhead. The hole, the one that I'd widened ever so slightly, finally morphed, flexed, stretched, and ultimately sealed itself.

"No!" the woman next to me yelled, reaching out for what was gone. "How do we get back now?" she cried.

Her gray captor snickered. "You don't."

I'm tripping. That's all this is. I'm in the hospital. No doubt Dimitri and his thugs worked me over pretty good. I'm on medicine and in a coma or whatever. I didn't float in the air, and I certainly didn't see a hole in anything over my head. There's no fabric over the earth, anyway. They don't have lightning leashes. This lady isn't even real, and neither are the gray men. I'm having a crazy, drug-induced hallucination. Fabric doesn't soak into skin. None of this stuff could possibly happen. When I wake up, if I wake up, I promise to call Doc. I'll do anything. I'll get straight.

The portly gray man did not mess around. This might be just a dream, but in it, he was the leader of the pair. The pecking order had long been established. "Let's get them to the gate, Gus."

Gus, the tall, skinny man with a goatee that matched his gray skin, didn't even argue. "We'll make a mint tonight, Chester. Bet the Reddies will be more than happy to entertain the pair of us."

"They better be," Chester snickered, rubbing his stomach as if he'd eaten too much. "Been a long go since we caught a pair."

The woman who walked beside me bawled. She'd been crying since the hole in the sky closed. Her tears dripped onto the electric collar around her neck, immediately sizzling them into tiny puffs of steam. The grassy field we landed in was peppered with large boulders, and the surface of a small pond glittered in the distance.

"What's your name?" I asked her.

"Pamela."

"Why aren't we gray?"

Chester snorted, but answered, "You haven't been here long enough."

"And where exactly is here? Oz?"

Gus nudged Chester. "This ain't no wonderland, doll." Gus was an idiot and had obviously never seen *The Wizard of Oz* or *Alice in Wonderland*.

"It's Hell, right?" Pamela asked, bawling louder. "We died and now we're in Hell."

"It ain't Hell, either." Chester slapped Gus on the chest. "We didn't properly introduce their new home. Ladies, welcome to Purgatory."

CHAPTER

FIVE

Slimy snot began running from Pamela's nose, oozing close to her upper lip, but Pam wasn't worried about it, so why should I be? She shook all over as she stumbled, trying to keep up with Chester. I decided I wasn't going to freak out. This wasn't real. Eventually, I'd wake up from the coma and this nightmare would end.

"Pam, you need to calm down."

"I'm *not* going to calm down! We're in Purgatory! Don't you get it? We're not going back!" More tears sizzled on her crackling collar.

Okay, then. Have yourself a little bat shit crazy party, Pam.

I looked around, determined to enjoy the views of this so-called "Purgatory." Maybe Dante had been in a coma. Maybe he had a crazy dream like this one before he wrote the *Divine Comedy*. I hadn't read the entire thing, but my high school English teacher was obsessed with his work. She had illustrations and posters of artist renderings of what they imagined the characters and levels of Purgatory looked like. One was a stepped mountain with a different deadly sin on each level. If this was Purgatory, there were no mountains here.

Leaving the field behind us, we carved a path through a maze of abandoned houses. In the distance loomed an imposing cityscape, where skyscrapers jutted into the sky like any city you'd see on Earth. Everything was coated in varying shades of gray.

We followed the concrete road past homes and down a long hill. No people were outside their homes. No cars were being driven. Could one drive a rust-bucket in Purgatory? Probably not. Where would they get gasoline?

"Where's everyone else?" I asked.

Chester answered, "In the city. Most people don't live on the outskirts."

"And we're walking through the outskirts? These...neighborhoods are the outskirts?"

"You're a bright one," he snickered, nudging Gus, who looked back at me and laughed.

Pam just blubbered beside me.

"Are there more cities?"

Chester nodded. "All over. They're abandoned, though. This is the only one that's alive."

Alive? It seemed dead to me. Of course, it was fitting if this really was Purgatory. Alleys were littered with dumpsters and puddles, reminding me of my last trip to The Castle. Townhomes sat empty; the curtains and blinds in the windows shut securely, while some doors were left wide open. There were no animals here, either. I expected to hear dogs barking, or perhaps see some cats slinking in the shadows, looking for food. Maybe they were in the city, too. Or maybe animals just didn't come here.

"Why'd you come and get us? Isn't it risky leaving this place to go through the hole into our world?"

"You're full of questions, girl," Gus answered.

"You would be, too."

His brows kissed one another. "Suppose I would. It *is* a risk to leave, but if we catch a floater, it's more than worth it."

"Did you just call us floaters?"

Gus smirked. "Ironic, eh? Just like shit in a bowl, you are."

"Fuck you, Gus." I kept walking behind him. "Anyone ever tell you you're a dick?"

He shot a nasty look my way, or maybe that was his happy face. I couldn't tell.

Pamela wept. She lamented over the people she left behind, pleading with Gus and Chester to release her, to let her go back home.

"Please, I have two little boys. They need me. Their father works nights. I need to help my elderly mother. My family depends on me. I have to go back. Please!"

I kept quiet for once, letting her work the pity angle. I didn't have anyone to go back to. No one cared if I was here, or in the hospital bed fighting for every breath. No one cared if I lived or died. But I wasn't above lying and creating a worse sob story if it worked for her. Even though I doubted it would. I had a feeling that Chester and Gus didn't care about the sad lives of 'floaters.'

The streetlights were busted out, chunks of plastic and glass lying beneath them on the asphalt. It wouldn't have mattered if they were lit. Nothing could brighten the dull in this place. Except the graffiti—which was everywhere, and it, too, was comprised of gray pigments, though the words themselves were colorful and mostly consisted of four letters. Pamela gasped when she read a few of them.

"What kind of place is this?" She began hiccupping in earnest.

Gus just laughed. "This is the bad part of town."

"I haven't seen a good part yet," I smarted off.

Chester smiled and quickly tugged my leash tight. The lightning burned the back of my neck with a sickening fizzing sound. "I'm starting to think you don't like me, Chester—a fact that hurts my feelings."

He stopped and tilted his head. "You're the strangest floater I've ever seen. Most are like her." He jutted his chin toward Pam, who swiped the snot on her face with the heel of her palm.

"You'd prefer a hot mess over joyfully complacent?"

His nose wrinkled. "No, I guess not. Come on. We ain't got all day."

There was no sun. Maybe it was already night in this place. How would you be able to tell? Did time even matter? A minute could have passed on Earth, or maybe a week, a year.

Chester stiffened. "Crossing the boundary with two will be interesting."

"I've never done it," said Gus, his tone serious.

"Me either," replied Chester.

"I thought you said you'd caught two floaters before, but it had been a while?" The men shrugged at me in turn. Liars. Lying bastards. They'd never caught two at once. Not that this was real…but, still. How hard could passing a boundary be? *Don't mind us, we're just out for a stroll across the boundary.*

"So, you gonna tell us what the boundary is and how it'll affect us?"

Pamela made a high-pitched shrieking noise from her throat. "Are we going to die?" she wailed.

I snorted. "Pretty sure we're already mostly dead."

"I died in a car wreck! It wasn't even my fault. You? You're some psycho. You look like you've been in a horror movie. What did you do? Slit your wrists? Take a hand full of pills?"

Checking my wrists to make sure, I saw there were no marks. I narrowed my eyes at her, grinding to a stop, which made Gus stop. Chester and Pam did, too. "I'm the only one here on your side, lady," I retorted. "I may be handling this situation differently than you, but I'm waist deep in this shit regardless."

She inhaled some more hiccups. "Y-you act like this is a joke, but this is really happening! It's not a dream."

"How do you know?"

"I've pinched myself. I have real tears. I can't get relief from this heavy stone of dread that's crushing my chest. Don't you feel it? Don't you feel the gray, the evil, seeping into your soul?"

"Is that what we are?" I snapped. "Because souls don't cry! Souls don't have hair or skin that burns! They're like ghosts, and, though they may float, they don't get dragged with lightning leashes!"

She shook her head, stumbling over a manhole cover. "I didn't think so either, but it's like we changed somehow. We were in the hospital, in our bodies, and then we weren't, and then we were taken and brought here..."

Pam prattled on in nonsensical rabbit trails, earning a few sharp tugs from Chester. I pretended to listen. This nightmare had to be close to over.

Caws echoed between the abandoned buildings as a murder of crows swirled overhead. "Where did all of those come from?" I said to myself.

"They won't hurt ya, but this complicates things. The Keeper's near," Gus muttered. "If we hurry, we can rush through the gates."

"The Keeper?"

"Yeah. The Keeper of Crows."

That explained everything. Not.

Chester and Gus slowed their steps and reeled us in close as they looked around at the rooftops and in the alleys. Their eyes scanned the windows of the apartment complexes, darting from one place to the next. Pamela was shaking all over.

"What are you looking for?" she said in a low voice.

"A thorn in our sides."

"Great. The Keeper and his crows. Fun times," I added sarcastically. "Now, if you could just wake me up now and send me back to reality, I would really appreciate it."

Pam nodded like a bobble-head doll on crack. "Yeah. Send us back. Won't it anger the 'Keeper' if you cross the border with us?" Her finger quotations were too much.

Chester sneered, searching for the thorn in his side who kept the crows. "It's a boundary, not a border," he corrected, and then added, "The Keeper's days are numbered here. I'm not worried 'bout the likes of him. A payday like this is worth the chance. Two floaters. How'd we luck out on that?"

"Maybe the Keeper likes it here. Maybe he's like, the Bird Man of Purgatory. I'd be reluctant to give up such an illustrious title," I defended, as I pictured an old man in an overcoat, hobbling along with a cane and a bag of bread, a trail of crows in his wake. I felt sorry for him. Especially if guys like Gus and Chester were mean to him.

A shimmer ahead revealed a previously unseen stone wall with an iron gate, at least two stories high and reminiscent of medieval times. If my high school English teacher was right, it was called a portcullis.

Pamela began to hyperventilate, her squeaks rising in pitch with each breath. "Where? How?" she asked incredulously.

"Raise the gate. We have two," Gus said in a low voice. Would they even hear him? My question was answered when the metal gate began to rise, its spiked bottom revealed and lifted high. The crows began to caw loudly, swooping down at our heads, and Pam and I reflexively raised our arms to guard ourselves. Death by crow. That would be a tragedy, even in a nightmare. A flurry of dark feathers swirled through the churning air. Maybe that was why they called them a murder...and not a gaggle, or a flock.

A tug on my leash told me to move. Chester wasted no time getting inside the wall, and Gus and Pamela were fast on our heels. But we were met with another wall; the second taller, thicker, and stronger than the first.

"This is The Killing Field. Watch yourself," warned Gus, his body taut, eyes focused on the tops of the wall.

"Killing F-Field?" Pam stuttered.

Thirty feet away was a gate that mirrored the one we just walked through. Was this some sort of joke? Like a McDonald's located on a corner adjacent to another McDonald's? Would a scary clown jump out from the shadows next?

The gray sky grew angry and bottom-heavy clouds swirled overhead. "Can it rain here?" I asked idly.

Pamela's mouth gaped open. "We're in something called 'The Killing Field' and you're wondering about the weather? What is *wrong* with you?"

She certainly was a scolder. A crybaby, too. Gus and Chester ignored us, easing step by step toward the next gate.

"Open up," Gus requested.

For a moment, there was nothing, and then the ground shook beneath our feet.

"Earthquake!" Pamela screamed, dropping to her knees and bracing herself against the soil. I stood, watching everything unfold. More feathers rained down in a macabre, yet beautiful torrent. The wind swirled. If I had hair, it would have whipped in all directions.

Gus and Chester looked like they were about to piss themselves. "Open the doorway!" Chester hollered. The gate did not rise. He ran toward it, hauling me along with him, singing my neck with each long pump of his arm. "Damn it all to hell! Open this bloody thing now! The Keeper is coming."

"He's already here. We cannot open it for you and we cannot help you," came a deep and ominous voice. "The Keeper has sealed the gate."

Chester's jowls began to quiver. "No, not like this. I can't go like this." He whipped around and his eyes went wide at something behind me. I expected to see something enormous, skeletal, and wrapped in black, or maybe not skeletal at all; maybe a monster whose skin oozed with pus and venom.

I turned to look over my shoulder and saw a guy with dark, messy black hair jump down from the top of the wall we'd passed through. I gasped. He wasn't a giant, but his demeanor led me to believe he just might be. His jeans were worn and bore holes at the knees and thighs. And my God, looking up, I found the V of his hips, which were as bare as the muscles that lined his stomach like soldiers in formation. Sweet holy mother of eight packs.

Tattoos crawled up his skin, morphing and changing as he approached Chester, who pulled Pam in front of him like the coward he was.

"Let her go." Three words, each one weighing more than the one that came before it. And then a promise. "And I'll make it fast." The Keeper closed his fists into tight balls and watched Chester with eagle-sharp eyes.

When Chester shoved Pamela toward him, the guy caught her by the upper arms and whispered something in her ear. The lightning disappeared from around her throat and she calmed immediately, a sweet sigh falling from her lips. Pamela moved to the wall, where she stood with arms folded in front of her. She waited, complacent as a child.

"What did he give her?" I asked, confounded. Dark eyes fastened on me for a second before Chester tore his attention away with one word, uttered like a curse.

"Keeper," spat Chester.

"Chester. What did I tell you would happen the next time you trafficked a soul?" He raised a dark eyebrow. It was pierced with a thin, silver ring. There were small, black ear gauges in his ears.

Chester backed toward me and Gus, looking back at his partner in crime for help. Gus pulled me in front of him, using me like a human shield, the same way Chester had done Pamela.

"Didn't work for him, Gus. Better listen to the Keeper," I told him, really not wanting his clammy hands on my upper arms anymore. I pulled away from him, but he tugged me back with a jerk.

"Shut your dog mouth, bitch!"

"That was redundant."

The Keeper reached behind him and produced a sword. Where the hell had he been keeping that thing? There were no straps on him. I knew this because he would look magnificent in leather of any kind. However, there was nothing but skin and jeans, and it wasn't a thin, short knife. This was a broadsword, and Keeper looked like he knew the way to Mordor. I'd follow his ass out of here. Raking my eyes up and down him, I thought, *I'd follow his ass anywhere.*

His eyes snapped to mine and he smirked as if he knew exactly what I was thinking, and that I was enjoying every second of ogling him.

I grinned back. If I was stuck in Hell, at least it was with him. I could have some fun with him…

CHAPTER SIX

Keeper stared at me and I stared back. For the first time, I realized that he wasn't bathed in gray shadow. He was beautiful, with suntanned skin and dark chocolate hair. His eyes were as blue as a clear sky in summer. Weren't they dark brown earlier?

Our eyes were in a standoff. I vowed I wouldn't look away first, and then he lost the fight by looking down ever so slightly to the lightning forking around my neck. Keeper snarled his lip and stalked toward Chester, making it look like the simplest thing in the world to dispatch him. The tip of Keeper's sword sliced into Chester's chest and the man went down like a sack of potatoes. The slice began to shimmer bright white, and a matching puff of smoke released from it. Keeper took in a deep breath and blew the puff into the sky.

Chester's body began to crumble and then disintegrated, turning to a fine ash. Keeper took a second breath and blew the delicate particles away from us. My fingers started to shake violently. He just blew him away. Literally.

Pamela watched the entire affair as though she were entranced in a favorite television show. She didn't blubber or shake; she just smiled slightly and intently watched every move Keeper made. I would have been a happy spectator, too, if the asshole holding me in front of him would give up and let me go.

Gus tried to grab me by the hair, but I didn't have enough for him to keep hold of. He cursed, trying again, raking his grubby fingernails against my tender scar.

"Ouch, you dirty fuck! Get your hands off my head!"

He pulled me tight, fisting the leash, and his rancid breath hit my face. "You're going to regret calling me that."

Gus gasped, his eyes going wide. Looking down, I saw the tip of Keeper's blade puncturing his side. I laughed as his grip relaxed. Keeper got him, after all.

The dark-haired guy laughed as he jerked the blade from Gus's body, raking across his rib bones. "Should have learned to keep your eye on the true threat, Gustavus."

Gus fell, gasping like a fish out of water, until his eyes unfocused and stared at the sky above. I could see the crows still circling in the reflection of his cornea. A puff, like Chester's, released from the brightly glowing wound and Keeper, leveling his eyes on me, blew it away. It flew into the air where a crow dove down to swallow it up.

Gus also turned into an ashy husk. Keeper puffed his cheeks, blew in his direction, and he was gone. With one breath, Gus just ceased to exist.

"What just happened?" I stammered. "Did the crow eat his soul?"

Keeper, crouched low, stood up and leaned in to me. What was he doing? I pushed at his chest, wincing in pain as I touched him. He was as hot as a branding iron. He whispered something in a language I didn't understand, had never heard. The lightning noose disintegrated, but unlike Pamela, my nerves were anything but calmed. They were firing like crazy. I looked at my palm to make sure it didn't consume the lightning like it did the fabric, but nothing was there. No char marks, burns—nothing, but my skin still crackled with awareness. Was it me? Or was it Keeper? Was it what he uttered? There was power in the words. The tattoos along his neck, some sort of script, had danced.

He stared at me accusingly. "Why isn't it working?" he whispered to himself.

"What? That spell or whatever? Try it again. I want to feel as high as Pam does." I grinned. "And then maybe you and I can ditch her and go have some *real* fun."

Keeper frowned, staring at me accusingly. "I didn't make a mistake. It simply doesn't work on you. And I have better things to do with my time than to entertain a simple girl."

"Number one: I'm not simple. Number two: Do you always give up so easily? It's worth another shot. Maybe you mispronounced something." Even witches made mistakes, or was he a warlock? Wizard?

Looking to the sky, he closed his eyes and spoke more of the language that sounded like honey tasted, smooth and sweet. I waited to feel euphoria, but caught nothing but the whiff of his frustration. Keeper cooed at his birds, circling lazily above us. The crows swooped down by the hundreds and landed on the ground around us. He stroked the feathers of those closest to him, whistling short tones to them. When he raised his hands, they took flight again, swirling protectively overhead.

With a flick of his wrist, the gate we'd been able to pass through opened. Who opened it the first time?

"I did," he answered.

My eyes bulged from my head. Could he hear me?

"I can."

What was this?

He snorted, motioning for Pam. "Time to go." She followed him, blushing like a school girl, watching him under fluttering lashes. Eww. Where had thoughts of her husband and two kids disappeared to?

Keeper smirked, ticking his head toward the gate. Why couldn't I be in the same pathetic shape as Pamela? She looked like she'd taken a few Valium and a couple of shots of Love Potion No. 9.

We stepped out of the gates, retracing our path though the dilapidation. "Where are we going?" I asked.

Keeper never slowed. His broadsword stuck to his back somehow. It must have been magic. This dream was awesome. I needed to remember every detail and write it down as soon as I woke. It would make a great book. I could be an author, sell a million books, and become independently wealthy.

Keeper was also fast; he didn't waste time, words, or steps. I followed behind him, scuttling to keep up because my feet were bare and tender. I looked at his back and noticed that each shoulder blade sported a thick, raised scab that crawled down his back several inches. A few droplets of dried blood rained down from each one. The healed mixing with the freshly torn. What happened to him?

The muscles of his back tensed and he stopped for a moment before shooting an irritated look my way and steering Pamela toward the right. There was no way to determine direction here.

No sun.

No moon.

No stars.

Nothing but gray.

And then there was him. The Keeper of Crows was in magnificent, masculine color.

———

We walked through yards where the tufts of grass were as tall as my thigh, up hillsides, through more yards, and across a creek with stones that barely protruded from the water's surface. It was the first time I'd seen a creek without flowing water. It was still as a lake, not a ripple on the surface, and the water was sleek and deadly as mercury. My legs felt like they were made of lead, or tree trunks. Something too heavy to lift much longer. "Can we stop?"

I hated to be the weak link, but I was dying. My body somehow wasn't ready for all of this. Discreetly, I sniffed my arm pit. It didn't stink yet, but it would. Sweat was popping up all over my skin.

"Physically, you might feel weak. It depends on the state of your earthly body. But it takes a lot of strength to ask for help," he said, looking me over from head to toe. If I wasn't so tired, I'd have flirted more, but I was too busy dying again. "We can stop for a few minutes."

The crows from The Killing Field were still following us. When we stopped, they perched on the branches of a nearby tree, leafless and skeletal-looking. Soon there were as many birds as there should have been leaves. They groomed their feathers and rested. I wondered how often they got the chance to take a breather.

"Not often."

This whole telepathy thing was creepy. *Can you read Pamela's mind? You haven't answered anything from her.*

He sat at the base of the tree of crows, leaning his back against it. I sat on a rock across from him and Pamela settled beside me, happily picking at the dry, dead grass along the base. She hummed an awful rendition of *Wind Beneath My Wings.* I wasn't going to survive this woman's crazy.

Maybe he couldn't hear me anymore. He didn't answer me.

Keeper watched his flock, perched above him dutifully. "Why do they do that?" I asked.

His eyes snapped to mine. "They are obedient."

Maybe he was into that sort of thing. In that case, I wasn't sure the Keeper and I would work. I refused to give men power. I'd seen the train wreck that could cause.

"You tell them to sit there?" My left eyebrow popped up on its own. How could he possibly control wild animals?

"They aren't wild." He snapped his finger once and the entire murder took flight. The beating of their wings was deafening. They swirled in circular patterns overhead, like scavengers scenting a dead animal, but faster. Their movements were sharp and precise.

Keeper stood, his frame powerful and taut, and looked to the woods beyond us. "We need to go."

"Do we have to?" asked Pamela in a childlike voice. "I really want to stay with you."

He smiled at her, glorious as the sunrise. "We have to get you back home."

She gets to wake up? I pushed myself to stand. "Me too, right?" I smiled. He was going to help me leave this place, too. Right?

Keeper's smile faded to one of irritation. His jaw muscle worked back and forth. "Of course," he answered curtly.

Why was he so pissy with me and so sweet to Pam? It was rubbing me the wrong way.

Striding into the forest, we followed him blindly. Tweedle Dumb kept bumping into me as she danced through the trees. Where was whimpering Pamela? I preferred her to the Disney version I was faced with now.

A constant overcast sky closer to the city was one thing, but in the forest, it made everything dark. Shaded versions of reality twisted and climbed from the land. Large, unearthed roots made traveling difficult. Pamela had no trouble twisting through the tangled vines, and

Keeper blazed a trail as if they weren't there at all, as if he were made of stone.

"When I go home, will I be the same?" Pam asked.

Keeper shook his head. "You will be forever changed in small ways or large. Most remember portions of the journey."

"What about my body?" she asked.

"It will recover if we can return you soon, though you'll be in considerable pain, given your condition. He smiled at her again. It seemed all his smiles were reserved for her.

"How can you tell that by looking at her, or me?" I interrupted, making sure my hospital gown dipped low in the front, drawing his eyes toward my breasts for a second.

Completely unaffected, his eyes fell to the forest floor as he ducked beneath a thicket. "I've seen many souls cross the threshold, and each one bears a resemblance to their earthly body. As such, I can guess what your recovery will be like."

Great. He can guess. He probably thought I would heal up and remember my journey and blah, blah, blah.

"I don't think that at all. In fact," he stopped, letting me catch up to him. "I can't get a read on you. My pleas don't work to cloud your mind."

Pleas? Not spells? Maybe he wasn't a wizard.

To that he snorted, so I continued my interrogation.

"You can hear my thoughts, but you don't know if I'll recover."

Keeper shrugged. "You may not. This may be the next step in your journey. You wouldn't be the first brought here against her will, only to find out that this is where you would have ended up in a few days anyway."

A single crow let out a caw as Keeper held a vine overhead for us to duck beneath. "We should hurry. Follow him," he instructed, pointing to the bird leading the others, and us.

"Where is he leading us?" I panted, struggling to keep up. Sweat beaded on my forehead, upper lip, lower back, between my breasts, and everywhere in between those places.

"A fissure is about to appear. He's telling us where." Keeper extended his fingers and then balled his fists, rushing after the bird. I was losing the battle. Somehow, Pamela could keep up just fine. She ducked under, jumped over, curved around, and stepped through the brush like it was nothing more than a field of delicate hay, swaying in the wind, more like water than plant and soil.

The two of them rushed ahead, leaving me in the shade. The crows followed their leader as well. A singular ebony feather fluttered toward me, and I caught it in my hand and held it up. The feathers shimmered. They sparkled black as coal, as rich as the fabric that had melted into my hand. I watched the feather harden, melt, and re-harden. Black held every color of the rainbow and for a moment, I could see them as separates and not as one.

"Keep up!" Keeper yelled over his shoulder.

I was trying. Before the feather fell, I was pushing hard toward them, but I stopped. I couldn't move my legs any farther. They turned to stone. I looked down to confirm it, but only saw flesh, so colorful against the shadow of this place. So foreign.

"Bring her," ordered Keeper from over the next hill. Thousands of birds swooped from the sky, swirling around and lifting me off the ground. "No!" I screamed, until I realized they weren't attacking. They never touched me with their beaks or wings. I was levitating several feet off the ground and they were moving me, as if they were of one force and mind. The forest, as quickly as it began past the few houses at the outer edges of the city, disappeared. The crows deposited me gently onto the ground at the edge of a steep cliff. Far below was a ravine with jagged rocks and a flowing river of gray, frothy water swirling around them.

I collapsed, my mouth in a silent scream as pain tore through my body. Blinking away tears, I panted until the spell passed. "What the hell was that?" I rasped. Keeper and Pamela hadn't seen what happened. "Didn't you feel that?" I muttered. It was like being torn in half from the head down, but it passed as quickly as it came. The spell was gone. Maybe something happened to my body on Earth. If he was telling the truth, that could be it…

"It's coming," Keeper said, watching the sky.

Pamela squealed in excitement, rubbing her hands together rapidly. "I'm going home," she said. "I can't wait. I want to see my children, and my husband and my mother. She's still alive, you know." I didn't, but I just nodded and tried to smile. Her excitement vanished in an instant. "You're not coming, are you?" she asked, sadness seeping into her voice.

"Of course I am. My hospital room is right next to yours. We'll go back together and then we can eat bland oatmeal and red Jell-O as we heal up. The nurses will make sure we have lunch dates."

She smiled, but the outer corner of her eyes didn't crinkle. She looked at the sky beyond Keeper as he kneeled on the edge of the rock cliff. He should really scoot back.

A sizzling sound, like some giant amp was being electrified, filled the air. The sky faded to black and the black began to churn and sparkle. "I'll try to remember you," she said wistfully.

When the tearing sound began, I covered my ears, feeling something warm and wet cover my fingers and palms. When I pulled them away, blood covered my skin, dripping down my wrists toward my elbows and reversing their tracks when I eased my arms down again. Bright white light shone through a tiny, vertical slit in the ebbing black mass.

"Pamela. Come." Keeper watched as she obeyed, walking toward him. He motioned for one of his flock. "Take her across the divide."

Pamela followed the crow near the edge of the cliff. She was even crazier than the Keeper, going that close. There was nothing between the cliff and the tear but a trip to the bottom of that gorge, nothing but death. The crow hovered as if caught in a strong gust of air. Its wings didn't beat, just stayed extended. Then it began to move forward, beating its wings once, twice. Pamela took another step.

I reached out for her. "Pamela. Don't do it. You'll fall!"

Keeper's eyes dared me to speak again. Screw him. "You will die. Look down! Don't step out there. This is a trap. He's trapping you." Why would he do this? Maybe the Keeper of Crows was more dangerous than Gus and Chester put together. What if he was sending her somewhere worse?

The fissure began to crackle; the light no longer a strong beam, but shattering into filtered shafts like sunbeams through clouds stretching to the ground. Pam stepped off the edge of the cliff with complete faith in the crow she followed. The fowl disappeared through the fissure, and then Pamela disappeared, too. There was no sound, just an alteration in the light for a split-second as she passed through.

"Your turn," Keeper said, standing and extending his hand to me. "Hurry up. It's going to close soon."

"I'm afraid!" I stared at the blood dripping down my arms. His eye followed and I could see the questions in them. That scared me more than anything. If the Keeper of Crows didn't know why my ears bled at the sound of the ripping fabric, why would he want me to go near it? And if I stepped off this cliff, I would fall. I could feel it. I wasn't like Pamela.

"You must be sensitive to the sound, but the fissure is the only way to cross the divide! You have to let me help you. This is the only way back home." His brows touched one another. "You have to trust me. I did not let her fall, and I promise I will not let you fall."

I already had. I'd fallen straight into Hell. Heights and me? We loathed each other. Not only did he want me to follow his bird, but he also wanted me to step off a fucking cliff into thin air. I didn't have that kind of faith. Not in him. Not in crows. Not in anything.

I paced back and forth in a frustrated path. The air began to sizzle again. "Hurry!"

"No!"

He stalked toward me and grabbed my wrist. I beat on his knuckles as hard as I could, bruising my own. "What are you doing? Let me go!"

"Time to go home, Carmen."

Tears warmed my cheeks. I shook my head back and forth. "I don't want to go like this. I don't want to step off the edge."

"This is the only way," he said simply.

The fissure's light began to fade. He motioned to a crow and then did the unforgiveable. He dragged me off the cliff's edge. My feet dug into the soil, pebbles trickling to the ravine below, bouncing off rocky cliffs and into the churning water. "No!"

His crow disappeared into the fading light. As Keeper pulled me toward the barrier, stepping beside the fissure himself, he shoved me toward the bright slice of light. I cursed him as he pushed my back.

I couldn't pass through. The light repelled me, like it was positively charged and I was negative. I didn't disappear like Pamela, a flutter of shadow. It wasn't my fault. I should've been pushed through. He certainly pushed hard enough, but I might as well have been trying to shove my way through a brick wall. I knew then that the only wall between me and Earth was myself.

It was the fabric. It wouldn't let me pass. Not even the tip of my pinky. An invisible barrier stopped me from going home. Keeper released my hand and stepped away from me. Looking down, hovering in the air, I panicked. The fissure snapped closed behind him. I couldn't breathe. Not enough air. Nothing. And then I fell.

My hospital gown flapped in the wind. I clawed for something, even the jutting rocks, anything that would break my fall, but I found nothing. A strong hand found mine and Keeper's voice split through the whistling air. "Come."

The sudden descent stopped. For a moment, we floated in a tight, dark tunnel of air, the outside of which was comprised of flashes of beating black feathers. Then the crows raised us, out of the ravine, out of the air, onto the land. I collapsed in a heap of overwhelming fear and liquid aggravation.

Keeper sat next to me, wrapping his arms around his knees.

"Why? Why wouldn't it let me through?" I croaked, trying to calm myself. Sitting up straight, I rubbed my arms quickly.

"You're supposed to be here, though I don't understand it."

"Is it the blackness inside me?"

He shook his head. "Everyone sins. You're no darker inside than anyone else who crosses, Carmen."

"I'm not talking about my soul or sins, or whatever. I'm talking about the stuff back there, the fabric or veil, or whatever Gus called it. When he pulled me through, I grabbed it—the sides of the opening—and then it ripped and a piece tore off. When I opened my hand, it soaked into my palm."

Keeper laughed, a deep chortle that caught me off guard.

Pushing myself to my feet, I stood and walked away, back toward the forest that I doubted I'd ever find my way out of. His footsteps soon followed me. "You aren't serious," he asserted. "No soul is strong enough to tear the veil."

The hell I'm not.

He placed his thumbs on my temples and stroked gently, speaking in the language I didn't understand and closing his eyes gently, the long lashes fanning his cheeks. His tattoos fluttered wildly on his chest. I clasped his wrists and tried to pull away from him, but he was in some sort of trance.

His grip on my head tightened uncomfortably and then painfully. I jerked him hard, but nothing would snap him out of it. He squeezed tighter. I slapped the side of his face, a red streak blooming across his cheek. What the hell was this? I did the only thing I could think of to wake him. Maybe he was Sleeping Beauty. Pressing my lips to his, his thumbs released my head. His eyes were open wide as they churned in color; indigo, emerald, a deep purple that was almost black. An immediate sense of relief washed over me as his grip slackened.

"Don't ever do that again." He pointed his finger at me, moving several steps away.

I wheeled around on him, my finger in his face this time. "You were squeezing my head off! And what the hell was that? You were in a trance or something. Wake up. This is not a joke. I need you to send me back home. Is this some sick, twisted way that my body is saying it's staying in the coma or something?"

Shaking his head, he muttered, "No, this is much worse than that. I don't even know how it's possible."

"Why were you squeezing my freaking head so hard?" I rubbed my temples.

"I was watching your memory."

"Of the veil?"

"Yeah."

"You didn't believe me? I'm a lot of things, Keeper, but I'm not a liar. And stop reading my thoughts. Stop looking into my memories. If you don't know how to help, can you please find someone who can?"

He shook his head slightly. "I'll see if I can get some answers, but just remember that not every answer is the one you want or expect."

"You remember that, too," I warned him. Enough of this shit. I walked back into the woods. There had to be another way. If Keeper wouldn't help me, someone else would. He couldn't be the only person in this place who knew the way home.

CHAPTER
SEVEN

I didn't make it very far away from him before thorns clawed at the sad scrap of fabric barely covering me. Stupid hospital gowns, washed thin and threadbare. I was tangled to the point that it was going to tear completely away and my skin would be scratched. These things were like tiny rabid dogs, clawing at everything in their path. I hated dogs. And kids. And old people. And men. But especially Keepers and cawing birds. Those bastards were still swirling overhead.

"Want a puff of my soul, you freaks?" I taunted at the sky.

They cawed as one, loud and dramatically annoying.

Keeper emerged from the darkness, plucking the thorns from my gown. "You need better clothes." He didn't even get poked.

"What? You don't like my fashion sense?"

He huffed, remarking, "I've seen better," and then patiently tore away the offending briars and freed me.

I stared at his arms, with not even a bloody trickle pouring from his skin. Of course he would be good at not getting shredded. He was good at everything. He snorted as though he knew it was a fact, glancing at the torn fabric lying in tatters around me. I was pretty sure he'd gotten a good look at my ass in the process.

"I did," he said matter-of-factly.

Hope you liked it, bud.

"I like to see you so worked up." Keeper smiled and ticked his head. "This way. We need to be on guard. The fissure will draw attention from those we don't want to encounter."

"More assholes like Gus and Chester?"

He shook his head. "Worse. The Lessons are more frightening than any merchant, and Gus and Chester were small time, at that. The true merchants have great ships. They're like the pirates of your world."

"Pirates?"

"Of old, yes. They especially like booty," he said with a grin.

My mouth gaped open. "Holy shit. Did you just make a joke?" His smile was like a burst of sunshine, and his chuckle led the way out of the forest. I was determined to keep up with him and determined to hear the deep timbre of his laughter. It was one of the most beautiful sounds I'd ever heard. Happy looked good on the Keeper of Crows. I wanted to see him smile again.

As the undergrowth thinned, Keeper drew the sword from his back.

"What is it?" I whispered, struggling to keep up with him. The skin on the bottom of my bare feet stung with each step. The soles of my feet were sliced open from all of the twigs and briars. Dried blood mixed with fresh along the soles. Between my arms and feet, I was a bloody mess.

"Don't you smell him?"

"Smell who?"

"The demon."

"Demon? Like a real freaking demon?" I whisper-shrieked.

He motioned for me to come closer. A scent, like that of singed hair, assaulted my nose. I covered it with my hand and tried to blink my eyes. They stung like I was too close to a fire. Keeper stopped just inside the tree line and watched the field beyond, where an intense orange glow lit the gray. The grasses were on fire.

Do we need to run? I stared at Keeper, begging him to answer. He grabbed my hand and held it stiffly, as though it were painful for him to comfort me. Heat flamed between our intertwined fingers and electricity sparked between our palms. For a moment, I watched our hands, waiting for them to ignite, for smoke to pour from the space between them.

I hated fire. And smoke. And demons. Dimitri was a demon, straight from Hell. I knew getting blow from him was going to burn me and it did, in the worst way possible.

Keeper motioned for me to keep quiet, and as much as I wanted to watch him purse those full lips, I wanted to watch the demon even more.

An abnormally tall man, clad in an onyx suit that cost more than my father paid for his hand-tailored ones, approached a person who was kneeling in the center of the fiery circle. His wife-beater tank was stained beneath his arm pits, a darker shade of gray, just as dark as the sweatpants he wore. The middle-aged man blubbered, much like Pamela had when we were captured and dragged to this place.

"I promise, I didn't do it. I'd never do something like that to a child. It wasn't me."

My stomach turned. What did the bastard do? I didn't want kids, but damn. No kid should ever be hurt.

"You burned her with cigarettes, didn't you, Earl?" the demon teased, his voice hissing each *s*. "You liked her screams. You ate them up."

Earl's face shone with tears as the demon mercilessly pulled him to his feet. A wet stain spread down one leg of Earl's pants, stopping short of his knee.

"She was only three. Why would you hurt your own offspring? Such a vile creature, you are. The order has been handed down. Those like you must be taught a lesson. Those like you must atone. You will pay a penance before your final sentencing."

The hissing burned my ears. With my free hand, I blotted them to make sure they weren't pouring blood again. He hurt his own baby? Earl deserved to burn for that shit. I shifted my weight, still crouching, and Keeper's eyes flashed in warning.

Sorry.

My muscles were burning from holding the position so long. Keeper turned back to the scene, his silver blade reflecting the lapping flames.

The demon, slick and fluid, grabbed Earl's ears, each hand smashing them into his head. Black bands of thick tar webbed from his fingers as he eased them away from Earl.

"No!" Earl screamed. "I can't hear anything! Nothing. Nothing at all!"

"And so you shall remain. Hear. No. Evil." The demon laughed, deep and resonating. With a click of his finger, Earl fell into a trance and began to walk out of the circle, past the flames, and toward the abandoned, dilapidated homes dotting the valley below. He never looked back, just trudged forward in his piss-soaked pants.

"Keeper, did you enjoy the show?" the demon called out.

Keeper stood, letting go of my hand and motioning for me to stay put. I kept low. I'd done bad shit, too. Not as bad as Earl, but damn. I wanted to keep my hearing and dignity intact. The demon watched as Keeper approached him with slow, deliberate steps. He wasn't as dark as the demon, but Keeper's presence commanded attention.

"I did," Keeper replied, stepping into the flaming circle.

"You sent two home today."

"Yes," Keeper replied. "They were interfering."

"Merchants. It's what they do. They *interfere*, according to you."

"According to you, as well."

"At times," the demon conceded with a hiss. "You chased the fissure. Why do you waste your time, Keeper? You can never reach them all, never stop all of the souls smuggled across the barrier. Why bother?"

Keeper straightened. "It's my duty."

"You should have abandoned that sense of loyalty long ago. He sent you here. He. Abandoned. You. Perhaps He meant to teach you a lesson, hmm?"

"He appointed me to a task, and I will not abandon it until He tells me to do so." Keeper stood tall, but the demon shrank a fraction.

"Then you'll be busy chasing your tail for an eternity."

Keeper smiled. "I like chasing tails."

Damn him.

"Don't get too comfortable, Heliazar. The demons are losing more ground each day."

"Perhaps. On second thought, perhaps we gain more than you know." The demon gave a slight bow to Keeper and slowly sank into the earth, inch by inch, until he was gone and all that remained was a pile of bubbling tar on the ground. Keeper watched for a few moments and then motioned for me to leave the sanctity of my mostly-bare shrub.

I avoided the scorched grasses, the tar—all of it. My feet couldn't handle more. Keeper stared at me. "We need to find shelter and something for you to wear. Also, we should tend to your feet."

"Tend to my feet?"

"Yes," he said earnestly. "They are torn apart."

"Okay, I'd appreciate that, actually." A nice foot rub would feel like heaven. Maybe he'd want to rub me in other places.

He scoffed with a grin, ignoring my internal comment. "Was that sincerity I detected in your normally-sour tone?"

"I'm not sour."

He quirked an eyebrow.

"Not all the time, asshole."

"The residents of Purgatory will get a view of *your* asshole if you don't cover it soon." Clutching the torn fabric, polka dotted with blood, I tried to keep Purgatory's residents from any unwelcome views of my backside.

"Follow me. There is a safe home nearby. We can stay there for the night."

I didn't argue, just followed as best I could, albeit slowly. Tracking through a large field, back across the placid creek of molten silver and into a different neighborhood with larger homes, I walked behind Keeper. Was that his name? Keeper? Poor guy. No wonder he has emotional issues.

"I have no issues."

"You have control issues," I argued. "You control a billion birds, fella. Tell me that's not a sign of a control freak."

Keeper approached a two-story stone home. The texture of the sidewalk felt like sandpaper in a wound. Looking down and behind me, it was no wonder. I'd left bloody footprints all the way to the front door, which Keeper shouldered open.

"No key?"

He smiled slightly. "Keys aren't necessary here."

"No, why use house keys when you have brute force?"

He craned his head in a few directions.

"Do you hear something?" I asked.

"Other than your incessant questions and inner monologue?"

I raised one brow at him.

"No, but I was making sure. I'll check everything thoroughly in a minute, but this is a safe place. We'll spend the night here so you can rest." As he jogged up the steps, a gust of air rattled the windows of the house, followed by the sound of scratching and rustling from the roof. His freaking birds. They would tell every Lesson where to find us tonight – or today – whichever it was. Or maybe they were like a security system sign; a deterrent. *Keeper Systems. Do not enter or the birds will eat your soul.*

"It's the latter. No one will bother us, and from here I can call for help."

He jogged upstairs and back down, carrying a dark lump.

"You're calling for help?" I wondered who the Keeper of Crows called for back-up. Batman? He smiled, throwing the pile of dark clothing at me. I caught the pieces against my chest.

"Get dressed. I'll be back in a moment."

I smirked at him as I untied the top strands of my hospital gown. "You can stay and help, if you'd like." The cotton drifted down, the gown catching on my breasts. My nipples were sharp as the thorns in the forest we'd just climbed out of.

Keeper swallowed, not entirely unaffected. Easing the sliding glass door open, he stepped onto a balcony. I eased the panties on, my legs sore from I didn't even know what. How'd he know what size I was? And how'd he know the clothes were here? I fastened the bra and pulled the shirt on. Sitting on the couch, I pushed my feet through the pant legs, wincing as I forced my toes to point. The flesh flexed along with the movement, and something on the bottom of my foot began to bleed again. Buttoning my pants was easy; however, bending forward to roll the pant legs up at the bottom hurt like hell. The carpet underfoot was painted crimson.

Outside, Keeper called one of his birds. He spoke to it, and though I couldn't hear him, I wondered if he was using the language he'd spoken against the lightning leash, the same language that he'd controlled Pamela and tried to control me with. It was lyrical and beautiful. If only it had worked.

He stroked the bird's head and raised his hand, allowing it to fly into the air. He watched for a long moment, until I couldn't see the crow anymore and doubted he could, either. He turned and opened the door again, stepping inside.

"I will rinse and bandage your feet. They'll heal by morning."

There was no way they would heal by morning. Maybe in a week if I kept them clean and wrapped, but bandages were the first step in that process.

He smirked, having gotten his way, and ran up the steps. I could hear him rifling through cabinets, and then he returned with a thin, white towel and a bottle of water. Easily tearing the towel into strips of fabric, he wetted one with the water and settled next to me on the couch.

"Give me your foot."

Um. What if they smelled? "Honestly, I can do this."

"You can't. Give me your foot," he repeated patiently. I lifted my left leg, and when he grabbed my ankle, the electricity shot up my leg again. "Are you doing this on purpose?" he growled.

"Doing what?" I sat up and tried to take my foot from him.

"That jolt-thing… Never mind. Just sit still." He blotted my feet and tied strips of cloth so that the knots sat along the top of my foot in a long row. His skin was perfect, the tattoos stationary for now.

Shifting in his seat, I realized he'd heard me. *Sorry. It's just strange that they change.*

"It isn't strange for me. Give me your other foot, please."

I eased my left one down and lay back on the couch while he gently tended to the other. I expected his touch to be rough, like the beautiful exterior of him, but it was a whisper, a barely-there brush that didn't hurt at all. Under his breath, he uttered words in the beautiful language. I wondered if they were words of frustration. Would angry sentences sound beautiful when spoken by the Keeper of Crows?

When the bandages were finished, he gently sat my foot down and stood up.

"I'm hungry. Is there food in the fridge?"

He stared down at me. "We'll eat in the morning. For now, you should get some rest."

He didn't have to tell me twice. I was planning to sleep on the couch, when his arms scooped me up. Gently, he carried me up the steps to the first bedroom we came to and laid me on the mattress. The blankets had already been turned down.

Watching him walk away was the perfect end to a very long day, but it left me wanting. I could hear him moving around, but couldn't tell exactly where he was in the house. The safe house, he'd called it. But this place, if it truly was Purgatory, didn't make me feel safe at all. I was afraid. Would I ever be able to leave? Why was I here to begin with?

From the stranger's bed upstairs, I tossed a thought into the air. *I'm cold. Feel like warming me up?*

A growl from the room beside mine was my only response. I pictured him stretched out on the mattress, hands behind his head, dark hair falling into his eyes, broody look on his face…maybe with a hard-on, because now he was picturing me naked and he really did want to come into my room and warm me up.

"Go to sleep, Carmen."

I wiggled into the mattress to get more comfortable before drifting off.

CHAPTER

EIGHT

How long did I sleep? My back was stiff. I placed my feet on the floor, sitting up and yawning with a long stretch of my arms. When I eased onto my feet, there was no pain. I sat back down and peeked beneath one bandage. Nothing. No blood, no cuts, no holes or torn flesh. Just a shimmer, a dark shadow, beneath the skin. I wondered if his words healed me, but they didn't work to persuade me in any other way. The shadow was dark, which I assumed meant the veil inside had healed my feet. Did he tell it what to do? Staring at the bottoms of my feet where clean, new skin had grown over the gashes and holes... It was as if I'd never been hurt.

"How is this possible?"

One by one, I eased the bloodstained bandages from my feet, revealing fresh skin, new and pink and tender to the touch, but new all the same. I left the shredded pieces of fabric on the floor and padded to the door, going downstairs in search of my handsome new friend. Keeper was on the porch, gathering chunks of bread that littered the surface of the wood. He looked up at me and ticked his head for me to come outside.

"What is that?"

"Are you still hungry?" he asked, smirking.

"Yeah, but I'm not eating sky bread."

"Sky bread," he muttered. "It's manna."

Manna. Of course, it was manna. "You're kidding, right?"

He smirked. "I am not."

Keeper held a piece up to my lips, teasing me with the white ball of fluff. Maybe it would actually taste good.

"Eat. It will fill you for the day."

"Don't we need to bake it or something?" I asked.

He grinned. "It is perfect the way it is. Baking it would destroy it."

I reached up to take the piece from his fingers, but he tutted. "Open wide," he teased.

"That phrase can mean a great many things, Keeper. Be careful who you say it to."

His eyes narrowed and flicked down my body, making me all too aware that he liked what he saw, even though he fought it. Then he lowered the piece of manna into his hand where the other pieces lay in a pile. He extended the hand to me. "Take all of this. I'll get more for me."

He emptied his hand into both of my cupped ones. I raised the manna to my nose and smelled. It smelled sweet, but not like sugar; sort of like honey or honeysuckle. I couldn't place it. "What exactly does it taste like?"

"Like everything and nothing," he replied simply, his dark hair mussed from sleep last night.

"Did you sleep well?" I should have peeked into his bedroom, now that I thought about it.

"I don't sleep, but you slept deeply, which is good. In Purgatory, you have to rest in order to heal. You have to eat the manna provided to keep from starving. And right now, you need to tell me everything—again—so I can see if there's anything that can be done to allow you to pass through the divide. No detail is too small."

"I'm not wasting my time or yours rehashing it, and you've already seen my memory of it. Or so you say…"

"I did, but I can't wrap my head around it." He paused for a long moment, hands on his hips. "No wonder the merchants were frightened. No soul has ever physically torn the fabric before. Not even my kind."

"Keepers? As in plural? There are more of you?"

He frowned. "In a manner of speaking, yes, but I am the only one assigned to Purgatory indefinitely."

"Tough gig. Who did you piss off to get sent here?"

"Someone important," he answered honestly, taking a piece of the manna and chewing it.

I bit off a little chunk of manna to taste it and found that it was nothing short of amazing. With the consistency of a marshmallow, somehow it was rich and sweet, but not too sweet. There were hints of cinnamon and bread; like monkey bread, only completely white. Mmmmm. And it was filling. The handful of manna he gave me was too much. Three bites were all it took to fill me. I doubted that feeling of fullness would last the day, though.

Keeper smiled. "It will. I promise." Promises... Promises were important to people. Were they important to Keepers? And who was he, really?

"Is that your name? Keeper?"

"I do not give my name to those I don't know well."

"Why not?"

"It's not wise," he said, chewing another piece.

Pulling out a pack of cigarettes from his pocket, he searched for something.

"Looking for a lighter?"

"Or matches. I usually have both." His eyes narrowed. "Did you take them from me?"

Well, bristle my feathers. "Hell, no!" I answered indignantly. "I'm not a thief. And why would I want your lighter?"

"I had it yesterday." He searched his pockets again and then started looking around the house. They probably fell out of his jeans when the birds carried us. They were probably teetering on a rock ledge along that God-forsaken cliff. Just a little gust and they'd be gone.

"Never mind," he said, pulling a small neon green lighter from his back pocket. "I found it."

Well, wasn't he nice to have apologized for accusing me of stealing? "Why are you smoking, and how in the hell do you get cigarettes here? Are there convenience stores?" Maybe it was a black-market thing, like the soul traffickers. Maybe Keeper got them in exchange for people.

He snorted. "I have them delivered from Earth, and another shipment should arrive in a day or so."

"Brilliant. Can you see if they can score a Pepsi?"

He ticked his head. "Caffeine is bad for your body."

"And cigarettes are healthy?"

"Not for you, but for me there are no ill effects. I like the taste, and it's become a habit."

"Can I have a smoke?" Watching him guardedly, I wondered what he would expect in return. I remembered the last time I bummed smokes. In all fairness, I'd offered the blow job. It was a trade, and at the time I thought it was fair.

Keeper threw the pack of smokes and lighter onto the couch cushions. He bared his teeth and walked away angrily, pacing over the carpet of the house. He was going to wear a path. I knew what he saw in my mind, but his anger was confusing. I wasn't angry about it. I really had no feelings about it whatsoever. I wanted smokes. The guy wanted a blowjob. What was the problem?

"You... What you did for him? He didn't... appreciate it. He was just using you."

"I was also using him. Or do you not get that? I wanted cigarettes. I got cigarettes. End of story." Judgmental asshole.

"You're worth more than that," he said, his voice gritty with emotion. The muscle in his jaw flared rapidly.

"*I* decide what I'm worth. Not you. Not that guy. No one. *I* decide."

Keeper glared at me and then, even though his demeanor hadn't calmed, he used a soothing voice and artfully changed the subject. "There has to be more to the story. A soul can't tear the fabric of the divide. The veil was torn once, but not by the hand of a human soul," he said, trying to figure out what I'd done. But I didn't understand it either. It just did. It tore off and freaking disappeared into my hand.

"Let me see it again," he said, standing up and grabbing my head, his thumbs at my temple and his fingers rubbing my scalp.

"Not so rough this time," I warned. This time it wasn't unpleasant. His touch was whisper soft, and if I had hair I'd have moaned embarrassingly loud. His touch was something I could easily become addicted to, better than cocaine, but perhaps more costly because I loved every soft stroke of his skin on mine. *This must be a dream*, I thought, closing my eyes and reveling in the feel of him.

"You aren't dreaming. This place is real," Keeper said softly.

"It doesn't feel real. Life doesn't feel like this. This is perfect," I said, looking up at him. His eyes swirled a soft caramel. "Why do they change?" He knew exactly what I was referring to.

"They reflect emotion." He had mood eyes.

"Why do your tattoos change?"

"They aren't tattoos, and they reflect the language I speak and the words that I need. They are reflections of the pleas I utter."

His thumbs massaged my temples and I melted into him. "Remember everything. Show me everything that led you here."

So I did. I took him back to when my life began to unravel at the seams. I remembered the paparazzi, the car accident, and the feeling of letting go. I remembered Doc and rehab and trying to escape Dimitri. The feeling of shattering bones and bruises so deep I would always be sore. The spikes of my hair upon my fingertips when I realized it was gone and the ridges and bumps of the staples and skin that lay cramped in between. I showed him the moment I realized I was the girl attached to the machines, laying in the bed effectively dead, the fabric or veil or whatever he wanted to call it and how I poked at it, my finger coming away clean. Giving him the moment of Pamela's abduction and then mine, I showed him how I fought them, how I didn't go down without a fight—I'd fought Dimitri and his thugs, too. No matter who or what I fought, it never did any good, but I did it to show that I wouldn't buckle before I broke. I showed him how the fabric tore, and then the fear in Gus's eyes and the overwhelming gray that found me as the swirling black mass soaked into my body and awakened me to this place. I showed him the gate and The Killing Field and the moment I saw him.

His body, so close to mine, went rigid. "Thank you," he whispered, easing his fingers away from me. When he touched my face, there was no spark. It didn't hurt or anything. Maybe we were past it.

"This is beyond my knowledge. I don't understand." The strained lines in his face showed how difficult it was to even admit it.

"The veil thing you talk about – is it a bad thing that I tore it?"

"Most likely, yes," he replied. "But it was so small a piece." His eyes, now ebony, snapped to mine. "Those men who hurt you, why did they do it?"

"I'm not the type of girl who deserves Heaven, Keeper. I was mean and did some very bad things."

"Every human does. Most waste the gifts they were given."

"Can you see life on Earth from here?"

"No. I can't leave this place. I haven't for a long time," he said, turning his back to me. Snapping his fingers, the crows swirled to the ground, pecking at the leftover manna.

I wanted to ask him what he was and how long he'd been here. Watching his back stiffen, I knew he heard my silent questions. He didn't want to answer, and maybe I shouldn't even think those things. Curiosity killed me a few times before. I still hadn't learned my lesson, apparently. The Lesson, the man with his ears melted by the demon, flashed into my mind. Would I suffer a similar fate?

"You won't."

"How can you be so sure? If the veil wasn't supposed to be torn, how do you know I won't become just like them?"

He leaned against the deck railing. "I don't feel it," he said, rubbing the muscle over his heart.

"What do you feel?" I asked, watching him rub his chest, his face contorted in emotions so deep, I couldn't wrap my head around them.

"I feel you, but it's so confusing. I'm not sure that what I'm feeling is accurate. My gifts don't seem to work on you."

"Does every Lesson lose their hearing?" I asked, toying with the fleshy bottom of my ear.

"No, some lose their sight. Others lose their ability to speak. Their mouths are sealed."

My chest tightened. "Hear no evil."

Keeper smiled. "Speak no evil, see no evil. Smart girl."

With a mirthless laugh, I told him, "No one's ever accused me of being smart."

His jaw ticked. "Don't put yourself down, Carmen Kennedy."

"Easy for you to say, Keeper." I took a deep breath. "What's on tap for today?" He could tell I was done talking about me and this crazy situation, and he graciously let me change the subject.

"We lay low and wait for help to arrive."

"Will help have a name?"

Keeper smirked. "Perhaps."

"Asshole."

Then he laughed, wholeheartedly. Keeper liked being called an asshole.

"I can think of a few ways to fill our time," I suggested.

"No," he said sternly and walked out the balcony door.

CHAPTER

NINE

In what I thought was the afternoon, it began to rain. It rained hard, the drops blown sideways from the gusts of wind that accompanied it. Keeper ran outside into the deluge, getting drenched immediately, but it didn't deter him.

"Come on!" he yelled, stripping himself of his clothes. With his back to me, I watched his hands scrub over his body. Every inch. And I couldn't tear my eyes away from him. Every inch of him was sculpted, powerful, and intimidating. He'd been chiseled from stone, I was sure of it. The only part that wasn't perfect were the two vertical scars slashing through his shoulder blades.

His body tensed, hearing my thoughts. I didn't dislike the scars at all. Scars were important. It meant bad stuff happened. Scars were the remnants of terrible things, but also proof that a person had survived them. I slid the pad of my finger over the large scar on my head, the skin around it still puckered and tender to the touch.

He wasn't naked for long, unfortunately, because just a few minutes after it began, the rain stopped pouring. Keeper gathered his clothes, tucking them strategically in front of him. I hadn't gotten a peek at *that* yet, but damn, if it matched the rest of him...

He was smirking when he walked through the door, fishing his cigarette packet from his dripping, tragically well-positioned pants.

I pointed a (sexually) frustrated finger at the window. "What the hell was that?"

"The cleansing."

"The cleansing. Oh. Well, why didn't you just say so? Does it come at this time every day, like the manna?"

"It does."

"Well, I know when to bathe tomorrow, then."

He looked at me and earnestly said, "You smell good."

"Oh, I smell good. Well, I'd like to get clean too, buddy. So, when 'the cleansing' comes again, I'll go get naked with you. Unless you want me to strip down now..."

"I told you to come. And I waved for you."

Water sluiced down his body, making him look like a delectable, juicy, fresh piece of man-flesh. Damn it.

"I'll be back," he said, walking to the steps. The muscles in his ass alone... My God. If *this* was Purgatory, maybe I should stay.

When he came back down, I was sitting on the couch, yet again. I'd snooped through every cabinet, closet, and room and found nothing interesting at all. Who had lived here?

"It mirrors someone's home in your world."

"But why? Why the city? Why the homes and manna and rain?"

"The city was built from one man's imagination, and this house came from another's. Some things stay, some go. Eventually, this house will fade away. The owner stayed here for a long time, but has moved on."

"To Heaven or Hell?"

"Does it matter?"

Did it? We were using the house now. That mattered. A chick lived here. She had a black Labrador retriever and a nail polish fetish, given the obscene amount of tiny bottles under the bathroom sink. She was my size. How did he know we were the same size?

"I can sense these things."

"You can sense them?"

"You repeat my questions often."

Hmm. He had a point there. But I still couldn't wrap my mind around this place. This dream was the weirdest and longest I'd ever had.

Keeper wore a long-sleeved black Henley, its sleeves pushed up to reveal muscular forearms and the tattoos that covered them. Dark jeans fit him like they were made for him.

"Where'd you get the clothes? I didn't see men's clothing in any of the closets."

"I asked for them."

"Whom did you ask?"

He rolled his eyes and strode toward me, reaching out for my hands. "Stand up."

Uh.

"Stand. Up," he said more softly.

I stood and placed my hands in his. He lowered his head, bringing our mouths precariously close together. Lightning struck between the pair of us.

"Do you feel that?" he slowly whispered.

"The electricity?" I was breathless, lightheaded. I could feel him everywhere. The spark. The connection. Him.

"Yes."

"Then, yes. I feel it."

Keeper's eyes fastened onto mine, swirls of violet and blue. "It's real. This home is real. You are not dreaming."

"But it can't be real. I saw my body. I'm not in it anymore."

He nodded. "You aren't in your earthen body anymore; you're in a body made only for this place. You are in Purgatory. It's a reality with its own rules. Earth's rules do not apply here. If you can accept that, you can survive here. If you refuse, you may lose your mind before your soul makes its way back to your body. Do you understand? If you lose your mind, you'll never find your way back to your body and you'll be lost for good. You have to keep a grasp on who you are and what happened to you, even though it's painful."

Remembering was part of the punishment of being here. Swallowing, I tried to pull my hands away. His lips were perfect, the bottom slightly plumper than the top.

"I'll try," I said, pleading with him to understand. It just made no sense.

"It doesn't make sense," he answered my unspoken thoughts. "None of this does. Especially not you."

"Why don't I make sense? The fabric? I'm telling you, my soul was like a sponge. Somehow, it just soaked it up."

Keeper smiled.

"This place is so strange, but I can honestly say I've seen weirder here," I added. I mean, hello, the tears or fissures themselves were creepy as hell. All of a sudden, a sharp sting ran up my spine. I jumped into him and Keeper caught me, holding me tight to him. It felt like the lightning leash was stinging me, or a lightning whip was cracking across my spine.

"Aaah!" I winced. He held me upright, fingers digging into my hips.

"What's happening?" he gritted.

"I don't know! *You* should know!"

He held me up as another surge forked up my spine, tearing a scream from my throat, and then he looked up to the ceiling.

"It's not possible." His irises turned dark and began to swirl and ooze like oil, hints of lavender, teal, and deep brown roiling within. "How did you know it was coming?"

"What? What was coming?"

"I only now sensed it. Come outside."

He pulled me along behind him, my back alive with sharp, stinging bursts of something more powerful than I was.

Out on the deck, the crows cawed and swirled into a funnel. The film of fabric appeared, swirling angrily. The noise, the screeching, ripping, ear-damaging sound came from above us. RIGHT above us. The fabric had torn apart.

"Is this your version of help?" I asked hopefully.

"No, this is you."

"*Me?*"

"You did this. You mentioned the fabric of the veil, and then you mentioned it tearing and separating. Holy... You envisioned it. You *caused* this fissure!"

The wind swirled as angrily as Keeper's eyes, as frenzied as his birds. They watched the flapping edges of the fabric, watched the gaping hole to see what or who would pass through it. But no one did.

"Close it!" he yelled over the sound of the wind and wings.

"I can't!"

"You can! Think it. Imagine it closing!"

Toward the fissure, I screamed, "Close, you fucking thing!"

He frowned at me but watched incredulously as the fabric begin to swirl, congeal, and repair the wound I'd caused. The scar was present for a fraction of a second before it disappeared, along with the veil itself. Keeper's jaw gaped open as he looked over at me.

"That was one way to do it."

"I didn't know what to say! I don't think it was me in the first place."

"It was you," he said, relaxing his stance. The crows circled more slowly and began to land in the yard and on the roof of the house. A few perched on the dead limbs of a nearby tree. Cawing at each other more calmly, they settled down. So did he.

I pinched my lip as he cast a wary glance in my direction, but there was something else in those tumultuous eyes. Intrigue, maybe?

"You are dangerous," he said simply, resting his forearms on the deck rail. If I was dangerous, then the Keeper of Crows was terrifying. I'd seen what he could do. He ignored the mental comment and barreled toward me with more.

"If the ruler of the city knew of your power, he would use you. But I swear on my life, I'll keep you safe. I'll help you find a way out of here."

"No one is using me ever again," I bit out.

"Never say never, Carmen Kennedy."

CHAPTER

TEN

My feathers had been ruffled. No one was using me, whether I had some sort of power to open fissures or not. Besides that, I thought he was insane. *I didn't cause a fissure,* I thought solemnly. *I can't tear the veil. I'm just a soul here.* I watched Keeper as he stood deep in thought, arms braced against the deck railing. I was almost able to hear the gears turning in his mind as the sounds of night fell around us and the unearthly bugs sang their sad songs.

The crows rested all around us; some on the tree limbs of a large tree in the back yard, some on the roof's peak, while still others lay on the ground, nestled into the overgrown tufts of gray grass. It was a moment of calm. A moment to catch our breath after such a strange event this evening. And calm moments in Purgatory, I learned, were fleeting.

Keeper suddenly stiffened, shoving me behind him toward the sliding glass door and the shelter of the safe house. "Get inside." The low, warning timbre of his voice set me on edge.

"Why? What's wrong?" Peeking over his shoulder, I saw what worried him. A Lesson, this one a male built like a wall of angry, hulking muscle. His eyes were gone and the sockets that once held them dripped tar onto his heaving chest.

See no evil. Why didn't the demon bind him so he could do no evil?

"Please go inside and secure all of the doors," Keeper requested calmly.

"I don't think I want to be inside," I admitted on a whisper, inching closer to his back. Not to mention that he was the one who told me no one needed keys in this place.

He looked over his shoulder at me, a perplexed expression wrinkling his forehead just slightly. "You will be safe. I wouldn't send you into danger, but I will keep you from it, or it from you."

Swallowing down my fear, I opened the door and backed into the house, watching Keeper jump up onto the railing, standing tall and raising his arms in the air. The crows swirled around the Lesson, disorienting the beast.

Keeper jumped off the balcony and then I couldn't see him anymore. I locked the glass door and ran to the front door to lock it, too. The windows were beyond my control. Most were stuck either up or down, and those that were up wouldn't close no matter how hard I pushed. They were frozen. Maybe it was how the person who lived there made them or remembered them, and they brought the whole thing here like this. Maybe it couldn't change.

From the window, I watched as the birds carried the threat away, dragging the Lesson away from the approaching Keeper. But then I saw the rest of the Lessons waiting nearby and wondered how there would ever be enough crows to combat them all. There were at least a hundred, some without eyes, others with tar dripping from their ears, and others with sealed black spots where their mouths had once been.

I ran to the kitchen, searching for a butcher knife— anything I could use as a weapon. Keeper would need help with this hellish army.

The ones who couldn't speak? They were the most dangerous, I learned. Because while the others had control of their voices and screamed and bellowed, the ones with no mouth were unable to make any sound whatsoever. Just as I reminded myself of the formidable threat, I realized I shouldn't speak of the devil. He would appear.

Two hands grabbed my throat from behind, wrenching me to the side and throwing me against the refrigerator. My head swam with black dots, but the pain in my ankle kept me lucid. Fuck. Me. This guy was strong. "Keeper!" I bellowed.

The Lesson needed to be taught a lesson, and I was in no shape to give him one. The windows burst open, angry wind swirling inside along with a torrent of crows. Feathers, once light and delicate as air, soft as down, were driven toward the silent monster. They skewered him, sharp as needles, each embedding into his flesh until he was covered, stumbling toward an escape he wouldn't find.

I covered my head with my forearms as he passed me by, my mind buzzing with a strange static. A soft touch on my shoulder made me jump. "It's me," Keeper said softly, crouching at my side.

"Did you do that to him? Did you have the crows kill him?"

He didn't answer right away and didn't look me in the eye when he answered. "Yes."

I raised up from my knees and hugged his neck harder than was necessary. He saved me from that creature. I was still shaking from head to toe when he cupped his hands and blew toward the Lesson, his body turning to ash and blowing away. I didn't watch this time to see if his soul was gulped down by one of Keeper's crows. I was a coward.

"Are there more?" I asked tentatively.

"No, they've been dealt with."

He wasn't completely honest. Keeper didn't merely *deal* with Lessons; he eradicated them. "Thank you," I told him, still holding his neck in a tight grip. I couldn't bring myself to let him go.

"How did he sneak up on you?" he asked gently.

"I was looking for a knife or something, and I guess with all the commotion outside, I didn't hear him. The carpet must have muffled his feet, or maybe I was deafened by the blood pulsing through my ears. It was terrifying, watching you jump up on the rail and face them all. I didn't want you to do it alone."

His hands found my waist and I gasped.

"I've never had a soul defend me," he admitted, his voice laced with a mixture of confusion and awe. I mewled when his fingers slid under the cotton hem of my shirt and grazed my sides. Every time he touched me, an arc of electricity sparked between us, not simply attraction or even lust. And it hurt a little, to be honest.

"It does. It's like a sting for me too," he said softly. "But it's not unpleasant, just strange."

I nodded, pinching my bottom lip.

I'd never felt love from anyone. Not even my mother or father. And with men, I'd felt frantic hands and teeth tugging at my lips, been groped and fucked against walls, but whatever this was…it was new.

"Seeing your thoughts is torture," he said, pulling away from me.

"Well then stop invading my mind," I retorted. My arms fell uselessly to my thighs.

His jaw worked back and forth angrily. "I don't like that men have touched you that way, that harshly."

"It's how things are now, and I didn't expect tenderness from any of them. I'm the girl who uses sex to get what she wants. I don't fuck just to make a man happy, and I'm definitely not the type a man brings home to meet his mother. I'm not marriage material, and I never will be. I'm not built for that," I breathed against the skin of his jaw. He wouldn't look me in the eye, wouldn't turn his head toward me despite the lack of space between us. "But tenderness sounds beautiful coming from your lips. If you turn your head, you can show me how nice you would be." And I wished he would, with everything in me. I wished he would place his lips on mine. Would the spark ignite us both?

He didn't turn his head. Despite every cell in my body willing him to, he refused. Keeper blew out a tense breath and I stepped back, allowing him to breathe.

"What's the matter?" I asked. What was holding him back?

He cleared his throat, lacing his fingers behind his head. "I don't understand you."

"That makes two of us."

"I also don't understand what happened here tonight. The Lessons have never attacked. They've never been coordinated before. This is a big problem."

"Why are they attacking you now? Power in numbers or something?"

When Keeper looked up, I knew what he was going to say before his mouth opened. His eyes swirled a rich, clover green. "They weren't attacking me. They were coming for you."

"Why? What could they possibly want with me? I'm screwed," I said, crossing my arms over my chest. "I'm going to be dragged to Hell one way or another, aren't I?"

Keeper pursed his lips, his features hardening. "I won't let them have you."

He called one of his crows and it landed on his extended finger. Holding it close, whispering in his secret language, he gave it a message. The crow cawed once and flew behind his brothers, but instead of landing on the yard below in the gray grass, or on the branches of the dead tree, he climbed into the cloudy gray sky and his dark beak punched through the veil, like pulling panty hose too tight and having it spring back to its original form, the crow escaping through the tiny puncture.

Would I ever get used to seeing that?

"I don't know," Keeper answered.

I might never get used to him being in my head. At least I wasn't shy or embarrassed. For the most part, I was an open book. It was actually freeing. He knew the real me; not the version of me I occasionally projected to civilized society.

"It's refreshing," he admitted. "All the other souls try to hide their inner thoughts. You don't even try to block them."

"Why bother? Can't you hear them anyway?"

"I can. Souls can't shield their thoughts. They don't have that ability while they are healing or learning. Too much going on in their minds."

A bubbling sound came from across the room where the Lesson fell. The feathers had begun to soften into a tar-like substance. They bubbled and boiled, reducing his body to nothing more than a slick, black puddle. Why didn't he turn to dust like the others Keeper killed?

"Lessons are different. The demons who make them use a substance found only in Hell. It's not tar, like on Earth. It's a mixture of dark, tormented souls."

Dark souls. In one's ears, eyes, or mouth. I wasn't sure which was worse: this ending, or one like Gus and Chester's where a simple puff was all that remained until a bird gobbled it up.

"Neither is preferable."

"Is there another way, Keeper?"

"There is. Souls who rest, or who learn from the mistakes made in their earthly life, have a much simpler and beautiful transition. I hope you get to see that one day."

Pursing my lips, I stared at the puddle. "I hope so, too."

I doubted beauty or hope could exist in this place, but at the same time desperately wanted to be proven wrong.

CHAPTER

ELEVEN

I didn't remember falling asleep or moving to the bed. It was as if I sat on the couch and suddenly wasn't there anymore, like I ceased to be. Only I awoke in Purgatory again, surrounded by gray and the telltale sounds of crows on the roof above the room in which I lay. Keeper must have helped me to the bedroom. The mattress was soft enough, although sunken in places. The pillows smelled like mildew, but they were better than nothing, and sleeping on the couch near the Lesson puddle wasn't gonna happen.

Stretching, I sat up and looked out the window, watching the manna rain down from the heavens. This afternoon, when the cleansing rain poured from the sky, I was going to get clean. Padding to the door and down the steps, I found Keeper on the deck again, gathering the soft pillows of nourishment.

"I didn't think you were ever going to wake up," he said, raking his chocolate brown eyes over me.

"Awww, that's so sweet of you to be concerned," I teased with a grin.

He shook his head. "No, I tried to wake you several times and couldn't. It was as if you were gone."

A shiver ran up my spine, the hairs on my neck standing at attention.

"What's that?" I looked to the sky.

He stood and shielded his eyes. "I see nothing."

I plucked a piece of manna off the railing of the deck and popped it in my mouth, letting it disintegrate.

"Wait, you felt that?" he asked.

"What?" I said around another piece. "What did I feel?" My eyes searched the yard for more Lessons. Would those bastards attack again?

Just then, a crow returned through the veil and flew straight to Keeper, perching on his outstretched finger. "Thank you," he said softly.

"Why are you thanking him? What did he do?"

Keeper cooed at his bird. "He delivered a message for me, and also returned a message to me." I watched the two stare at each other, Keeper stroking the oily feathers of the fowl as if it were a pet.

"What message?" I asked. "What's going on?"

"We will find out more this evening. Help will arrive then."

"This evening?"

"Yes," he said. "Until then, we stay put."

"What about the Lessons? Will they attack again?"

"They didn't overnight," he retorted.

"But they did yesterday, in a very coordinated way, which you said they hadn't done before, so how do we know they won't?"

Keeper smiled. "We have faith, and we stay here."

"Why should I trust you?" I asked, hand on my hip.

He snorted. "Whom else will you trust? A Lesson? Another merchant? You can trust them all the way to your demise."

"Why do the merchants want souls?"

"They sell them into slavery in exchange for favors or women. It's disgusting and the trade is thriving, despite my efforts to stop them. And it's not just souls dragged across the divide; now they're taking souls from the city. Nowhere is safe, and nothing is sacred," he explained, looking at the silhouette of the towering buildings in the distance.

"Was it ever safe?"

"It's been a long time since Purgatory was used for its purpose; a city to house those who needed rest, with the outskirts left to the Lessons and the walls to separate the two. Merchants are nothing but parasites looking to make a deal."

"You said they would trade souls for favors. What kind of favors?" My stomach churned as I wondered what Gus and Chester would have traded me and Pamela for.

Keeper smiled. "Favors are important here, as important as money is on Earth. For instance, they will give a soul to a gatekeeper in exchange for the gates to open for them another time—a more convenient time."

"What do the gatekeepers use the souls for?"

"They sell them to the Meat district."

My eyes bulged. "They *eat* them?"

"No!" he laughed. "Souls can't be consumed. The Meat district is much like the red light districts of Earth. It is a portion of the city where souls are forced into slavery, sometimes sexual in nature, but sometimes it is simply servitude."

I remembered Gus and Chester and the 'reddies' they mentioned, and my stomach churned. "That's awful. I thought sex trafficking was only an earthly issue."

He sighed. "I wish."

"You can't stop them?"

"I try, but I can't be everywhere at once, and my orders have changed. I guard the fissures and try to stop new souls from being brought across the divide; however, I can't stop them from kidnapping souls from within the city itself while I'm out here guarding the fissures."

"Which is the bigger problem? Souls being stolen from Purgatory or souls from Earth?"

"Earth, because those souls often aren't supposed to come here. That's why I have orders to protect them. Besides, many souls kidnapped from Purgatory have already lost themselves. They won't return to their bodies. They're mindless and easy to capture. But the merchants covet fresh souls from Earth. They're worth much more, because there's still fight left in them."

Someone felt the souls taken from within the city weren't worth protecting, but even if they lost their minds, they didn't deserve to be slaves.

He stared at the ground below us.

"Why is it only you and the crows?" I finally asked.

"That is the way."

"That is the way? Well, that way doesn't work anymore." He was exasperating.

He swallowed, his brows knitting together in anger. "I am finished answering your incessant questions." And with those biting words, he stormed inside, down the stairs and out the front door, leaving me wondering what the hell was going on with him.

Keeper didn't return in the afternoon, or what I thought was afternoon. He was sulking or pouting—or every other emasculating word I could mentally throw his direction. Asshole. But I wanted to get clean, so I stayed close to the back door and waited for the sky to open up. When the cleansing began, I stripped fast and ran into the deluge like a kid, scrubbing fast, kicking the fast-forming puddles and whooping, scaring the crows around me that otherwise didn't seem to mind the rain one single bit. That was weird for birds, right?

Can they fly with wet wings?

"They can," a masculine voice answered from right behind me.

I stared into his eyes, the rain carving rivers down his face. His eyes, swirling sapphire, never left mine, even for a second. We stood so close that I could feel the warmth radiate from him, but our bare skin never touched. It was a different kind of torture to keep myself from reaching out for him.

He narrowed his eyes, silently telling me not to touch him. But why come back at the exact time he knew I'd be naked and cleaning myself off?

"Did you come back for the show?" I shouted as the rain slowed.

"I was never far, but the show was...interesting. You act as free as a child."

"I had fun."

He smiled. "It looked fun."

"Fun usually is. You should try it sometime." I stood taller, pushing my breasts out for him to notice, and he did. His fingers might as well have pinched my nipples because they ached, straining toward him. And that was just with his eyes on me.

"Perhaps I will," he mused, finally raking his eyes over the rest of me. Of all the men who'd seen me naked, tasted me, his eyes on me, even without his hands on my body, was more intense than all of them put together. "You're beautiful, Carmen."

Remembering the way I looked before I ended up in that hospital bed, a patchwork mess of bruises and torn flesh, was difficult and painful in a way I didn't expect. My hair was always styled. My clothes were expensive, even if risqué. I was pretty at one time. I was beautiful. But now? I looked like I'd been run over by a train.

"I was," I answered dejectedly.

"You are," he said adamantly. "And you are brave. When the Lessons came I told you to stay inside, and yet you went in search of a weapon. You were going to come help me."

I nodded. "I was. You shouldn't have to fight them alone, Keeper."

He crossed the space between us, lifting his hand and tipping my head up. The rain stopped completely as we stood there, staring at one another. His face dipped lower and I strained to get closer, rejoicing that I would finally feel him, kiss him, and touch him. But then his eyes tightened at the corners, transforming from royal blue to black in an instant. He set his jaw and used his body to cover me. "Get dressed quickly and get inside."

"What is it?" I spun around but saw nothing. My heart pounded in my chest.

"Go!"

I ran for it, leaving my clothes beneath the porch. There were more inside. I bolted up the stairs and into the bedroom, where I searched quickly through the drawers for a bra and panties. Throwing open the closet door, I found jeans and a t-shirt.

Jogging back downstairs, I stopped in my tracks. Keeper was arguing with someone. I heard his voice, angry and sharp in its tone, yet still beautiful. He was speaking the language I loved. Two sets of eyes, almost red in color, turned in my direction. Keeper's entire body was taut and so was his...brother's?

"We aren't brothers," Keeper barked.

The other man, who looked eerily similar to my new friend, smirked, revealing a dimple in his left cheek—a dimple that Keeper didn't have. Loose dark curls brushed his shoulders. Those were the only true differences that I could see. Same height, weight, and build. Same mood-ring eyes.

"She's thought that a few times. What is a mood ring?" Keeper asked.

"It's a trinket that turns different colors depending on the person's body temperature, but according to the packaging, it varies with their feelings. I will bring you one when I return," his near twin promised. "Here are more cigarettes," he said, offering two packs to Keeper.

Keeper turned toward me, and then quickly, his feet closed the space between us. "Do I look like a fool?"

Our guest – whom I decided to call 'Help' – positioned himself between us, somehow faster than Keeper in that moment.

"Pardon?" I ticked my head back.

"This entire thing – you coming across, tearing the veil, acting innocent in it all. Have you been playing me for a fool?" Keeper stepped toward me, mouth open for another assault.

"She doesn't know," Help interjected.

"And how do you know that?" Keeper growled at his friend, who I now knew was definitely not his brother.

"Because I can see it. There is no malice in her. While *he* is malignant, she is innocent. Look at her."

Keeper fastened his eyes on me. They swirled to crimson and then faded to a dark blue before turning crystalline once more. "You're right," he admitted, his entire posture relaxing. He looked like he was ready for battle seconds earlier, but against me? And who was the tumor in this whole thing? Help said, 'he is malignant.' Who the hell was *he*?

And who was this mysterious friend, anyway? Someone who could procure mood rings and cross the veil, or divide, or whatever weird word they called the barrier today. Looking at Help, I asked, "Who are you— and before you say you can't tell me, I want your damn name!"

Help amusedly looked from me to Keeper.

"She calls me Help and you Keeper? Why have you not given her your name?"

"Because I don't understand her."

"You are too out of touch with the souls of Earth. She makes more sense than most. Don't you, Carmen?" Help turned his head to the side, quirking a dark brow. "She is honest and forthcoming, if somewhat crude. She values honesty. You should be open and forthcoming with her."

"I have no idea how my soul compares to anyone else's, but my attitude is pretty normal these days." I wasn't an asshole most days, but I had issues. Keeper did too, and he *was* an asshole every day, so boo for him.

"She calls you an asshole!" Help cackled, clutching his stomach.

"He *is* an asshole," I said, meaning every syllable. "And he won't give me his name because he doesn't trust me. I just can't figure out why."

Keeper crossed his arms over his chest, brows knitted in confusion. "Why do you think I don't trust you?"

"Uh…" I started ticking the reasons off on my fingers. "You won't tell me your name because I'm not worthy, or whatever. Every answer you give me is cryptic, and you get pissed when I ask too many questions. You won't let me out of your sight, even when you pretend to. Remember the cleansing?" It was my turn to raise my brows.

Help coughed to cover his laughter after Keeper slugged him.

"I am *not* 'Help'," Help said. "My name is Gabriel."

Fitting. He was smoldering hot, with his dark clothing and rocker hair. The name Gabriel suited him.

"What suits me?" Keeper asked, his lips pulling up at the corners.

"I wouldn't *trust* myself to give you a name."

He huffed. "You're infuriating."

I smiled flirtatiously. "You didn't find me infuriating a few minutes ago."

Gabriel nudged him hard. "Give her your name. If you trust her, and you should, she'll need to trust you as well. Especially now that we know why she is here."

I sucked in a sharp breath. "You know why I'm here?"

The men exchanged a look.

"I will be back soon. I have to relay the information. You should find a safer place for her. He knows she's here." Gabriel raked his hair back. "He'll come for her. The only question is when."

"Handle the human I showed you, or better yet, bring him here so that I can take care of him myself."

Gabriel smiled. "You might be a little behind the times, but you're still the most fun."

Keeper wasn't a person I'd describe as fun.

"It's the asshole in him," Gabriel said with a wink before stepping forward and walking up a staircase made of invisible steps, easily crossing the divide when it appeared before him—in the damn living room. Gabriel didn't need a fissure. He punched through the same way the crow did. Why couldn't Keeper do the same and leave this hell hole?

Keeper cleared his throat and held his hand out for me to shake. Warily, I took hold of it. "Carmen Elaine Kennedy," he began. "My name is Michael."

CHAPTER

TWELVE

"Michael?" I asked, my mind catching on. Or at least I thought it was.

Keeper inclined his head, too long pieces of hair falling into his eyes.

"Gabriel?" I looked to the spot at which he vanished.

He inclined his head a second time.

"*The* Michael and Gabriel?"

Keeper nodded and simply said, "Yes."

"Angels?"

A smile tugged at Keeper's normally stern lips. "Archangels," he corrected. Of course, he was an archangel. In Purgatory. Talking to my soul because it was stuck here. And in this place of gray and shadow, it seemed to fit for some strange reason. He seemed to belong to this place and it to him.

"Why crows?" I wondered aloud, raking my eyes over him. He was delicious.

"I'm not delicious," he said with a grin.

"You totally are. You look like a dark-haired, hot emo-guy, all tatted up and sexy."

Then the Keeper of Crows smiled and I could see he was more angel than I'd imagined. In that moment, I knew I was in trouble. Since he could read my mind, he knew it, too. But being a gentleman, he didn't even make fun of me for having a crush on him. Were his pleas finally sinking in? Was the Keeper-crack taking hold of me? I hoped so, with every ounce of me, I hoped so. The Lessons were terrifying, and if I never saw another one again, it would be too soon.

"I'm worried about the wrong person overhearing our conversation. Not the Lessons, and not merchants. There are worse things in Purgatory, most of whom work for a very evil man."

He led me to the couch, his warm hand singing the small of my back. I sank into the worn cushions and he sat beside me, leaving enough distance between us that I could turn and point my knee toward him.

"I'm really confused. Gabriel didn't exactly clear things up."

"I know. Where to begin..." He exhaled heavily, gathering his thoughts. "Crows," he started, "have always ushered souls to and from Purgatory."

"So, why are you here?"

"When Christ was crucified, the veil was torn completely in two. The archangels hurried to repair it, but it was difficult to mend. The fabric was stretched tightly, thin over the Earth. After several years, it was clear that the fissures that happened occasionally due to the strain were here to stay. It wasn't safe for souls anymore."

"Were you sent here to guard Purgatory and help souls?"

He smiled lightly, his shoulders relaxing. "Mostly," he hedged. There was more to the story, but he didn't want to discuss the fine details just yet. I had other questions, so I asked one of those.

"You had wings, right? What did they look like?"

His smile faded. "I did. The crows I command were born from my wings. They had to become part of me, and they are obedient to me alone. I've seen them watch you, though. It's strange. It's like they know you're a part of the veil."

"Better watch out. I might take your crows away, Michael."

Shaking his head playfully, he silently told me that wouldn't happen. I imagined him, the way he looked before he came to this place: dark hair, morphing tattoos, oil slick feathers in great wings that arced behind him, holding a broadsword and kicking demon ass. He would have been fierce, but then again, he still was. He was intimidating.

"I'm not, and I don't know that I really looked the way you're imagining."

With complete sincerity, I looked into his eyes, softening into caramel. "On behalf of all womankind, I hope you looked *exactly* the way I imagine."

When he laughed, the room was filled with a presence that was larger than the air and all the objects in it. Then he sat back and sighed. "I do miss them, though. My wings."

"I bet you do. I imagine that was really hard to accept."

He swallowed. "It was."

"So, can I ask a really nosy and rude question?"

"You may ask, but I will choose whether or not to answer it."

"Okay. Who were you and Gabriel talking about, and why do you think he's coming for me?"

The Keeper, Michael, threaded his fingers together and pursed his lips into a tight line. "What do you know about your father?"

"I know he's a lying bastard who hated my mother, hates me, and can't seem to keep his dick out of any woman half his age who pays him the slightest bit of attention. He's just...incapable of most human emotion," I said, feeling glad to have that out in the open.

"He is also a crosser."

"A crosser? What's that?" I asked, although my gut said I wouldn't like his answer. My gut didn't lie.

"When the veil was torn, certain souls escaped from Purgatory and walked the earth. You see, some who come here, like you, have bodies waiting for their souls to return. Others who come here had bodies who have passed away. Their soul has nowhere to go but to Heaven or Hell. If a soul with no body escaped and walked among the living, they would appear ghostly, like an apparition. That was what most people assumed: that the dead walked among them. It wasn't exactly the case."

I couldn't even form a rational thought.

My father was a crosser. His soul was an escapee.

"But he has a body. On Earth, he has a body. He's young and real. This is...it makes no sense, Michael."

"He took one. It's not the first one he's taken, but if he takes over a body, he can live normally on Earth. He can have a life, a family. He's taken many lives in order to walk among you. He's had numerous families over the years. Your father is one of the most dangerous beings among the realms."

Of course, he was. My father was a bastard. I raked my hands through my hair, frustrated. This couldn't be real.

Could it?

"And his name isn't Warren Kennedy."

I huffed. "What is it?"

"Malchazze."

Several minutes of trying to absorb the gravity of the situation later, and my internal freak-out still hadn't subsided, not in the least. "So, he's evil? Then send him to Hell." I wouldn't lose sleep over it.

Michael frowned. "I can't without the order."

"Well who can send him? Who can give the order?"

"No one here."

"Then get someone to help!" I screamed in exasperation. "Ask someone to come and banish him. Ask your freaky demon friend to drag him down through the tar."

Michael stood and walked to the sliding glass door. "I have no demon friends," he hissed, composing himself again before speaking. "Demons approve of his actions here. If souls aren't rested, if the Lessons learn nothing, then the souls are forfeited to Hell. And he's made it easy for them to work the system. Purgatory was intended to be a place of rest; a place for souls to learn what they did wrong, and to complete their journeys. Lessons aren't supposed to be here. They don't belong here. But demons are using Purgatory for their own purposes. The Lessons the demons bring belong in Hell—like the man you saw punished—but now Purgatory is just another layer of Hell for some people, another realm of torture until they descend. That's not the way it was meant to be."

"What is my father doing here? If he can live on Earth, why cross back and forth? What's in it for him?" Because there had to be something lucrative for Father to give it his attention.

Michael was silent for a long moment.

"What's going on, Michael?"

He turned around and pinned his eyes on me, royal purple and roiling. "He's establishing an empire."

"He's making an empire. A kingdom in Purgatory?"

"Yes, and right now, I cannot stop him."

"But Purgatory wasn't meant to be ruled. Right?"

"Right," he agreed, turning his back to me again.

"How is he—?"

Suddenly, Michael ran toward me, lifting me up and racing toward the steps. "Upstairs! Lock the door, move furniture in front of it, just don't let anything in until I say. Okay?"

I nodded. Looking past him out the glass front door, I saw a Lesson. This one had no mouth, just skin stretched taut over where his mouth should be. When the creature tried to smile, his cheek bones stretched the skin further, revealing purple and blue veins that forked across his pale face. His eyes, every part of them, were black. Soulless. Evil.

He pressed his hands against the glass, fingertips leaving black smudges across it. Michael released a deep, reverberating growl before running toward the Lesson and leaping across the couch. The door shattered when he burst through it, but the Lesson's throat was in his fist in a fraction of a second. I could swear time stood still, and that the shards and splinters of glass were still falling as I took my first step upstairs.

"RUN!" he yelled. It was hard for a girl to run without knowing what she was running from, so I looked past him again. Big mistake.

Lessons. Some with ears and eyes that oozed black tar-like fluid, and some like the one Michael held with his feet flailing above the ground—no mouth at all. They were all over the yard, running toward the back porch and Michael. He needed help!

"No! Carmen, no! This is my purpose! Go upstairs, now!"

No way, Michael. You can't handle all of them. There are twice as many as last time!

I looked for a weapon and found a broom in the corner. Better than nothing.

In an instant, there was a loud caw from outside as the crows came to defend their master, individually and as one ferocious group. Feathers rained from the sky, and each time one touched a Lesson, the Lesson's skin began to sizzle and steam from the contact. The ones who could yell, did. The ones who couldn't, jerked and writhed on the ground. Then the crows began to swoop down in groups of thousands, carrying the Lessons away, their screams rising into the air as they were taken into a vortex of flying dark feathers and sharp beaks.

Michael stepped outside, watching the melee unfold. I relaxed my grip on the broom handle and lowered it to my waist. Bad move.

It grabbed me from behind, somehow having snuck up behind me. He didn't make a sound, because he couldn't. He had no mouth. I tried to hit him with the broom, but he was at a weird angle and I couldn't get leverage. Looking over my shoulder, I could taste the sulfur on his fingers as they covered my lips, just before I parted them and bit down hard. He slammed my head into the drywall as I screamed for Michael. A very angry Keeper rushing to help me was a powerful sight to behold.

He lifted the Lesson with one hand, crushing his throat with a sickening series of cracks and pops. "You chose to follow the wrong leader," Michael told him, calling his crows as he carried him out the back door, glass crunching beneath his boots. The crows carried the Lesson away and Michael strode to me, his hands feeling my body for damage. Up and down. Around. "Are you hurt?" he said frantically, his eyes wild.

Feral.

"I'm not hurt."

I was panting, my breaths fueled by adrenaline and his hands on my body. He finally began to relax his muscles, but didn't take his hands away from me.

"You could have been killed," he breathed against the column of my throat.

"I'm fine."

"You shouldn't try to defend me. It's my job to defend you."

"Am I your assignment?"

He didn't answer, just held me.

"Am I your assignment, Michael?"

"No," he admitted, tilting his head so that his lips hovered over mine.

"Good," I breathed. And then I waited, hoping he would lower his lips to…

And when he finally closed the distance, his breath hot on my lips, I thought the Lessons would be safer. Because Michael, the way his eyes swirled, the way his muscles rippled beneath the skin…he was far more of a threat.

I could lose my heart to him.

As soon as I thought the words, I felt the connection sever. He stepped away, raking hands through his hair.

"You can't. I can't." He liked that word. *Can't.*

I hated it.

Keeper retreated to his room, and then I heard the lock engage. If he thought I was a girl who gave up easily, he was mistaken.

CHAPTER THIRTEEN

I woke in the dingy gray bedroom with a headache that stabbed straight to the core of my brain. A single crow stood guard on the bedrail at my feet. He didn't make a sound except for shuffling his feet from one side to the other. I groaned and let my head fall back onto my pillow. No gray light filtered in through the disgustingly dirty window. The bitter taste of Hell lingered on my tongue.

Michael appeared at the doorway.

"I collected the manna this morning. Are you hungry?"

"What time is it?"

"Nearly sunset. We're about to have a visitor soon." I slept all day?

"Who?" I sat up and swung my legs to the side of the bed before I realized they were bare. "Uh, did you undress me?"

"You've slept without jeans on since coming here. I thought you'd be more comfortable. You fell asleep on the couch, so yes. You slept much of the day, but that's good. You needed it," he said, refusing to look me in the eyes. I decided to mess with him.

"You saw my ass again, didn't you?"

He smiled and shook his head. "I wasn't looking."

"Wasn't looking or wasn't interested?"

He grabbed hold of the top of the doorframe and blew out a harsh breath. "I can't be interested, Carmen. I shouldn't have let you believe otherwise. For that, I'm truly sorry."

"That's an interesting choice of words, Michael," I purred. "You said you *can't* be, not that you *aren't.*"

"Angels are forbidden from being intimate with humans, and I can't afford to be distracted."

"Am I human?"

He swallowed thickly. "I believe so, yes. But whatever you are, the answer is the same. Angels are forbidden from being intimate with souls, humans, other angels, with anything at all. Our sole purpose, the reason we were created, was to serve."

I wished he could serve me. I was frustrated as hell, and it wasn't because of the Lessons and their feeble attacks. It was because I was tantalizingly close to an Adonis all day long and had to endure looking at his beautiful face and physique. It was torturous, really. Maybe I was being taught a lesson of my own. Would someone squish tar onto my eyes if I kept ogling him? Maybe it would be a just sentence. I couldn't manage to tear them away from him.

I was so going to Hell.

He chuckled. "You aren't. And for the record, it's not easy for me either." He left with a wink and a grin, leaving me sitting on the bed, a frustrated, hot, flustered mess of a woman.

Closing my eyes, I pictured him returning to the room, shirtless, with his jeans hugging his hips, deliciously revealing the V I knew lurked beneath his clothes. I'd stand up from the bed and walk to him, waiting for his eyes to finish undressing me, and then I'd rub my hands over his chest, shoulders, back...pulling him close to me and our bodies would touch. They would ignite us both, a fire that had been smoldering beneath the surface, now fed with oxygen, sparking back to life, flames licking at both of us. I'd drop to my knees and unbutton his pants, unzip them inch by inch, and free him from the confining clothes he wore. I'd take him in my hand, stroking him, and then take him into the warmth of my mouth, drawing him in deep. He would groan and his thighs, hard as stone beneath my fingers, would tremble as I raked my nails over his skin, the skin that was like velvet.

His head would crane back as I brought him closer and closer to the brink...

"Carmen," a growl of warning came from downstairs. The pictures on the walls quivered in response and so did I.

I'd stand and pull the t-shirt over my head, letting it billow to the floor at our feet as he stepped from his pants. Guiding him to the bed, I'd watch as he fell back on the mattress and then I would climb up, straddle him, and rake my breasts all the way up his torso, reveling in the rumble that came from his chest. His eyes would turn every color under the heavens. Gold, silver, amethyst, emerald, sapphire, ruby… His tattoos would churn and I would sink down onto him, slowly, torturously…

"Carmen!" My eyes snapped open.

"Yes?" I asked throatily.

"Stop it. Our visitor is almost here. And he can also see and hear your…thoughts."

Damn it. I was so close, too. I eased my hands from my panties and sat up.

"Get dressed," Michael barked. He was cranky. If he'd let me help him with that, he'd be less of a grouch.

"Carmen?" a familiar voice called from downstairs. "I brought you a present."

Michael's deep growl reverberated through the floorboards underfoot as I rushed down the steps to see a writhing figure, clad in what used to be a three-thousand-dollar suit. It had been shredded to ribbons. When Gabriel picked the figure up by the back collar and turned him to face me, I almost peed a little. Gabriel had brought me a present, all right. Dimitri's icy eyes locked onto mine with laser precision before he began spewing Russian words I couldn't decipher, but understood anyway.

Michael took one look at me and his face contorted with anger. He grabbed me by the elbow and pulled me back up the stairs. I wrenched my arm away.

"What the hell is your problem?" I demanded.

"Pants, Carmen. Put some clothes on before coming back downstairs."

I looked down at my tan, bare legs and rolled my eyes at him. "I have nice legs, I'll have you know."

He stalked toward me, backing me up the stairs faster than I thought my feet could carry me. At the landing, my back hit the wall as he stalked forward. So close.

"I *do* know." His fingers slipped up the outside of my thigh and I gasped from the feel of him. Electric. "I know your body. Every curve, every bone, every hair on your head, and every shade in your eyes. I know you have nice legs, Carmen," he panted. "I just don't want *them* to know." He stabbed a finger toward my bedroom door.

I swallowed. "Fine. I'll get dressed."

"Fine," he growled.

After he slammed the door shut, I yelled, "Fine!" just for good measure. Michael struck me as someone who always had to have the last word, but I showed him.

I tugged the denim over my heels and shimmied it up over my hips, buttoning and then zipping, before making my way downstairs. I grinned at Gabriel, who beamed back at me.

"I trust you like your gift, Carmen?"

"I absolutely love it."

Dimitri began yelling again, angrily thrashing against Gabriel's steel grip. I eased toward him. Could I have a lightning leash, or maybe a whip made of the same? I'd teach Dimitri a lesson he'd never forget before frying his pathetic ass straight to Hell.

Gabriel inclined his head and suddenly Dimitri was sucked across the room, plastered against the wall, held by what I first thought was an invisible force. Then a familiar crackling sound filled my ears. Lightning.

It bolted across the skin of his neck, searing tender flesh and making Dimitri pant, puffs of air inflating and then deflating his cheeks rapidly. Two lightning cuffs forked across his ankles. His wide eyes watched as I approached.

"What do you want?" he panted in defiance of his restraints.

I stepped toward him, fingers clenching in rage. "Your head on a fucking pike would be a good start, Dimitri."

Michael pushed me aside. "You know Warren Kennedy?"

Dimitri laughed. "You figured it out, then? Your own father paid me to nearly kill you. 'Put her as close to death as you can, Dimitri, but do not cross that line,' he said."

"Why would you take orders from my father?" I spat.

"I am a businessman. He paid me enough to keep me comfortable for years."

Michael tore the shirt over his head, his tattoos angrily morphing all over him. Gabriel's eyes flashed dark before he did the same, revealing similar markings that ebbed and flowed, a furious, dangerous tide of dark ichor.

A loud snap came from behind Gabriel as his wings unfurled, hindered by the ceiling about us, each the gray-white color of a dove. They looked as though they emanated light, lit from within their hollows. I imagined Michael's wings, what they would have looked like; dark as the night and holding every color within. Powerful and menacing.

Dimitri's smug look disintegrated into terror. "What the hell is this?" he mumbled.

Gabriel looked menacing, despite having seemed so nice when I first met him. Michael would have been even more terrifying with wings. Maybe that was why he didn't have them anymore. I couldn't help but take a step back from the furious angels. Rage rippled through their muscles, and for a fraction of a second, I was afraid, afraid for myself and afraid for Dimitri. However, the worry for him faded as quickly as it began when I thought of the dark car pulling up in front of the gate after the taillights from the cab I rode home in faded in the distance. Of the deeply tinted window rolling down, and the feeling of knowing what would come next. Dimitri didn't visit people in the hospital—or rehab—out of the goodness of his heart. *Get in the car...*

Something passed between the two angels, and then Michael turned to Gabriel. "Show me."

Gabriel sneered at Dimitri and grabbed Michael's temples before lowering his head. Michael stared, unfocused, at the wall above his friend's curly hair. He was seeing something, his eyes darting back and forth angrily as he took in the scene Gabriel laid out. A low growl began deep in the hollow of his chest, and soon Michael couldn't contain it anymore. He let out a howl that was so loud, I had to cover my ears. And then the archangel unleashed all hell on Dimitri.

Bones cracked. Skin split and tore. Bruises blossomed. Blood oozed.

"Let him down," he panted to Gabriel when he finished his initial assault.

Dimitri fell into a bloody heap on the floor, his face unrecognizable. He tried to push himself up, but Michael kicked him to the floor. Blood drizzled from Dimitri's mouth and nose.

"I saw what you did to her—what you let them do to her. You will spend an eternity regretting every second of it. Do you hear me?"

A groan fell from Dimitri's mouth as he collapsed, blood falling in threads to the floor below. Michael turned to Gabriel, looking as if he'd just gone for a light jog instead of having beat a man to a pulp. "Make him a triple."

"A triple? Do you have authority for that?" Gabriel asked, confused.

"I just said make him a triple."

With one last glance at Michael, Gabriel knelt by Dimitri, rolling his body over. Only the subtle rise and fall of Dimitri's chest indicated he was alive. Gabriel covered Dimitri's eyes, speaking in the language Michael used, and then he covered Dimitri's ears. Black tar filled both sets of cavities. He laid a hand over Dimitri's mouth and it sealed, a thin layer of skin immediately growing over his lips.

See no evil.

Hear no evil.

Speak no evil.

A triple.

I just hoped it prevented him from *doing* evil.

Dimitri deserved to be a triple, but my heart ached for Michael. Would he get in trouble for doing what he did? He did it to avenge me.

"I did it because that man," he angrily pointed to Dimitri, "deserves to burn, but I want him to suffer first." Michael just did the same thing he hated the demons for doing, and he did it for me. I just hoped this wouldn't eat away at him and somehow turn him against me. But whatever he saw, it was worse than what I remembered. The kicks and punches, I felt them, saw them coming and had no way to defend myself against them – but what else was there?

"What did you see?" I asked, brows knitted together.

Michael shook his head, a crystalline tear falling from one of his eyes. "You have so many things working against you, Carmen. That is one burden I will bear for you." He was crying. For me. The archangel wept with a silent strength I didn't understand.

Gabriel eased Dimitri from the floor and carried him outside, but I couldn't look away from the clear, wet streaks running down Michael's cheek.

Did angels often cry?

"Sometimes," he answered, a matching tear falling on the other side.

"I'm sorry," I whispered, stepping to him and wiping his face.

"You have no reason to be," he whispered back. And then I did something monumentally stupid. I stepped up on my tippy toes and placed a soft kiss on his lips.

His eyes darkened to a rich toffee and then he smashed his lips onto mine, claiming them with the same intensity that he radiated from morning to night. Nipping and tugging, licking and breathing into me an intoxicating flavor I wasn't sure I ever wanted to stop tasting. My fingers pulled him closer and closer until there was too much space between us and my lips were left aching and swollen from the sweet assault.

With a shove, he pushed me away from him and began pacing.

He pointed his finger at me. "You're not supposed to kiss me," his voice broke as he pinched his bottom lip.

"But—"

His face turned to stone. So did his voice. "Never again, Carmen."

Gabriel stood at the back door, watching with his mouth agape as Michael stomped around him and disappeared outside.

"Did I hurt him?" I asked Gabriel when I was sure Michael was out of earshot.

"Not physically, no, but you can't treat him like a human man. He isn't one. And if he and you were to... Well, he would no longer be an archangel."

I let out a frustrated noise and threw my hands in the air. "Why is everything so either or, black and white, with no shades of gray in this fucking gray world?" I said, swiping tears of frustration from my eyes.

Gabriel sighed. "I'm not sure."

CHAPTER

FOURTEEN

I didn't tell Michael about my new nightmare, but since he could read my thoughts, he probably knew about it anyway. Dimitri was in my father's pocket on Earth. Father paid him to nearly kill me, he'd said. But now that he was a Lesson, Dimitri could be controlled and manipulated by my father here in Purgatory. He was a triple, and that made him a triple threat.

Gabriel stared out the back door, as if waiting for someone or something. It was morning and the manna would fall anytime now. Michael had come back at some point, because I heard him speaking with Gabriel in the language of the angels. Their discussion got heated, and then he left again.

"Why are we here?" I asked him.

Gabriel turned, leaned back against the wall beside the door, and crossed his arms over his chest. "Philosophically?"

I laughed slightly. "I should rephrase. Why are we hiding out in this house? You're an archangel. Michael is an archangel who controls an entire legion of crows. Why aren't we storming the city, righting wrongs, and kicking my father's ass?"

"It isn't that simple, Carmen."

"Isn't it? Isn't it that simple? Why make it any more complicated than it has to be?"

He sighed. "We are given orders, and we don't resort to vigilantism—unless we're told to."

Oh, really? I thought. Perhaps he didn't understand the concept of vigilantism. Vigilantes don't take orders; they act. Like Michael did when he punished Dimitri.

"What do you call making Dimitri a triple, then?"

Gabriel's lips thinned into tight lines of flesh.

I had him, and he knew it.

"Are you always this bold in your thoughts? What happened to women being meek?"

"A thousand or so years," I answered.

"We've been told to keep you in the outskirts, but maybe a new safe house is in order." It might have been the shattered front and balcony doors, or maybe Dimitri's blood staining the floor beside the tar of the Lessons, but this house certainly didn't look safe anymore. "You shouldn't have contact of any kind with Malchazze."

"I don't want to have contact with him."

Gabriel pushed off the wall, dropping his fists to his side. "We will deal with your father when we're given instructions, or if he attacks first. Believe me, nothing

144

would bring me greater pleasure than to end him slowly and send him to the demons he uses to do his dirty work. They would enjoy his torment, as well."

"How is he so powerful?"

Gabriel closed his eyes. "Crossers were never supposed to exist. The threshold wasn't meant to be breached by a soul. When the veil tore and the barrier was compromised, we worked feverishly to mend it and round up those who had escaped into the earthen realm. But there was a problem we never anticipated. Those who breached were endowed with the power to create fissures and cross back and forth along the divide as they pleased. Your father took it one step further. He began to build a following here. His powers to control the Lessons are recently acquired ones, but he is more dangerous now than he ever has been."

"He's trying to establish an empire on Earth, too." I thought of his fake smile, caked-on orange make-up, and his jubilant face as it waved to hungry crowds, starving for his lies.

"Are there more of him? You said *those* who breached…"

Gabriel blew out a breath. "Malchazze is the only crosser still in existence, but only because he killed the others so they didn't interfere with his plans to create a kingdom. However, he has infused some souls with the power to cross when fissures naturally occur."

"The merchants?"

Gabriel nodded. "The only catch is that those he infuses have to wait for naturally-occurring fissures, or for him to make one for them. So far he hasn't been able to make more crossers, but it may just be a matter of time.

Some suspect he is part of the veil, which until you came here, I thought was only a myth."

My mind flicked back to Gus and Chester. Why would anyone want to give them power to cross the barrier of Purgatory? My father sure did, possibly because they were weak and would follow orders. That had to be it.

"But I'm different. I can't leave. I can't cross the divide. The veil won't let me. So that means he can't be part of the veil."

"I'm not sure how it works for him," Gabriel admitted.

"Do you know why I'm bound here?"

Shaking his head, he pursed his lips. "I honestly don't know."

If Gabriel didn't know and neither did Michael, that meant the only one who did know was my father, and I doubted he would offer up the knowledge out of the kindness of his black heart. If Malchazze was using a body, the body of my natural father, it wasn't genetic. Maybe it was some sort of karma at work. Maybe I wasn't able to leave simply because he could.

An electric jolt ran through my body and I grabbed the nearest wall to steady myself. "What was that?" I looked overhead. Could earthquakes happen here? I half expected the second floor to crash down on top of us.

"You felt that?" Gabriel strode to me and grabbed my elbows, forcing me to look at him.

"Of course I did," I stammered, glancing between his darkening eyes and the ceiling. "What was it?"

"That," he began, "was a shudder. A crosser—your father—just left or returned to Purgatory."

A cacophony of crows heralded Michael's arrival. He ran through the back yard toward us, a dark angel who looked more vengeful than merciful.

I let my eyes unfocus, a scene unfolding in my mind. Would Michael kill me? Would he have to? Was I some sort of evil abomination? Malchazze's seed might not have made me, but his parenting skills molded me in ways I couldn't even begin to imagine. Would nature or nurture win out?

I could see him running toward me, manna and feathers falling all around us. He would unsheathe his sword and swing it at me with a precision I could neither escape nor run from. Michael would dispatch me with the same ease as he had with the merchants who dragged me into this hell. My soul would be eaten by his crows and he would blow the ashes of my gray body away with his breath.

Hands were shaking me when the scene vanished. I gasped as Michael shouted, "What's wrong? Carmen? What's the matter?"

His eyes were orange, like pumpkins on a fall day.

"I'm okay," I rasped, pulling away from him. *For now*, I thought.

"What happened to her?" he shouted at Gabriel.

Gabriel did not respond right away, only shook his head slowly. "She felt the shudder."

Michael growled and began pacing the floor. "She feels everything, she knows before I do that a fissure is going to occur, and she can split the veil! She can *make* them. Did you know that?"

Gabriel's mouth gaped open. "I did not."

"She *is* the veil," Michael whispered.

But he was wrong. "I'm not. I'm not the veil. I'm a drug addicted rich kid from Beverly Hills who was pulled into this fucking place by two assholes with lightning leashes. I didn't ask for any of this shit!" I screamed.

"Your father orchestrated it all. I doubt he knew you could or would rip the veil itself, though."

Gabriel agreed with Michael. "He couldn't have anticipated that little twist." His lips curved up in a mixture of amusement and pity. I didn't need either.

"What do I do? Michael?" He stopped pacing and stared at me, but said nothing, offered no solution. "Gabriel? What am I supposed to do?"

A crow landed on Michael's shoulder and cawed loudly, and then it flew and perched on my shoulder. My body was stiff as a board. Would the bird peck at my eyes if I moved?

Michael looked quickly to Gabriel and shouted something in the language they shared. I couldn't understand them, but Gabriel quickly walked away, up the invisible steps and out of Purgatory.

The crow took flight, disappearing along with Gabriel.

"He explained more about your father?" Michael asked.

"Some, but I still don't understand how he has the power to establish an empire here. Just because he can walk between worlds, how does he have influence over Lessons?"

Michael closed his eyes. "Because he sides with Satan. Carmen, your father isn't just a crosser or a soul. He is the antichrist."

My heart hurt just hearing the word, because my heart knew it was true. It felt it. I sank to the floor, held my knees, and rocked. Michael didn't try to comfort me because there was no comfort to be had. He didn't touch me because it was too dangerous. But he stayed in the room. He waited until all my tears were gone, until I was spent and ready to rest. Again.

CHAPTER

FIFTEEN

The crows began cawing outside, becoming more frantic as they swirled, darted, and dove toward the ground. "We have to leave this place," Michael said.

"More Lessons?" I didn't have the mental strength to deal with them yet.

"No, a bigger threat."

I instinctively knew who he meant. My father ruined everything he touched. He was a poison; a cancerous tumor, whose tentacles were strong and far-reaching. They twisted and grazed and took root where they didn't belong. He was ruining the world on Earth, and if elected, would have more opportunity to wreak havoc. He was ruining souls here. He had probably trapped the soul of my real father in order to steal his body. Malchazze had to be stopped. And if the archangels wouldn't stop him...

"I would," Michael answered my thoughts sincerely. "And when given the order, I will, Carmen. I promise you that."

Michael's words were a vow, but it was only as good as the possibility that it might actually happen. If he never got the order, he wouldn't do anything other than stop merchants and guard fissures.

"Your promise means nothing. You may never get the order. I can't rely on maybe, Michael."

Dimitri's tar-filled face floated through my mind. *He did it for me. He broke the rules, making him a triple. He kissed me...*

Michael walked to the front door, flinging it open, the handle embedding into the siding of the house. He could've just stepped through the empty metal frame. "We need to move. Malchazze is searching for you himself."

I shivered. "How do you know?"

The crows cawed as one; a flying security system.

"Oh. Okay. I need to find some shoes."

I found a pair of boots yesterday and had placed them beside the door, on top of the shards of glass. I pulled them on and stomped after him. He led me through yards and into the forest, but I didn't make it far before my body started to tire. Michael growled when it was clear I couldn't keep up. As hot as he was, he was impatient and it was wearing on me, just as each step made my body more tired.

"The crows will carry you," he said simply.

I threw my hands up. "I don't *want* them to carry me. I want to walk at my own pace. I want my body to fucking work!" A hot tear fell from my left eye.

Michael was before me in an instant. "Your body will work when it heals. Until then, Carmen, please let me help you. Let the crows help you."

I turned so he didn't see me cry, although he could hear it. Hell, he could probably smell my tears, but he wouldn't see them. "Fine."

Suddenly in front of me, he brushed the tear from my cheek. "Don't cry."

"Why does it even matter?" my voice shuddered.

"It breaks my heart," he said softly, running his fingers through the short strands of my hair. "I care for you, and I can't bear to see you so upset. I need to make sure you're safe, and right now, safe is far away from here. My crows can carry you. Just think of them as an extension of me. They are my wings."

I sniffed and did my best to keep my hands plastered to my sides, despite the fact that I wanted to touch him, to hug him and pull him tightly against me. I knew it would hurt him, and hurting him was the last thing I wanted to do at the moment.

Some moments with Michael were tender and heartfelt. Others, he was angry and frustrated at me. I wanted to curl up in this gentle moment and stay. It would make Purgatory much more comfortable. However, this place wasn't meant for comfort, not anymore, so we had to go. I could see it in his eyes. He wanted to tell me, but didn't want to push. I opened my mouth first.

"Let them help me."

Within seconds, I was surrounded by a murder so large in number, they encapsulated me within their swirling mass and carried me quickly through the forest, setting me gently down on a rocky outcrop near an angry, frothing river of silver water.

Michael was quiet for several long moments. When he broke his silence, his words sliced me in two. "Thank you for trusting me, and for allowing them to help you."

"I let *you* help me, Michael."

He smiled sadly. "I know."

"Why does this have to be so hard? Why does everything have to be so complicated?"

"Is it not the same on Earth?"

"Oh, no. It's completely complicated there, but this is on a completely different level."

He smiled. "Because of your father or because of me?"

"Because of him. Because of you and how... and how I feel about you. How can I feel anything? That's the part that's so confusing. I've known lust. This isn't it."

"What's between us is infused; lust threaded with passion, but it isn't only passion. Those emotions fizzle and burn out as fast as they ignite. They burn brightly for a moment, but that moment is all there is."

"I want more than just a moment with you," I admitted.

He cursed and chucked a stone into the river. It sank along with my heart. "I wish for the same, but I can't give you more than what I am. I hope you can understand."

Of course, I could understand. He didn't want to go to Hell, and I didn't want him to go to Hell or be placed in harm's way just because I'd developed feelings for him. This was a stressful situation. Emotions were high. That was all this was. *If I could go home, I might forget him*, I told myself, but my heart knew it was a lie. My brain knew it was a lie, but I had to tell it anyway.

He changed the subject to a much graver one. "Your mother is here."

I choked on the air in this place. "Where?"

"In the city. I went to find her. That's where I was."

"She isn't with him. Please tell me she isn't with my father."

He shook his head. "She isn't."

"Good."

"But she isn't in a good place, either."

"Can I see her?" I asked, hoping for a small sliver of brightness.

"Not yet."

Not yet. Of course, not yet. What did it all mean? The angrier I became, the more the veil just beyond my fingertips began to shimmer. Its oily texture thickened until I reached out for it, sticking my finger inside again. Then, an epiphany.

"Can I make it stronger? What if I could seal it for good?" I mumbled.

"We've tried."

"As amazing as you are, you don't have a piece of it inside you, archangel."

He smirked. "I've gone from Keeper, to Michael, and now you refer to me as archangel, as if it's an insult to be such a thing."

I stared at the veil. "Maybe it is. Are archangels the highest-ranking angels?" He was quiet, his fists clenching. That was what I thought. "Look, maybe the veil just needs to be solidified. Before it tore, it was strong. Nothing could cross the barrier then, right?"

"Right," he conceded for a moment before opening his fat mouth. "But, Carmen, it's been stretched too thin for too long. There is no repairing it beyond what has already been done."

"Says you."

He began pacing, hands on his hips where I knew the delicious V of his abdomen was hiding, lying in wait. The man was sin incarnate, a forbidden fruit dangling in front of womankind. He was the ultimate temptation.

"Stop thinking such things about me!" he shouted, raking his hands through his hair. "You are the most frustrating creature I've ever encountered. You think about my body incessantly!"

"Thank you," I answered smugly. "But in my defense, it's a magnificent body."

"It wasn't meant as a compliment."

"I took it as one just the same."

Michael growled, lyrically instructing one of his fowl friends and sending it from his finger into the air. It returned a moment later with his message. That was fast.

"We can't ever be anything to one another. Don't you get it?"

"I do," I said calmly, counteracting his anger. I completely got it. I finally felt something positive, and it was forbidden. Story of my life.

Another earthquake, the hair on my arms standing on end until the ground underfoot stopped shaking. I clung to a rock, waiting for an aftershock.

"What are you doing?" Michael asked, his head tilted to the side.

"Making sure I hold onto something. I'm not used to this."

"That was a shudder. It's not a real quake."

I scoffed. "It feels real enough to me." My God, I sounded like Pamela. I wondered if she had woken up at the hospital, had a miraculous recovery, and was now spending as much time with her two kids and husband as was humanly possible. I wondered if she remembered this. Me. Any of it.

"She probably will. She may even remember you."

I raked my hands down the legs of my jeans. "You had her feeling all happy. She probably thinks the medicine made her have strange dreams of hot guys and crows and some hella-crazy bitch who laughed through it all."

He smiled. "Maybe."

Something occurred to me in that moment. "My father can use the Lessons. Can he use me?"

Michael stilled. "We aren't sure."

"You aren't sure. When will we know?"

"If you come into contact with him, but we don't want that to happen."

"How big is Purgatory?"

His brows kissed one another. "Why?"

"We've been running around the homes in the outskirts, through this gnarled forest, and along cliffs that are taller than sky scrapers. We've seen rivers that run silver and carve through valleys, and canyons that are bigger than the Rio Grande. I can't help but wonder what else is out there, or if anything is. Does Purgatory just end? Will we eventually wind up in the city no matter which direction we go? How much longer can we run? He's coming, and eventually he'll find me, Michael. We can't keep this up. I can't keep up."

"We run until there is no other choice, Carmen, and then we keep running. But yes, eventually everything leads back into the city of Purgatory. We must stay one step ahead."

I didn't want to tell him that I was no runner. My body was torn. My soul was tired. I needed to rest for the fight that was coming swiftly.

"I know," he replied to my thoughts. "You can rest now. I will watch over you."

"I'm glad someone is," I said on a yawn, my body shutting down even though I didn't want it to tap out just yet.

A deep, dark abyss awaited behind the lids of my eyes. I sank into its warmth and slept, dreaming that Michael folded me into his arms, holding me against him until I woke.

CHAPTER SIXTEEN

"Carmen?" a far-away voice whispered. It sounded like Gabriel. "Don't give up. You must breathe."

My chest felt heavy, like a boulder was crushing me.

I couldn't lift my arms.

Beeping.

Female and male voices shouting things I couldn't understand.

I felt a thumb swipe my hair. "Breathe," he whispered. "You have to take a breath."

Finally, my chest expanded. "Good girl." Another swipe across my hair. "Keep breathing. You'll be fine in a few minutes. I got here in time."

Soft, warm lips pressed against my temple. A thumb caressed my hair.

CHAPTER

SEVENTEEN

When I woke, I felt like a semi had crashed into me, I stayed plastered to the grill of the giant truck for fifty or so miles, and then slid onto the pavement where all eighteen tires rolled over my body. Thump. Thump. Thump… I hurt everywhere.

"Don't move," Keeper grumped. Keeper was in a bad mood and so was I. Then he smirked. "I thought I was 'archangel' now."

"You're whatever my mind can conjure at the moment. Deal with it." I was lying on my back, staring at the light gray clouds in the darker gray sky, watching the feathers gently rain down from the heavens. If the veil was so close, how were the birds able to fly up there?

"They're magical," he teased.

"Is that a smile I hear?" I hadn't seen his teeth in far too long, not since he graced Pamela with the mega-watt pearly whites. But I kept my gaze on the sky because if I saw that sight, I'd melt into a puddle of goo. My body wouldn't be able to hold its form. I was sure of it.

"Gabriel should be back soon. He sent word that he's on his way."

"Does he always have to check in with you? Is that a Keeper power trip, or is he just being polite?"

Michael chuckled. Damn that sound.

"I heard him when I was sleeping."

"Heard who?" I could almost feel Michael tense at my words.

"Gabriel. He kept telling me to breathe and said he'd gotten there in time, or something like that. Was he here?"

Michael was quiet, so I finally turned my head to look at him. Every muscle in his body was rigid. "No."

"What is it?"

"Gabriel has some explaining to do." He pushed up off the rock he was perched on and began to pace again, muttering beautiful, angelic curses, or so it sounded.

Gabriel, true to his word, stepped down from the sky. He looked like he belonged to it, or it to him. I wasn't sure which.

He smiled broadly when he saw me blink. "You're awake."

"Sort of," I deadpanned.

"You're alive."

"That's arguable," was my reply.

He crouched down beside me. He was wearing khakis and a polo shirt, the top two buttons undone. The fabric was bright yellow and his skin shone like he'd been near the equator for a few weeks, basking in the sun's rays and daring skin cancer to mess with his hotness. His eyes flashed royal purple. Apparently, Gabriel liked compliments.

"She heard you," Michael said, as Gabriel watched him walk back and forth along the rocks on the river bank. The sounds of the water crashing on and around the rocks was somehow comforting.

"Heard me what?" Gabriel asked, his smile falling away.

"You were telling her to breathe. What exactly happened to her?"

Gabriel stood up and shoved his hands in his pockets. I wanted to sit up and be a part of the conversation, but I needed help to do so. I attempted to lift my head, but found it was far too heavy. I'd need lots of help.

Michael came toward me and gathered me in his arms, sat on a rock, and helped me sit up. On his lap. I should be tired much more often.

He smiled for a moment.

Gabriel didn't. His facial features hardened. "The shudder you felt yesterday, Carmen, was your father crossing the divide. I followed him to work and at first it seemed like business as usual, so I let my guard down. He took the opportunity while I wasn't watching and made his move. I didn't locate him fast enough, and he found you in the hospital."

Michael's grip on me tightened. "What did he do?"

Gabriel looked ashamed when he told me, "He turned off your IV and the ventilator, but when he saw me at the door, he disappeared. I thought he'd crossed again, but—"

"He did. We felt the shudder from here," Michael told him. "He's getting desperate. If he ends her earthly life, she'll be stuck here for a time. He obviously doesn't know she *can't* leave. That's both a blessing and a curse, but he won't stop. He wants her and he'll stop at nothing until he has her. He's waiting for us to slip up, to make a mistake so he can take her away."

"My mother," I gasped, squirming. Michael held me still. "He's going to go after her. He knows I love her more than almost anything in the world."

"You found her mother?" Gabriel asked, eyes wide. "Why didn't you tell me?"

"It wasn't the time," Michael said cryptically.

"We need to seek her out and bring her here where she can be safe," Gabriel asserted.

"I agree," I told them. Gabriel nodded, acknowledging my concerns.

"It's not that simple," Michael hedged.

"Where is she?" Gabriel asked, his eyes turning molten.

"The Meat Market. She's a slave," Michael answered, but he wouldn't look at me. He stared at Gabriel, the muscle ticking in his jaw.

"What kind of slave?" I whispered.

All of a sudden I couldn't breathe again. Something was wrong – on Earth – with my body.

"Nothing is wrong," he whispered, grazing my forehead with the stubble on his chin. Manna began to rain down around us, dropping softly onto the rocks and flowing down the river. It bounced off tree branches and onto the ground. The crows feasted.

There was something wrong. I couldn't breathe.

"You can. I know you're upset, but I vow that I will release your mother from this servitude." He looked meaningfully at Gabriel. "I need you to guard her with your life." Michael eased me off his lap and onto the cold, gritty rock beneath it.

Gabriel inclined his head. The two spoke in angel, their voices and facial features hardening into stone in an instant. Just like that, Michael clucked his tongue and the crows flew in circles around him, whisking him into the air and away from us in an instant.

My stomach roiled as I watched him disappear into the leafy canopy. "Will he be okay?"

"In the city? Yes. And your mother will be fine as soon as he convinces her owner to free her."

"What's he going to have to do to convince them?"

"Anything necessary," he said.

Tears filled with aggravation and helplessness fell from my eyes. I couldn't stem the flow.

"I hate to see you cry," Gabriel said softly as he watched me, unblinking.

"They're hurting her. She's being used. Her soul, her body. My father hated her so much that she ended up taking her life to get away from him, but that wasn't enough for him. He sent her here and threw her to the wolves, and now they're tearing her apart." I let out a frustrated scream, clenching my fists. If my father was standing in front of me right now, I'd beat him to a pulp; just like he sent his puppets to beat me. Fast. Frenzied. Unmerciful.

My poor mother died a slow, agonizing death that started long before she decided to finally escape him. Most people thought she was troubled or selfish for taking her life, but I thought she was brave as hell. She knew there was no way out, no way she could possibly escape him, and so she gave him no say in the matter. She went out her own way. I only wished that she'd taken me with her. Just driven off a cliff or something. I swiped my eyes.

"Don't wish for death, Carmen."

"I can't help it. Maybe it's the situation, or maybe it's the God-awful gray of this place, but it's seeping into me. Slow like poison, but just as deadly." I stared at my arms, still tan and freckled. No gray to be seen on me… Yet.

Gabriel stared at the sky. "Michael will make them all pay."

"The way he did Dimitri?" The scene flashed through my mind, brilliant and bloody.

"Yes."

I tried to smile. "Good."

I hoped they all died. I hoped his crows sent sharp feathers into them all, or pecked their eyes out, making them Lessons, swooping their bodies to the outskirts. Maybe Keeper would strangle or beat them. No matter how it happened, I hoped the ones who hurt my mother suffered. I hoped for a second, for a minute or an hour, Michael made them feel her pain, even just an ounce of it. Those cowards would be crushed under the weight of the burdens they made her bear. They needed to feel it.

"Can Michael hear me now?"

He shook his head. "Only when he is near."

I didn't want him to hear what I was thinking about those bastards. He might do something we'd both regret. Besides, I wanted my chance at them. Alone.

Gabriel swallowed. "You are fearless."

"I'm really not."

He nodded slowly. "Do you plan to confront your father?"

"As soon as I'm able, but I can't do anything as long as walking across a few yards makes me so tired, my legs can't hold my body up."

"Healing will take some time."

I picked at my cuticle. "I don't have the luxury of time, Gabriel. I need help." I wondered if he would have the same reaction Michael did about my solution for the veil...

"What about it?" he asked.

"What if I was able to strengthen or harden it?"

He shook his head and began giving me the same story Michael did. It was as strong as any angel could make it, and I was certainly no angel. But the veil was a part of me now. What if I could trap my father in Purgatory, ensuring he wouldn't be able to cross the divide and crush anyone else with his depravity?

Gabriel crossed his arms over his chest, standing and looking out at the churning, colorless water. "Michael would never agree to let you try."

"I know."

"You'd have to be certain that your father was here, contained in this realm."

"I know that, too."

He sighed. "You'd also have to make sure that everyone else who doesn't belong here is out of the realm." His eyes turned a bright green, like the first leaves of spring.

"Can I block my thoughts from him?" I asked, curious.

"From your father or from Michael?"

"Both."

Gabriel blew out a slow breath, his cheeks inflating dramatically. "Michael is going to be angry, but there is a way." He reached to the ground beneath him and found a small pebble. If pebbles were going to keep me from revealing my thoughts, I'd fill my pockets with them.

He smiled and held the stone with both hands, cupping them to form a cavern. He muttered some unintelligible words, and then blew into the hole toward the rock. When Gabriel opened his hands, the stone was white, sparkling like the veil's pale opposite. The rock changed shape, its borders expanding and receding slightly. "Angel stone," he announced, holding the stone out for me to hold.

"What exactly do I do with this... rock?"

"Keep it on your person. If you wish to block your thoughts, simply rub it. Keep contact with it while blocking, and let go when you are okay with the angel hearing you. It's that simple."

"It seems too good to be true, and in the earthen realm, that's usually the case, Gabriel."

"You don't trust me?" He clasped his chest as though hurt. "But I'm an angel!"

"You're also male, so my trust is something you'll have to earn. With the exception of Michael, every man I've dealt with recently has tried to kill me, or worse."

Gabriel kicked the pebbles underfoot. "There is something else I can do to help. Michael doesn't know I can do it, though."

"What?"

"I can strengthen you."

Adrenaline coursed through me. "Do it. Do it right now."

"I can't make you completely whole, but I can help bolster your recovery time."

"I want you to help me," I begged. "Please, Gabriel. I'm worthless in the shape I'm in. I wouldn't stand a chance—against a Lesson or Malchazze."

He looked guiltily at me. "Michael would not approve."

"Michael doesn't want me to approach him. If I'm weak, he knows he can keep me from my father, but Father isn't one who likes to be told no, Gabriel, and I can't face him like this. He'll hurt me, and I won't be able to fight back."

Gabriel grabbed my hand. "Do not breathe a word of this to Michael."

"I won't," I promised.

He opened his mouth and I heard his angelic words, the lilting rise and fall of them. I felt my body mending, the skin repairing itself, the bruises fading, the bones... I felt amazing.

Gabriel stepped back from me, releasing my hand. "That is all I can do."

"Thank you."

"Thank me by being strong enough to stop your father."

"I'm going to try my best." When I threw my arms around his neck, he let me hug him. He didn't flinch or tell me I couldn't touch him; he just stroked my back like he'd done it a thousand times before. For one, blissful moment, I felt comfortable and calm.

CHAPTER EIGHTEEN

Clutching the Angel stone in my pocket, I thought about the veil. It was liquid, but I needed it to be impenetrable as stone and strong as titanium. Gabriel busied himself while gathering manna for us both. If I went through with this, Father would have to be here—in Purgatory. Gabriel would have to leave. And Michael... I couldn't trap him here forever, so I had to figure out a way to make him cross over. Would he leave without orders to do so? Could I force him to? He was in danger. Gus and Chester had mentioned that there were plans to take Keeper out. My father was going to kill him if the isolation of this place didn't.

Do I want him to go? The answer was no, but I didn't want him sealed here, either.

The change in the veil, if I could manage to do it at all, would likely be permanent. For me, for Father, for all of us.

"If I could seal the veil, could souls still pass over?"

Gabriel shrugged. "I would think so, but I'm not sure. Assuming you could repair what's been damaged, perhaps you could also make a way for it to work the way it was intended to, or at the very least, make it passable only from Earth to Purgatory—a one-way ticket with no return flights." He smiled.

I let go of the stone when he handed me a handful of puffy white goodness.

Did angels fly commercially?

He laughed heartily. "I have once before. Recently."

"Why would you need to fly on a plane?"

"It depends on the assignment. For a few weeks, I was charged with guarding an important dignitary. His life had been threatened."

"By a human?" I asked.

He shook his head. "No, a powerful demon in the hierarchy of things. He wanted to sway an election by removing one of the persons running for office. We typically don't interfere with the lives of humans because of their inherent free will, but we also don't allow demons, or crossers, to manipulate people or politics on Earth. They would manipulate everything if they could. Demons would love to make Earth a veritable Hell for the living."

"Give 'em an inch, they'll take a mile?"

He sat down on the rock beside me. "Exactly."

"You must be busy all the time. Is there something you should be doing right now? An assignment you're missing or slacking on because of me?"

He popped a piece of manna in his mouth and chewed. "Not at the moment. Right now, it seems Michael needs me, and that is my current assignment—to help him in any way I can."

I had to know... "Will he ever be able to leave this place?"

Gabriel's eyes turned the saddest deep blue I'd ever seen, and I got my answer in the form of that weary indigo. "Not without orders."

"Can you ask for new orders for him? Do you have a superior, or can you plead on his behalf?"

Gabriel stopped chewing and swallowed. His mouth opened as if he wanted to speak, but couldn't find the words. "You care for him."

My face heated at the words. "I do," I answered sincerely. "I know I'm not supposed to, but I also think it's wrong that he's stuck here and has been for so long."

"It hasn't been very long, Carmen. Not in the great sense of time. We've been alive since before the creation of the universe. We will live forever, unless the Creator decides otherwise."

"Has the Creator ever done that? Has he ever killed an angel?" A shiver crawled up my spine.

"Lucifer lives," was his response.

My palm was sweating around the Angel stone, so I released it into my pocket. I didn't want Michael to get in trouble for my stupid feelings. They were unreliable at best. But I did care that he was here, that he'd lost his wings and gained a murder of crows. He'd done nothing but help me, avenge me, and keep me safe. He was trying to save my mother this very moment. It was hard not to be attracted to someone who would do that, and who looked the way he did.

Gabriel chuckled beneath his breath. "I do the same thing. I save souls every day, but you don't look at me the same way."

"I know."

He smiled and handed me more manna. Mine had already disappeared into my belly. It was delicious. Don't judge.

"You know you and he can never be, right?"

"Yeah, I know." My heart sank. Boy, did I ever know. I mean, what girl fell in lust with an archangel?

"Lust?" Gabriel questioned.

"Definitely lust."

"Are you certain it isn't love? Love looks different when she first shows her face, from what I've seen. Humans are blessed with the ability to love, but angels can't experience it, Carmen," he said pointedly.

I chewed my manna, hoping Michael was safe, that his crows were going all gangsta, and that my mother would be returned safely to me and finally get some peace. Love? I wouldn't know anything about it. No one had ever thought I was worthy of it. I'd seen plenty of lust, though.

Gabriel's hand stilled on mine. "I have news of your mother. She is safe, but you will only get to see her for a moment," he said, standing and pulling me up.

"Why? Why only a moment?"

He looked to the sky, searching the gray for something that contrasted. I did the same. A few seconds later, a swirl of birds appeared, traveling quickly toward us.

The crows brought Mom straight to me. Her make-up was heavy and exaggerated, and though it was colorless, it was dark and trashy and nothing my mother would have worn. Her clothes consisted of what looked like a pillowcase with holes at the arms. It was dingy and bore the stains of her imprisonment and mistreatment. I rushed to her, steadying her as she held her head in her hands. "Mom? Are you okay?" Tears rushed down my cheeks.

She raised her head, her big brown eyes locking onto mine. "Carmen?"

"Yes, Mom, it's me. Are you okay?" I repeated.

"I don't understand." She looked around us, bewildered. The river. The trees. The rocks and pebbles beneath her feet. Mom looked at Gabriel and then at the crows, now roosting in the treetops just beyond us.

"I know. It's hard for me to understand, too."

She hugged my neck and I squeezed her with all the strength I had, holding her as she sobbed.

"He said I have to leave now," she said in a tear-soaked voice.

"Who?" I looked over her shoulder at Gabriel. "Where are you taking her?"

"I love you, Carmen. I'm so sorry that he clouded that love for you, and that I let him."

I held tightly to her, clutching her dark brown hair in my hands. She couldn't leave if I didn't let go. She cried against my shoulder.

"I'll miss you so much. Please remember to follow your heart. You're the strongest and the only one who can stop him," she whispered. With that, she straightened, pulling away from me and taking a step backwards, wiping her tears. She looked ten years older than the last time I saw her when she was still alive, still walking the hallway, searching for more liquor to ease the pain that creased her face. But she was herself, her *old* self, before Malchazze and addiction took the light from her eyes. The light was back. I couldn't stop staring at it.

When Mom placed her hand in Gabriel's, he looked at me sadly.

"Mom?"

I could see the apology all over his face, but still didn't understand what was happening.

"Wait, can't we have more time?" I yelled to Gabriel.

He turned away from me slowly and led her forward, and then he took a step upward into the air. She followed.

"Mom, stay! Just for a few more minutes. Please!"

She turned to look at me, the light in her eyes clouded with tears. Blurry, but still visible.

"Please let her stay!" I begged. "Gabriel, please?"

Step by step, they ascended until they disappeared entirely.

"Mom!"

I collapsed onto the rocks, flinging an angry handful into the churning water. *Why did she leave? Where did she have to go? Why didn't we have more time?*

Michael's hand found my shoulder. He crouched behind me soundlessly and then sat down with me.

"I know it may not make sense to you right now, but she has been saved. I pleaded for her to be granted entrance into Heaven."

My eyes widened. "You did?"

"Given the circumstances, with your father being who he is and with the knowledge of what he did to her, on Earth and in Purgatory, entrance was granted. Immediately."

At the same time my heart broke, it was full. Mom was finally getting what she deserved: an eternity of happiness. She deserved it after dealing with my father, sipping his poison for so long.

"I watched a movie once that said suicides can't get into heaven."

"Sometimes they can't, but the circumstances that led her to that decision were considered. Your father was sending her to a shrink who prescribed a drug to her that he knew had a high likelihood of causing suicidal thoughts and actions. Your father's company was responsible for manufacturing it. He used favors to get it approved by the FDA, and your mother was in the first human trial. In effect, she was his first guinea pig. We believe you also took the drug while in rehab."

"Doc?" That knocked the breath from me.

Michael nodded. "One of your father's many friends," he spat.

I could feel my body deflate. How far was my father's reach?

"Far and wide, Carmen. He's very powerful, more so in this era than any other, and in both realms as well."

"That sucks."

He stared at the water. "I know."

I clutched the Angel stone. If it weren't smooth, it would have sliced me open the same way my father did. *He has to be stopped. I have to stop him. It has to be me*, I thought to myself, knowing Michael couldn't hear.

We sat near the water until the cleansing rain fell that afternoon. Michael stood up and walked toward the trees. I held tightly to the stone, hoping Gabriel hadn't lied about its powers. Could angels lie?

If he could hear my thoughts while I clutched the rock, Michael never let on. Shivering in soaked clothing, he approached with dried branches from the forest floor, arranged a rock circle on the river bank, and stacked the wood. "The fire will warm you."

"Don't suppose you have a lighter?" I teased.

He smirked. "I don't need one."

He held his finger out and a flame appeared at the end. The fire slowly began to consume the dry bark, licking its way up the stack of wood.

"That was sexy," I said, meaning every word.

Michael grinned, but didn't reply. I pondered the contour of his mouth; soft, pillowy bottom lip, strong, stern top lip. Lips that knew how to move over those of a woman... instinctually.

His eyes flashed a deep crimson. "Stop."

Clutching the Angel stone, I couldn't help but laugh. His eyes were like a damn traffic light. "Sorry, I will. I'm... sorry." I giggled.

"What is so funny?" he growled, stalking toward me.

I took a step back. The Keeper of Crows might just be Michael to me, but he was all archangel to everyone else, and at times when he was all worked up like this, if he had wings, I'd have fallen at his feet and begged him for mercy.

"Your thoughts are erratic. I can't read you. Are you laughing at my lips, or at my ability to wield them, Carmen?" His face was an inch from mine. He'd moved so fast, my mind couldn't process what I saw.

"Uh...neither?"

"Is that a question or an assertion?"

I didn't know which it was, because my mind felt tingly when he was this close. I just wanted him to press those lips to mine and show me how skilled he was with them. Then, suddenly he did. And it was heavenly. His lips captured mine and his teeth scraped against my flesh as they nipped and pulled my bottom lip, taking it and making it their captive. My entire body was on fire. My eyes fluttered closed, but I was sure he'd used his fiery finger to ignite me. When his hands found my waist and reeled me in, my knees buckled. When his fingers urged my head forward, I wished I had hair for him to pull. When he finally broke away, panting just like I was, my heart shattered.

He pointed a finger at me accusingly. "You..."

"*Me?*"

"You tempt me!" he yelled.

"Well you tempt me, too! You're like sex on a stick dipped in butter!"

His brows furrowed. "Sex on a stick dipped in...?"

"BUTTER!" I yelled, turning my back to him. I crossed my arms over my thundering heart to keep it from leaping out of my chest and beating him to death. He was so frustrating!

Then he laughed. His deep, rumbling laughter filled the space between us and I wanted him to stop. I picked up a handful of pebbles and launched them at him. He stopped chuckling immediately, his eyes turning a playful shade of pink. I knew I was in trouble. Turning as fast as I could, I took off running from him, but he caught me in only a few feet.

"What are you doing to me?" he rasped into my ear.

"I could ask you the same thing."

———

The following day, with the crows keeping watch overhead, I pushed myself off the boulder I'd been sitting on.

"Let's go swimming," I suggested, ticking my head toward the river.

"Can you swim?" he asked.

"I grew up in California," was my answer. His brows touched. "Of course I can swim, archangel. Probably better than you."

He stripped to his boxer briefs without another word, and the way his eyes flitted over my body gave me goosebumps. I stripped to my bra and panties and was about to remove them when he stopped me.

"Leave them on."

Squashing my disappointment, I walked over to the edge of the river, placed my feet on the slick rocks, and let the icy, gray water wash over my feet. "It's cold!"

"Did you expect bath water?" he teased, waltzing in until the silver water lapped at his waist. I didn't realize until then that it wasn't gray water; it was silver like mercury, like the water in the streams that was so still, it didn't seem to flow at all. But this churned angrily, or maybe it was happy, because it wasn't still. It was alive.

"Come on," he said, splashing silver across my thighs, stomach, and chest. I giggled as he sank into the water to his neck, re-emerging and looking like the tin man of angels. He looked down at his skin and chuckled. "I do look like a tin man."

I stepped into the water, my feet finding rocks beneath the surface. "Do me a favor, Keeper. If you ever make it out of this place, make sure to look up 'The Wizard of Oz'."

The creases in his face broke my heart. He didn't think he would ever leave Purgatory.

"Can you ask for a new assignment?" I asked tentatively.

"I have."

"Can you clean up the problems here so they'll let you leave?"

He shook his head. "I'm not allowed to interfere. My only order is to guard the fissures and try to stop merchants."

"Why? Doesn't anyone care about what Malchazze is doing? Don't they care about the demons dumping Lessons here? That my father can control them? The trafficking? The souls kidnapped from this place and then sold? What about those souls? They matter, too."

"I know they do, and I truly wish I had answers to your questions, because then my own would be answered. I've spent years asking the same things, begging for a change in orders, begging to help the situation, and the answer has always been no."

The silver water lapped at my thighs, drawing his attention. I kept walking toward him.

"There's a tension between you and Gabriel, even though he and you are friendly to one another. I can tell there's a long history there and some loyalty, but I feel the air thicken when you and he are in the same room. Why is that?"

Michael blew out a heavy breath. "We haven't always seen eye-to-eye on things. The archangels were created at the same time. We've been together through battles, times of peace, and difficulties you probably couldn't even fathom. Of all the archangels, Gabriel and I were closest."

"Were?"

"Sometimes siblings squabble."

"It seems like more than that, Michael." Another step toward him. The water swirled around my waist and ribs.

"I don't want to talk about it."

I nodded. "Okay."

He smiled. "I thought you'd keep pressing me for an answer until I exploded."

I smiled, looking down at the water sloshing onto my chest. "This isn't toxic, right?"

"No, it's safe, but I'm surprised you're able to withstand the current. You've been so tired lately."

"It *is* strong—the water, I mean."

He nodded. "It is." He wasn't looking at the water.

CHAPTER NINETEEN

The manna fell and I told Michael to sit and relax while I gathered it. Were his eyes on my ass? Yes. Did I like it? Absolutely. I emptied my cupped hands into his and went back for more. He could eat a ton of this stuff, but it filled me up quickly. I never got hungry before it was time for the manna to fall again.

"Tell me a good memory from your childhood," he asked out of the blue.

I popped a piece of velvety fluff into my mouth, thinking of what to tell him. "Okay. Once when I was in elementary school, maybe first grade, my mom said I didn't have to go to school that day. She helped me dress and brush my teeth and hair, and then she packed a cooler with food while I gathered toys to take with me. We drove to the zoo and spent most of the morning exploring. It was empty because it was a weekday, and it was like we had all the exhibits, the whole place, to ourselves. We laughed and held hands and she bought me a stuffed penguin from the gift shop because they were my favorite animal. We ate lunch in the trunk of our car, picnic style, and drove to the beach where we just walked along the shore, toes in the sand, saltwater splashing our legs. It was the happiest day of my life."

"Your mother loved you."

"She did that day," I said, looking away from him.

He watched me gather a few more pieces of manna. "She loved you every day. Malchazze is skilled at crushing souls, Carmen, and she was another victim of his, as were you. But she did love you."

Hot tears burned my eyes. "I never thought so until now," I admitted, my throat clogged with emotion. "Seeing her, normal, was the best gift in the world, but watching her walk away, even to Heaven, was the hardest thing I've ever had to do. It's like getting a shiny new present on Christmas morning and having it ripped from your hands five seconds later."

"Should I not have brought her back? I thought it was what you'd have wanted."

"No! Please don't think I didn't appreciate it; I just miss her and I'm a mess. I'm sorry."

"Don't apologize. Sometimes, I'm not sure I understand all of the emotions you, and humans in general, feel. I read people and situations wrong sometimes."

"Bringing my mother here was the right thing to do. I wouldn't have traded that minute for anything in the world, Michael. Thank you for helping her and for letting me say goodbye."

He was quiet, staring at the pebbles beneath his bent legs. "You're an amazing person, Carmen."

"I'm not. I'm actually a really shitty person, Michael. If you had someone else to compare me to, you wouldn't say such a thing."

"I would. I've seen countless souls over the eons, Carmen, but none have shone brighter than you."

Maybe I had half of an excuse for being a bad person. I was raised by the antichrist, after all, so maybe that pardoned my attitude toward life and love.

"You are the most loving person I've seen. You don't love many people, but those you love, you love fiercely, with everything you are. What could be more sacrificing than that?" he asked.

"Sacrificing everything you are for hundreds of people you don't know and who don't care to know you…that's what *you* do. Every single day. That's what you do here, Michael. You may not recognize it, but the love in you is greater than anything *I've* ever seen."

CHAPTER TWENTY

For two days, we camped near the silver river. We swam in its cold water, watched it from the bank, let its churning water lull us to sleep.

Michael hovered around me. His crows flew around us and kept watch from their perches on the spindly branches above. There were no fissures. No shudders. No one crossed the boundary. Not even Gabriel returned.

It was too quiet, like the calm before the storm we both knew was coming. I hoped we could weather it.

We didn't kiss again. Michael didn't touch me. But we did talk. I told him about my life and he listened, his eyes changing colors with each detail offered. Sometimes I said things just to see what color they would turn next, but he quickly caught on to that game.

"You can hear my thoughts, but I can see your emotions," I told him. He didn't like that so much.

He thought he was putting distance between us, but it was me. I'd reeled him in and now had to throw him back. He needed a chance to swim. I just had to figure out a way to convince him to take the leap and leave this hellhole. I didn't know how long the veil would be sealed. It may need to be sealed forever. *If I can do it*, a tiny voice teased. Self-doubt was a bitch, and I wanted to squash her along with my father.

"Will you tell me about the city?" I pleaded. The only thing he would offer was that it was crowded, corrupt, and the castle my father had built overlooked it all.

So we ate, brooded, cleansed, watched the crows, and avoided each other. One night, under the faded gray sky that was only slightly darker than it was during the day, Michael came and sat beside me on the rocks. "You're still soaked."

It was hard to dry when there was no wind, no warmth, and the river splashed beside us, dampening everything all over again once it began to dry. "So are you," I said, trying not to look at him.

"You're upset with me," he said.

I was. It was pointless to lie.

"Why are you angry?"

"I'm not angry at you, Michael. I'm angry at our situation. And I'm sorry for even speaking about it. I know it can't be easy on you. These rules would have driven me crazy a long time ago."

"I wish things were different," he said, brushing my knuckles with his.

I hissed. "You know, I wish things were different, too. I wish I didn't feel this connection to you. I wish Mom was still here and Father wasn't the fucking antichrist, but he is. I wish I wasn't stuck in this awful, gray hellhole, but I am. I wish I could just stand beside you and stop staring at you, and I wish… I wish for once, someone found me worth it."

His brows knotted. "Worth what?" he breathed, his eyes turning sapphire.

"Worth everything," I admitted, turning my head from him.

He was quiet for a long moment and then he stood, I thought to walk away from me for good. He should wash his hands of me. I was far more trouble than I was worth. Ask anyone who'd ever known me.

"You are fearless," he whispered. "You are a soul, but you tore the veil because you were too stubborn to let merchants drag you through it. You fought, Carmen. Those animals who beat you, who did things… You fought. You never stopped fighting. Even when you looked as though you had lost consciousness, your fingers twitched, trying to stop them. You came to my defense against monsters you couldn't even begin to fathom. Twice."

"I didn't get to help you, though!" I cried.

"You tried! Don't you get it? No one…not a soul, not an angel, not even an archangel, has ever done that for me before. Ever." His breathing was labored as he looked at me, a pained look creasing his face. "Stand up," he commanded, whipping around so fast he blurred.

"Why?" I scanned the tree line, the water, the sky. Nothing. No Lessons lurked.

I stood and his hands clamped onto my waist, pulling me to him so fast, I didn't register his lips on mine, his tongue on mine until I was tasting him, moving in unison, the beginning of a deadly and dangerous dance.

Pulling away, I pushed against his chest. "No."

He pulled me to him again. "You are worth everything to me, Carmen. Rules be damned."

His hands roamed my back, breasts, ass, pulling me closer to him, so close I could feel every hard plane of him. Every angle. Every heartbeat. I pulled him closer still, trying to commit the feel to memory. One glorious moment.

He stripped me of my shirt and then his hands deftly unbuttoned my jeans and slid them down my legs, where they fell in a whisper to the pebbles below. His shirt and pants joined mine and then my bra and panties. He inhaled sharply when he saw me.

"You've seen me before," I said, gasping as his lips tugged my earlobe, his hot breath on my neck as he bit down.

"Never enough," he breathed. His hands found my folds and found out how much I wanted him, hot and slick. When he flicked my clit, I came hard, pulsing around the fingers he'd sunk inside me.

"We're going too far," I breathed against his chest.

"Not nearly far enough." He removed his boxer briefs and revealed himself to me. I stroked him. Long, hard, steel. "Carmen," he hissed.

Michael gently eased me to the ground. I expected him to be like the others, to have me face away from him, to take me from behind so he didn't have to look at me, but Michael wasn't like the men I'd been with before. He knelt between my legs, wrapping each around his back, and then he paused. He was having second thoughts.

I started to scramble toward my clothes.

"Stop," he said sternly.

I obeyed.

"I am not having second thoughts. I'm simply enjoying the view." He grinned, stroking the cheeks of my ass.

Letting out a pent-up breath, I pulled him to me with the strength of my calves, my heels bringing him closer. He rubbed against me, his length against my core, and I could swear that Purgatory burst into a rainbow of color, if only for a moment.

"Michael, I'm not worth the consequences you'll face."

"Yes, you are." It was a pledge, a vow. When he slid inside me, he was gentle, almost painfully so. His body echoed the promise he made, while mine accepted his vow and made one in return. Our slow rhythm turned feral, wanting, needing, never enough, not enough. He slammed into me and I rose my hips to meet each thrust, gritting my teeth to keep from crying out.

Growling, he looked into my eyes, his turning magenta. "Don't forget this moment. No matter what."

"No matter what," I echoed. I couldn't forget him or this if I tried.

"I want this to last forever," he breathed.

"I want to explode with you."

Garnering his strength and my body to him, we came together. Dark feathers rained down on top of us, tickling our sensitive skin. A sense of foreboding filled my marrow.

What did I do? What did I ask him to do?

———————

As Keeper checked on his murder and I slid my clothes back on one piece at a time, I heard rustling behind me from the direction of the forest. I expected Lessons, a hoard of demons. Something. But what I got was my father staring at me and motioning with one finger for me to follow him into the woods. I was conflicted, but I knew he might hurt Michael if I didn't obey him, and I couldn't let that happen.

"Use the Angel stone," the familiar, velvety voice ordered.

I grabbed hold of it and brought it out of my pocket. "How did you know I had it?"

"I have my sources."

Have you ever seen eyes that were vacuums; soulless orbs that showed no emotion? Serial killers, mass murderers, and terrorists all had those looks about them. So did my father. Those were the eyes of my father.

"I want you to come with me."

"To the city? What do you want? For me to become a sex slave like you made my mother?"

His face contorted in anger. "Your mother is a slave no more, but I'm sure you know that already."

"I sure as hell do. She's in a place where you'll never be able to hurt her again," I said triumphantly.

"Is that what the angels told you? Aww, naive isn't your color, Carmen. Suicides can't enter the gates of Heaven. It is forbidden."

Rage filled my veins, hot and fast. "My guess, Father, is that you know nothing about Heaven, and you never will."

"No, but you may have just cost Michael everything. He'll probably taste the fires of Hell because of you, and for that, I am forever in your debt."

My stomach churned and I vomited toward his polished shoes. Had I damned him?

Father stepped back from the frothy mess and continued, "You need to come with me to see what you stand to inherit from the labors of my hard work. You'll never understand this place unless you enter the city and stand in front of your people. The Keeper wants to keep you away. Why do you think that is?"

I glanced back toward the river, toward the swirl of crows above us, now angrily cawing. "They know you're here."

"He's coming. If you want to see your empire, take my hand," he said, offering his palm to me.

Gritting my teeth, I glanced over to see Michael running as fast as he could, a blur among the landscape. "Carmen! Don't trust him!"

I didn't trust Malchazze, but I couldn't risk Michael's fate any more than I already recklessly had. I had to see what he'd done, what he built while crossing the barrier. "I want to see the castle."

"Carmen, no!" Michael shouted, his face contorting in worry and pain.

As I placed my hand in my father's, we were spirited away.

CHAPTER TWENTY-ONE

The gray on my father's skin fit him. It suited him like the ashy tone was made for him and only him. He was the gloom of this place, I quickly learned. Did he leach all the color away, or was it simply a side effect of being in the presence of evil?

In a split second my feet hit a smooth, stone floor. The room itself was empty, the stones on the wall rougher in texture than those beneath my feet. Aside from a window adorned with white, fluttering curtains that hung the length of the wall, it was as empty as I felt, even standing next to someone else.

Was it a talent of his? Making a person feel more alone in his presence than they would if they were actually by themselves? Despite my roiling thoughts, Father didn't spare a glance in my direction. The stony expression on his face never faltered, so I was fairly sure he couldn't hear me. It was called Angel stone; not crosser stone or the stone of the antichrist, so it probably didn't work on him. He simply didn't care to listen.

He began walking toward the window. "Are you ready to look upon your subjects?"

"They're yours, not mine."

He grinned finally. "They will be yours. I will teach you everything."

"Why do you need a successor? Are you planning to leave this place?"

"No, I simply decided to give you a tiny slice of power, as is your birthright."

He moved through the curtains and into the light beyond it. When I touched the sheer fabric, parting it and stepping through, I found myself on a large balcony. It was like the most macabre fairy tale; an evil king ruling a land that wasn't meant to be ruled, asking his daughter to join him in his insatiable quest for power.

If he'd asked me to learn the pharmaceutical business, *that* would have been normal; simply a father passing down his knowledge to his only child. Only Father wasn't a normal father. He was the antichrist, evil incarnate, building an empire. Why he and his city hadn't already been leveled was something I couldn't understand.

I stared at him.

Father didn't look a day over forty-five. His salt-and-pepper hair was cut short. He looked the part of the sophisticated multi-millionaire instead of wearing long, tattered robes or cloaks that would better fit the scene. He smelled like the cologne he always wore on Earth, like exotic spices mixed with the sea, like money. I eased toward the edge, keeping a safe distance between us. He might try to kill me, shove me over the edge where I would plummet to my death.

His sharp eyes watched my movements. "I didn't bring you here to kill you, Carmen."

"But you nearly killed me to get me here, so pardon me if I don't exactly trust you. You've lied to me my entire life."

"Fair enough." He leaned his elbows on the stones along the edge of the balcony and peered down below him. "I'm sure you understand now that there was no other way for me to get you here. There are rules. Humans can't pass through, but souls can. I needed you in this form, and Dimitri was able to deliver you to me."

I followed his eyes and gasped. It was like looking at New York City from the top of the Empire State building. There were buildings everywhere, crumbling and tagged with graffiti. People—souls—walked along the streets. Some lingered in front of doors and alleyways.

He nodded his head to the scene in front of us. "That is the north end." Pointing behind us, he added, "South end is that way." Pointing to the left, he instructed, "And that is the west end. Those three are mostly comprised of ordinary souls. To the east is the Red District, more commonly referred to as the Meat Market. I trust that the Keeper told you all about that lovely place?"

I looked east and saw barely-clad women and the men who lingered around looking at them on the streets in broad daylight. There was a large platform filled with trembling souls. I could see their shapes distort even from this distance. The souls were terrified, and the horror of that place radiated everywhere else. It seemed like the Meat

Market was expanding, encroaching to the south as well. Business was booming. The thought of my mother in the thick of it all sickened me.

"Did you send Gus and Chester after me?"

"I didn't send them there for you, though I did grant them the power to cross over and gather a soul. The fact that you intervened was purely a convenient coincidence. They felt the fissure, crossed, and found the other soul. You got involved when you shouldn't have. Not that it would have mattered. I would have soon dispatched someone to get you anyway."

"You would have had to wait for a fissure."

"The one of whom I speak has no need of a fissure."

Michael said my father was the only crosser left. Either he was lying, or something worse than a crosser was coming after me.

"Oh, and that was a good touch, using Doc to poison me. I actually trusted him, so you shattered that faith. But then again, I guess that's what you're best at."

He smiled. He actually fucking smiled at me. "I hope you can see past all of the difficulty and appreciate what I've done. I could have sat here in Purgatory, minding my own business, but you don't know what it was like before. Purgatory was not a resting place, as I'm sure the angels tried to feed you. It was a lesser step up from Hell, and not a far one. Souls were being tortured."

"They still are, from the looks of it," I said, staring in the direction of the Meat Market. It was truly sad. All of it.

"There are problems, but nothing like it was before. Demons ruled this place, while the angels turned their heads and let them break souls, bit by bit. When the veil was torn, I saw an opportunity and took it. A few others did, too."

"Where are the others?" I asked.

He stood up straight and adjusted the lapels of his jacket, answering in a disinterested tone, "I ended them."

"There isn't room for more than one ruler, right?"

"Precisely."

"So do you plan to end me, too?"

He shook his head slowly. "If you don't give me a reason to, then no. Let me explain. I don't want you to succeed me; I want you to rule beneath me. When I win the presidency on Earth, I'll have to be gone for long periods of time. However, I can't risk losing all I've built here. I need you to manage it in my absence. You'll have just enough power to help, but not enough to hinder. I know you. You only care about yourself."

Oh, I wanted to hinder. I wanted to hinder him six feet into the soil. Wondering who in their right minds would be stupid enough to vote for a man like him, I remembered the crowds who came to hear him speak, to hear the lie-filled rhetoric. He told them what they wanted to hear. He would make sure they had jobs. He would make sure the country was secure, that their families would thrive and be safe. Promising that the government would help them with their every need, he ignored the questions about funding, his background, and his stances on turbulent issues, and charged ahead with empty promises, never answering how he would actually make them come true. And the people loved him for it. They loved hope, and that was what my father gave them. He was hope in a handsome suit, with sparkling white teeth and a boldly colored tie. If he could drag himself from the lower-middle class and come out on top of a multi-billion dollar industry, they could trust him to better their stance as well.

He would wave and kiss babies, pose for photo opportunities, and stand shoulder to shoulder with the average working-class man and woman. All the while, he hammered my mother into the ground, drugged her and programmed the detonator, waiting for her to self-destruct. He did the same to me.

There was no shortage of casualties where my father was concerned. If someone got in his way, they mysteriously disappeared. Did he drag them here? Enslave them? The blood pulsed angrily along the column of my throat. I clenched my hands and stared at the sky as it darkened, angry clouds building overhead. Then the crows came.

"You must have made quite an impression on the Keeper, Carmen. I'm pleasantly surprised. I've been trying to lure him here for years."

There it was. He was using me as Keeper bait. I wanted nothing more than for Michael to run as far from this man, this castle, and this city as possible. I never wanted him to stop or look back. He might turn into a pillar of salt. If I could keep my father from hurting him...

"Will I be able to cross the divide, too?" I asked.

"What?" He looked at me, his attention diverted from the circling birds above.

"When you give me power, can I cross back and forth?"

He crossed his arms, the suit jacket he wore bunching around his biceps. "You would stay here."

"What if the press asked where I was?" He loved media attention. My father prescribed to the ideal that there was no bad press. My car wreck? Everyone had problems. Send her to rehab and fix her. His affairs? He was trapped in a loveless marriage with an alcoholic. Why shouldn't he have the chance to be happy? Spin, spin, spin. It was all about the spin of things.

"Do you intend to keep my body alive on Earth?"

The crows descended slowly. Michael was in the city, but not in the castle yet. I couldn't feel him, his electricity.

"No, your earthly body will die. Your soul will then be free to remain in Purgatory."

"What if I want to see my friends?"

He smiled pityingly. "You have no friends, Carmen. You never have."

Unfortunately, he was right, and I had nothing to distract him with. Except for my mother.

"Why did you hurt Mom? Did you know she would kill herself? When she ended up here, why did you make her a slave?"

"I've lived for so long, and I've had many women, but your mother was the most difficult. Once the addictions kicked in, it was easier to manipulate her, but she determined her own fate by betraying me."

"You killed her! How could she possibly have betrayed *you*?" my voice rose, shaking with rage.

"She mailed information to the press – confidential documents she stole from my office, mind you – but I paid the newspapers enough to cover it all up. But none of that is important now. You need to decide whether you are with me or against me, Carmen. With one choice, your soul lives, and with the other, I dispatch it. Only angels can dispatch souls to either Heaven or Hell. I have no power over Heaven. I can only send you to be with your mother."

He thought Mom was in Hell, but he was fucking wrong. However, I had to make him think I was on his side. That way I could tear his kingdom completely apart.

A mass shriek from below drew our attention. "They're breaching the gates!" someone yelled. "Run!"

Father smirked. "It's time to end the segregation of this place. The Lessons deserve to live in the luxury that only the city can provide."

"The Lessons are in the city?" I suppressed a shudder, remembering the soulless eyes of the ones who still had them, the dripping tar and translucent, pale flesh, the veins rolling blue and purple beneath the surface. The stench of their gray flesh, the tip of each finger dark and decayed. The strength in their hands. They were people who should have no rest. Father was right about that. They should have gone straight to Hell where they belonged, but then he would have no army, no one to fight for him.

"I called them," he sneered. "The Keeper can't fight them all at once, and if he's distracted by you, I can finally get rid of him."

Father flicked his hand toward me, and in an instant I was transformed. A black, strapless silk ball gown hugged my body, the layers spilling away from my hips. Heavy diamonds hung from my ears and neck. My hair.... I had hair. Reaching a hand up, I expected to feel soft spikes of hair. Instead, I found that it was long and pinned to the crown of my head.

"How did you...?" I couldn't see it all, but before the accident that wasn't an accident, my hair was bleached blonde. Now the tendrils that hung in curls were dark as death, matching the strands my mother wore before age threaded her head with silver. "Thank you." I beamed at him, hoping he bought my bullshit.

He smiled in response.

I need the Lessons to leave the city, I thought, pinching my lip as the screams below continued.

Father was entranced with the firework show. The Lessons were killing souls everywhere, the wisps of what remained flying into the air, one after another.

A heavy thump came from behind. "Stop the Lessons. Call them back. Now," Michael commanded my father as his crows stood along the parapet wall, waiting for further instruction.

Father turned around, filling the air with a slow clap. "If I'd known you'd show up here with just a little nudge of the Lessons, I'd have done it years ago. Or is that why you're here? If you hadn't grown so attached to Carmen, I think you'd still be slinking along the outskirts, petting your birds."

A single crow cawed at him angrily, and soon they all joined the chorus.

CHAPTER

TWENTY-TWO

The two stared each other down for several long moments, and Michael again ordered Father to stop the Lessons. "Last chance," he warned. Shrieking and screams from the city below made my hair stand on end. The souls were under attack, and by the sounds of it, they weren't winning the battle.

"Did Michael tell you why he's here, Carmen? Your archangel is being taught a lesson of his own."

My mouth opened as I looked to the archangel. "What? What for?"

"For losing sight of what's important. For allowing a human to distract him, a woman, to be exact. He didn't lose his wings when he came to this place. They were stripped from him and turned into a curse that he will bear until he learns his lesson. The fact that he's fallen for you is proof that he's learned nothing at all. At this rate, he'll never leave." Father smiled, zeroing in on Michael. "I've been waiting to finish you for what feels like an eternity." In his hand, a black, glistening blade appeared. "Now, not only can I kill you, I can send you straight to Hell."

"The sword of Lucifer," Michael whispered, but nothing on the warrior's face indicated that he was frightened. "What did you offer him to get that? Your soul is already forfeit."

"Lucifer has helped me in ways you couldn't begin to understand, angel. And, for the record, it wasn't *my* soul I promised him," Father enunciated, glancing toward me.

Michael growled as he grabbed the hilt of the broadsword from his back, his tattoos churning tumultuously. The archangel was about to unleash Hell on my father. That part I didn't mind, but if Michael was struck with the sword of Lucifer... Michael was an angel, but with that sword, he would die. Could he truly be sent to Hell? Was Father telling the truth? I couldn't risk it. I couldn't live with that. I had to do something.

I rushed in between them, hands outstretched. Michael's eyes collided with mine, the dark irises fading to cornflower blue. With my mind, I called the fissure to appear. The Earth shook and the veil appeared, a fissure slicing through it, brightly lit from behind.

"I love you, Michael, but you can't stay here. Not anymore. You've given enough to this place." He tilted his head to the side, his eyes telling me he knew I was betraying him. "I'm sorry," I told him, my throat clogged with tears, and then I shoved him hard through the opening. He lost his balance and tumbled backward into the earthen realm, an angel without wings. I screamed into the sliver of light, "No matter what!"

He probably thought I'd been lying to him all along, that Malchazze controlled me only to get close to him and learn his secrets. Fighting back the tears that were forming, I focused on the real problem at hand. Maybe somehow, someday, Michael would understand and forgive me.

I had to free him. I had to protect him. I had to give him a life worth living, because it wasn't here. Michael was prepared to die for me, but I couldn't let that happen. He might think me worthy, but I knew I wasn't. Michael deserved to live. He couldn't defeat Malchazze without orders, but I could. And I had every intention of doing so.

Somehow, in a short span of time, my heart claimed the archangel who defended her, and she wouldn't survive if he didn't.

"It's true," Father marveled. "You are part of the veil…" His eyes sparkled with the possibilities my curse presented him. I watched as the birds swirled again, and with my mind, I called them, praying they would listen, hear, and obey.

Whether it was me or the fact that their master loved me, they came to my defense. The crows descended upon my father. I stuck my hands into the fabric of the veil and closed my eyes.

"Solidify. Become stone. I need you to close, to mend, and to stop letting evil pricks through this fabric. No more fissures. No more crossers. Michael should be freed. This has to stop." And just like that, everything went silent. The fabric no longer circulated around my hands. It became solid. It had become like stone, just as I'd asked. I had to break a few pieces off just to free my fingers. The crows stilled.

Father's mouth shook as it hung open in surprise. "What have you done?"

"I fixed the veil. Now, you're stuck here. You're trapped. Just like me."

He scrambled to his feet. "But how? Unseal it!"

I laughed, shaking my head. He wouldn't manipulate me any further. "I'm stronger than you ever could have made me. I am part of the veil now. It obeys me. And only me." I felt the cold seeping into my veins, feeding into my heart where it recirculated. Soon, frost was all I could feel. Frost and gray and emptiness.

The crows should dispatch you, send your soul where it belongs, I silently vowed. *I want to see the light fade from your eyes, the awareness as you are sent straight to Hell. And I want you to know that it's me sending you there.*

The birds angrily snapped at his face as by the thousands they swooped at him, sending sharp needles straight into his traitorous heart, a circle of dark feathers protruding from his chest. A wisp of smoke filtered from among the ebony vanes. It floated lazily until a crow, one of my crows, gulped it down and flew away with it. I left my father's prone body lying propped against the parapet stones, but I slid the sword of Lucifer out of his hand and walked away with it.

PART
TWO

CHAPTER
TWENTY-THREE

Michael

The ground shook so violently, I thought the balcony would break off the face of the castle and take us with it as it fell. I saw the fissure appear just behind me and knew it wasn't a coincidence. I thought it was Malchazze who made it. I was wrong.

I *trusted* her.

When I fell into Earth and slammed onto the ground in the middle of a lush, green park, no one paid attention. No one offered me a hand. Their eyes were glued to their phones, and even if they weren't, it was obvious that people didn't get involved with the affairs of others. Humans hadn't changed much at all in the last thousand years, despite their advances in technology. Over the years, Gabriel brought magazines and newspapers so I could keep up to date with the times, but seeing it with my own eyes was different. Purgatory's reflection had changed over the span of many years, the buildings growing so tall they nearly brushed the sky, but seeing this skyline in the distance was overwhelming.

I called the crows by instinct, but none had fallen through with me. I hoped Gabriel would hear my cry and come find me. It was the only way to right this. Until he arrived, I would walk, searching for a fissure to descend. Except…the world was calm. It was steady. There was no buzzing current looming overhead. And it was bright; the sun blindingly so. Trees were green, their leaves swaying happily. The sky was a heartbreaking color of blue.

The sword of Lucifer.

Not only was Carmen in danger, every angel in existence was. We had to stop Malchazze from using it on her and against us.

Gabriel suddenly appeared, walking through the park wearing jeans and a button-down, holding a newspaper and walking a five-pound poodle. "You rang?" he deadpanned.

"Why aren't you surprised?" I said, grabbing his striped shirt by the collar.

"Carmen *might* have mentioned closing the veil for good, and I *may* have told her she had to make sure her father was inside Purgatory…"

"And that I was out?"

"She figured that part out on her own."

I let him go, sorry that I'd frightened the dog. Its tail was tucked beneath him as he cowered at Gabriel's feet.

Crouching down, I held my hand out for him to sniff. "Sorry, fella."

His small nose flared rapidly as he took in my scent, which probably matched Gabriel's with the addition of cigarette. Speaking of...

He pulled a pack out of the pocket of his shirt. "They might be smashed now," he smarted. I watched as a girl jogged by, her ponytail swishing from side to side. A man was yelling into his cell phone from a nearby bench. An old woman sat across from him on the other side of the path, spreading birdseed at her feet.

"Why didn't the crows come with me?" I thought aloud.

Gabriel shook his head. "I'm not sure, but I'm worried about Carmen. She's still there with her father."

"He has the sword of Lucifer," I said quietly.

Gabriel's fists clenched around the leash. "How?"

"Malchazze promised him her soul."

"We have to get back in there. We have to help her."

"How?" I asked. How in the hell would we get through the stone barrier she'd erected between us?

"We have to make a plea. Just...let me get rid of the dog." He walked to the elderly bird lover and asked her to hold his leash for a moment, muttering in angel that she loves the dog and should take him home.

"That was uncalled for. She's too old to care for him."

Gabriel laughed. "The dog is old as well. They'll make great companions. You worry too much about small things when we have much greater things to worry about."

"When did we ever care this much about one soul?" I asked.

"She's a good person. Beneath her harsh words, she is good. Carmen didn't ask for any of this. She is an innocent."

Was she? "She shoved me out a fissure."

Gabriel threw his head back, laughing as he walked toward a thicket. "I bet she did. She certainly is a feisty one."

A growl erupted low in my chest. Not for the first time, I wondered if perhaps Gabriel cared for her in the same way I did.

"I don't. Our relationship is friendly, whereas yours is... passionate. Though, I worry that when we make our plea, that may be a determining factor and a negative one for Carmen."

"I won't lie about it, Gabriel."

"I should hope not. The truth will be known."

Away from human eyes, Gabriel took my hand. If I had wings, the contact wouldn't be necessary, but my wings were stuck in Purgatory with Carmen. I just hoped I could get them all out of there.

It had been far too long since I walked the streets of Heaven, golden and soft beneath the skin of my bare feet. The eyes of many angels caught on my form until they saw my face. They initially assumed I was among the fallen, that my wings had torn away when I fell from grace. In a way, I was. I fell, just not from Heaven. Many eons ago I was charged with protecting someone, and I failed because I was distracted; a distraction that I've paid for in spades.

I may not have fallen from Heaven into Hell, but being thrown into Purgatory was a hell in its own right. My wings were torn away when I entered that place, and the crows became my only companions.

Heaven knew I loved Carmen, and Heaven knew we'd physically sealed our union by making love. I knew the rules and that relations with humans were forbidden, so it was only a matter of time before punishment was meted out. This time, I hoped it earned me a one-way ticket back to Purgatory, back to her. Realistically, I knew it wouldn't be allowed, but someone had to get her out of there.

A light breeze stirred. I heard the moment my oldest friend sniffed the air. Gabriel's feet stilled and the smile he wore slowly slid from his lips. His countenance darkened as his wings violently shredded his shirt. Like a bull seeing the color red, his nostrils flared. "What did you do? I smell her on you."

"From your reaction, I'm assuming you already know."

His lips thinned. "I want to hear it from your lips. Tell me how you took advantage of her."

My shoulders, forgetting they bore no wings, flexed, tearing the scars open again. Red hot pain seared my flesh, two ribbons that would never heal. Two twin paths of warm blood trailed from the wounds. "I did not take advantage of her."

"Oh, because, let me guess," Gabriel mocked. "You love her. You've only known her for minutes, Michael. She's so young. She was raised by Malchazze. She's never had love or affection. You weren't the first she used to cool the ache in her heart, and you won't be the last.

Carmen is a spoiled child trapped in the body of a woman. She wields it well, but you should have known better."

"She deserves better than me, I know, but I was tired of pushing her away when I wanted nothing but her. Judge me if you must, but I won't yield. I love her." It was the only truth I did know.

Gabriel spat at my feet. "You know nothing of love. Love is putting someone else's needs above your own. You have only ever considered yourself since…"

"Say her name!" I roared.

"No."

"Say it. You want me to grovel? I will. I am sorry. Eulalia… My failure to protect her? That was an accident. I've paid years of penance for trying to help her mother when I should have been watching over her. You didn't know that, though, did you? You assumed I loved the woman, but I didn't. However, in trying to help Eulalia, I knew that her mother had to be helped first. She was possessed by a powerful demon, so I took her to a priest and held her down as he exorcised her. The act took two days; time enough for me to lose focus on my charge, and for the bastards to torture her thirteen-year-old body to death."

Gabriel's jaw ticked.

"I wonder why in Heaven they omitted that part of the story, Gabriel?"

He shook his head and then lunged, catching my throat in his hand. Within a second, he lowered me and wrapped Elysian cord around my wrists. "This time is different, Michael. This time you broke the rules knowing the consequence. This time, you chose to fall."

Shoving me forward, I glanced behind me at the beautiful gates, solid and made entirely of pearl, shining and welcoming. I'd almost made it inside them. But in that moment, I knew I'd never see them again.

Gabriel stretched his wings wide and lifted me off the ground. "There will be a tribunal. Tonight. And you will pay for hurting her."

I didn't hurt her; I loved her, but I'd pay all the same. Gabriel would never understand. He would never concede an inch of his position that he was right and I was wrong. His eyes only saw in black and white. Shades of gray were lost on him, worthless hues that clouded the eyes of the weak.

He was taking me to Marum, a secret, bottom-level domain of Heaven itself, where punishment would be decided and meted out by one of the seven angels charged with the task. It was why the fallen chose to leap to their possible deaths, onto the earthen plane. Marum was a place of nightmares for our kind, and mine was just beginning.

"You have to go to her, Gabriel."

I could hear his teeth grind together.

"She's still weak. Malchazze will kill her."

Gabriel smiled from above me. "But she isn't weak. I strengthened her. I gave her an Angel stone, as well."

That was why her mind had been so quiet. The stone cloaked her thoughts. "Why would you do that?" I roared, rage pulsing through my veins. I wanted to tear him apart, piece by piece, peeling away an inch of his flesh at a time.

"I did it to protect her from you, and to make her strong enough to physically fight for herself. It was the only way she could survive him."

"I can't feel her, Gabriel."

He shook his head as if cobwebs had formed within it. "Neither can I, but she sealed the veil. She did what she knew she was capable of doing. Carmen only needed someone to believe in her."

"And I suppose *you* were the one who bolstered her confidence?" I growled.

"Of course I did," he spat, lowering us through layers of clouds, each darker than the last. He let go of me and I fell to the ground, to the top of a snow-capped peak. Dark clouds swirled around menacingly.

"Kushiel!" Gabriel called out.

The clouds swirled faster until Kushiel's white wings appeared from the center of the storm. "You called?"

Gabriel smiled. "Michael has fornicated with a human. More specifically, with the daughter of Malchazze."

Kushiel's gaze was feline, predatory as he reached to his side, sliding his palm over the burning leather of his whip. It was made of hellfire, and only he could wield it and contain its power. He used it to break angels. I was next. "After the tribunal, you're mine," he promised.

I looked at Gabriel, whose prim look of satisfaction made me want to tear him apart, limb from limb. "Find a way to get to her."

"She controls the way in and out now," he said. "She has to open a doorway."

I shook my head, staring at the blood seeping red through the pure snow beneath my knees. "She's in danger. If you really care about her at all, as an innocent, please help her. Someone can help her or give you the power to do it."

He turned his back, flapping his wings once, twice. His feet lifted from the ground and I stood on my knees. "Help her!" I pleaded.

Gabriel wouldn't look at me. "Help. Her. Gabriel!"

Kushiel grinned at me before winking. "Don't get too comfortable."

I wouldn't. I was getting the hell out of Marum, one way or another. Conjuring flame, I willed it to burn the Elysian cord. The bitter wind, filled with bits of snow and frost swirled, extinguishing the flame every time I lit it. Rising to my feet, I started down the mountain. I had to get into the trees below, where the fire might stand a chance. It would take days to get there. Fear fueled my feet. Fear and love. I had to get to her before Malchazze could hurt her again.

Carmen

Slowly, Malchazze's body turned to ash, a flaking husk of a soul. I cupped my hands like I'd seen Michael do and blew a long breath at the corpse. It flecked away slowly, and then all the pieces of him took flight, disintegrating in the air before reaching the ground. A wave of nausea threatened to take me under. What would happen to the earthen body of the man Malchazze used to occupy? *What do I do now?*

Screaming and wailing from below the castle answered the thought. First, I would kick the Lessons out of the city, but not before allowing them to clean it up. *I wish I had something more comfortable to wear.* As I walked from the balcony, the sound of swishing and sighing fabric as it caressed the stone floor stopped. The corset was gone, as were the skirts. In its wake was a flexible, black, metallic second skin. Chain mail, but so fine it wasn't something a human could create. I jogged and it didn't hold me back. I swung my arms up and down, side to side. It hugged me, but allowed the movement. The fine hair along the back of my neck danced in delight. I reached up to find a high collar...of crow feathers.

I was the Keeper of Crows now.

Jogging down the stairs, I ran for the exit, for room to breathe. The castle was stifling in a way I didn't understand. Maybe it was Malchazze's lingering presence. I called to the sky for a single crow. When one looked down, I held a finger out, silently ordering it to land. When the bird's feet wrapped around my skin, it was a gentle hold.

I stroked its feathers, walking toward the breach in the wall where the Lessons were. I called them to stop and they obeyed. They were out of sight, but the commotion came to an abrupt halt. The screaming ended. The sounds of terror, already a memory.

"What is your name?" I asked the fowl.

One hundred eleven, it answered in my mind. They were numbered.

"How many of you exist?"

It stepped farther down my finger, perching near the second knuckle. *Seven thousand, seven hundred, seventy-seven.*

"Am I your Keeper?"

The bird cawed loudly once. All other swirling birds echoed above us.

My boots clacked loudly across the cobbled streets as I wound through the labyrinth. I was the Keeper of Crows. I was… the Keeper of Purgatory.

Souls peeked from windows in the buildings that rose into the sky. I heard every hushed whisper. They wondered who I was, how I'd killed Malchazze, why the crows answered to me, what had happened to the Keeper. The answer was simple. *I* happened. And it was time they knew who held the power.

I stood on the balcony and looked below. With my mind, I called the Lessons to the Meat district and told them to wait for me there. The streets were desolate, wrinkled gray paper tumbling down the streets. Foul-smelling liquid trickled along the sides into sewers. Waste. This part of the city was a wasteland. It was time to clean it up.

There was a square of concrete, cracked and bleeding weeds, each as gray as the pavement. The sky roiled along with my heart. This was where they hurt my mother. This was where they would pay for it.

Tar-filled eyes and ears, mouths covered with flesh, the Lessons waited as I climbed onto a fire escape to speak with them, to give them their orders.

"You are to hurt no ordinary soul. If you harm a single, innocent soul, I will end all of you. You are to take out the trash. And by 'trash', I mean anyone who owns, traffics, or tries to sell one of these souls as slaves, for sex or otherwise. You are to end the merchants. Send them all to Hell."

With that order, they went to work. Raiding the buildings, they dispatched the occupants according to my instructions. I felt the souls. They weren't being harmed. I could feel them all, I realized. Every single soul in Purgatory had a distinct taste, and I felt them on my tongue. The most bitter were bursting on it; those who traded people for sex and goods, those who hurt my mother. More fireworks. Wisps of light flew into the air, bursting, my crows swallowing them whole and then carrying them through the veil only because I allowed it. The veil was strong, but I made it flexible again. I wanted the garbage out of this place.

I didn't realize I'd unsealed it enough for an archangel to enter, but Gabriel landed on the ground in front of me, his broadsword raised and ready to slice through any threat. When he found none, his eyes landed on me. "What are you doing?" His eyes were wide. "Where is Malchazze? Michael said you were in danger."

"Michael was wrong." I felt the sword of Lucifer warming the bones of my spine. It ached to split Gabriel in two. "I don't need your help. Leave, Gabriel."

Gabriel's long hair curled across his face in the wake of the feathers and wings above. "Where is Malchazze? Did you end him?"

"We did—the birds killed him, actually." I climbed down from the fire escape and walked to him. His tattoos swirled, more gray than black like Michael's. They matched his wings, his eyes. A million questions rolled through his eyes, but I didn't want to answer a single one of them.

Gabriel looked to the castle above us, a sliver of dark stone peeking through the city streets. Muttering a curse, he listened to the buildings around us. "Why are the souls being dispatched so quickly?"

"I'm doing what no one else had the balls to do. I'm cleaning up Purgatory, starting with the garbage."

He looked at the tagged brick around us, and then at the ground, littered with glass and dark feathers. "Carmen, there are risks—"

From the street came a loud, echoing hiss. A snake, black and glittering as the veil itself slithered through the debris. Gabriel tensed, used his wings to propel him off the ground, and slashed at the serpent. The animal vanished in a haze of dark smoke, a sickening laugh filling the air.

"Seal the veil again," he commanded.

"Where will the souls go? Don't the crows have to carry them away?"

"They'll hold them until you unseal it, but please trust me when I say that was just a test. The next step is Lucifer showing up himself. That sword is bound to him, and him to it."

When his feet found the concrete, I finally relaxed enough to ask, "Is he okay?"

"Who?" Gabriel asked.

"Michael."

"He was okay when I left him." I didn't like the harshness of his voice.

"Are you angry about the Lessons?"

He sheathed the sword at his back. "I'm not angry with you, Carmen. I'm in awe. And I don't understand what just happened."

"You sound pissed."

He shook his head. "For so long, I've wondered who would be able to defeat your father, who would mend the horrors in Purgatory; make it what it once was and what it was intended to be. I thought Michael would do it."

"That's the trouble with you angels," I said, watching his head tick to the side. "You only know how to follow rules."

His eyes latched onto mine, roaring like a fierce storm. "Is that why Michael risked everything to break them with you? Did you trick him to make a point, Carmen?"

I swallowed. "Is he in trouble?"

"Of course he is! What you and he did... it's forbidden!"

The souls flew. The crows ate. The rain began to pour. The cleansing.

"He told you about that?"

Gabriel's laugh was hollow. "I could smell it. He didn't have to tell me."

"What did you do to him?" I screamed above the torrent of cleansing rain. "You're his only friend!"

Steam formed between us, tar bubbling between our feet. "Carmen! Run!"

Why? The question lodged in my throat as one of the most beautiful men I'd ever seen emerged from the molten asphalt. The scent of it burned my nose.

Brown hair, neatly cropped. A suit that cost more than my house, by the looks of it. An air of superiority. Roman nose, not crooked in the slightest, and full lips that were sinful as hell. He was gorgeous. He was dangerous. The sword cried out for him, the metal singing against my spine.

He was the devil.

CHAPTER TWENTY-FOUR

Gabriel's wings snapped out, the softness gone; steel weapons that protruded from his back to shield me from Lucifer. The devil wasn't what I expected at all. I thought he would be grotesque, a monster.

"I *am* a monster, Carmen. Never doubt that," he answered, a flirty smile on his face. His hair was dark as midnight, and truthfully, the devil was hot. He was insanely old, but looked young and vibrant. "Your father made a promise to me. Are you aware of it?"

"No," I lied. I knew Malchazze had promised him my soul, but what were the terms? I felt the pockets along my sides, coming up empty. My Angel stone was lost.

"Angel stone wouldn't block me from your thoughts, anyway. It would be no more useful than a pebble," he answered my unspoken thoughts. Lucifer crouched to pick one up off the ground and levitated it over to Gabriel, pausing in front of my face. When he realized I wasn't going to touch it, it fell back to the concrete. "The terms were as follows: He was given my sword and the use of it for five days."

"My father traded my soul so he could use a stupid sword for five days?"

"You can't bargain for the soul of another. It's forbidden," Gabriel spat from between his teeth.

I peered over his outstretched wings. "Is that true?" I asked Lucifer.

Incredulous, Gabriel asked, "You trust the devil to tell you what's true? I wouldn't lie to you, Carmen."

"Wouldn't you?" I asked. His tattoos roiled angrily over his back.

"Nevertheless," Lucifer said in a bored tone, "I need my sword."

"You need to leave," I answered. I heard Gabriel tighten his hold on the hilt. Metal against angel made a distinctive gritting sound.

"Return what's mine," the devil demanded. "Malchazze is dead. Time is up."

"Get. Out!" I screamed.

The crows ahead began to caw loudly as Lucifer's feline eyes slithered to mine. "Where is the Keeper of Crows?"

I stood taller, stepping out from behind Gabriel's wing. "You're looking at her, prick." I wanted to raise his own sword at him, but I wasn't confident enough to keep hold of it. If he could make a pebble float, he could certainly call the sword to him. He probably could have called it anyway, slicing through me if he wanted. Power radiated off him, like the shadows that curled around his form, ebbing and flowing, a suit of tortured souls, writhing, churning.

Delight danced in his eyes. "It's about time they sent a human female to do a male archangel's job."

I flipped him off and he laughed, clutching his stomach.

"I will be back. Keep the sword until then. I'll enjoy breaking you, but I *do* want you to have a fighting chance. It's the gentlemanly thing to do. Wouldn't you agree, Gabriel? She wouldn't stand a chance against me in this shape. You should help her, angel."

Gabriel answered with a growl that shook the windows in the buildings above us.

Lucifer waved as he sank back into the bubbling tar beneath his feet. "Soon," he promised. I had a distinct feeling that though the devil may lie, he would manage to keep this oath.

Gabriel cursed, the tip of his sword stabbing into the tar and meeting only cement. "You should have given it back to him."

"He would have killed you with it."

Gabriel swallowed thickly.

"And it wouldn't matter anyway. He wants this place. He knows I'm a weakness, and he'll make plans to take Purgatory as his own."

The Lessons slowly began to return to the square, lingering for further instruction. The only one I had? *Get out of the city. You belong in the outskirts. For now.*

Each turned and slowly began filing out of the city, more filtering from the buildings and joining those who were leaving. Shuffling feet. The crows above ate the few souls just dispatched and held them in their mouths.

"Seal the veil," Gabriel reminded.

"You should leave."

"I'm not leaving. Seal it."

"Archangels don't belong in Purgatory!" I yelled, angry at how long Michael had been left here with no other instruction but to watch his birds and the holes that tore in the veil. Why hadn't he taken this place from Malchazze? My father deserved to die a long time ago. The souls here? My mother? They certainly didn't deserve to be trafficked and debased.

White-hot anger sliced through me.

"Lucifer *will* come back. He will come for his sword, and if you aren't prepared, he'll kill you and take this place as his own," he answered.

"I can't stop him from doing that. It doesn't matter how much training I have. Standing against my coward of a father was easy, but standing against him?" I motioned to the ground where the tar had solidified. "*That's* impossible."

Gabriel sneered. "Do you know that Michael tried to kill Malchazze? Several times he came close. Without orders, I might add. I'm sure you're surprised to learn about that. But he couldn't stop him. His birds, his sword, nothing worked. An archangel, it seemed, could not harm the antichrist. But you did. You killed him."

"He might have been the antichrist to you, but to me, he was just a mean, callous bastard."

"He was also one of Lucifer's pets. The reason we couldn't end him was because Lucifer strengthened your father, guarding him against us. Archangels can't kill one another. It's not physically possible. Michael couldn't even command his crows to do so. He couldn't utter the words. But you, a soul, turned him into dust. Even if he was just a mean, callous bastard." Grinning, Gabriel folded his wings behind him. "We just have to convince you that Lucifer is the same."

I snorted. Never gonna happen.

"Seal the veil. You can open it later, right?"

"Right," I parroted, calling to the fabric, to the Earth beneath my feet. *Become stone. No one passes through. Not even Satan himself.*

"I want to see the castle—all of it."

Gabriel nodded. "We should note the exits, any hiding spots, where the weaponry is…"

I smiled. "You're a true soldier."

Gabriel brushed the hair off his shoulder. "When Lucifer returns for the sword, you'll be glad we're prepared."

"Why is the sword so important to him? Is it the one he left Heaven with?" It looked much like the ones the archangels sported, only black as obsidian.

"No, it's much more dangerous. This sword was created in Hell, forged from the metal spear that pierced Christ's side when he hung upon the cross. It probably contains trapped souls and more evil than either of us could ever wield. Even being around it is dangerous."

"Lucifer is more dangerous *with* the sword than without it? That's scary as hell." He seemed powerful without it. I couldn't imagine his deadly intent growing exponentially because of a simple blade.

"It isn't a simple blade, Carmen. And I'd love to keep him from getting his hands on it again."

"Take it to Heaven," I told him.

He shook his head. "It's been tarnished, and evil isn't welcome inside the gates." His eyes turned to the sky above.

"What? What are you thinking about?"

"There may be one safe place to store it, but it's risky." Something flashed over his eyes, gray-blue as storm clouds.

"When do you think he'll return? I've sealed the veil."

Gabriel snorted. "Lucifer is already searching for a weakness, no doubt. Not to attack just yet, but so he knows them before you do." A shiver of fear crawled up my spine. "He will come for it – soon – but I'll be ready for him. I'd love nothing more than to end him. It's been a millennia since he betrayed us all, but the wound still stings as if it's fresh."

We walked through the hallways, taking note of each room, its exits, the best areas in which to hide, and areas that were dangerous to stand near, like fireplaces. They were entry points as well, and demons could easily scale the tall chimneys.

"Do you think he'll come with demons?" I asked curiously.

"Lucifer doesn't need them, but he rarely fights alone."

Coward.

"Exactly."

There were rooms bursting with swords mounted ceiling to floor, empty rooms, rooms with rich furniture, and rooms with books flanking every wall. We were exiting the third library when a thought came to me.

"What if we hid it?" I asked, walking farther down the hall.

Gabriel eased out of the closet he was looking in. "Hid what?"

"The sword."

"How would we do that? It knows its owner. It would call to him, and he would know in an instant."

"What if we cloaked it in the veil?"

Gabriel stilled, his brows kissing. "Could you do that?"

"I think so."

His fingers reached over his head, spreading around the grip of his sword, and with a slicing noise, he freed it. "Try it."

He extended the blade, transferring it to my outstretched hands. I hoped I was right about being able to manipulate the fabric so freely. Would the veil allow me to use it that way? Even if it worked, would Lucifer be able to find it? Would it still call to its master? If he got it back, could he harm the veil with it? Open it up and spill the darkness upon the Earth?

"No, he couldn't," Gabriel answered honestly.

"How do you know?" The weight of the metal was heavy in my hands.

"Because he's tried before. The veil doesn't answer to him."

It answers to me.

Gabriel inclined his head. "See what you're capable of, Carmen."

I knew I needed to keep my wits about me unless I wanted to be Lucifer's puppet; the controller of the veil, a gatekeeper for evil.

I took a deep breath and stepped away from Gabriel, holding the archangel's sword in my hands. Closing my eyes, I imagined fabric, glittering like the night sky, wrapping around and around the glowing silver metal until every speck of it was concealed in darkness. When I opened them again, Gabriel's lips were parted. I was holding dark fabric, and when I willed it to, it became invisible.

"You can do it," he breathed in awe.

"O, ye of little faith, Gabriel," I teased.

CHAPTER TWENTY-FIVE

The next morning, I relaxed the veil so the manna could fall. The souls would go hungry otherwise. "We have to be on guard," Gabriel explained. "Lucifer will wait for an opening and take the first one he gets."

"I'll seal it as soon as the manna stops."

We watched the cloudlike puffs fall from the sky, and as soon as they stopped raining down on the city, I sealed the veil, making it harder than steel. I wasn't ready to face him again, but I knew he was lurking just beyond this realm. I could feel him there, just out of reach, taunting me. Gabriel was strung tight. He'd been training night and day. Archangels, it turned out, didn't need to sleep at all. He finally stopped the clanging and crashing last night after I screamed at him for keeping me awake.

"You're grouchy," he snipped. "I'm only trying to help you."

"Help me in the morning," I groaned, my muscles and body strained past the point of exhaustion. The longer the veil was solid, the more tired I became. I didn't know if Gabriel had put two and two together yet, but he soon would.

"Can you strengthen me, Gabriel?"

He wasn't happy about it, but he stepped forward and infused me with some of his power and energy. I felt better immediately, but was still wiped out. Leaving him, I traced the path to my room.

This morning, he watched as I descended the steps, clad in black, wearing the feathers of the crows perched on every windowsill in the castle. "It suits you," he finally rasped.

"What? Darkness?"

He nodded. "Yes."

"Don't get soft on me, Gabriel. You're the one who said angels can't feel."

Taking in a deep breath, he muttered to himself, "Perhaps I was wrong about him."

"You were," I answered callously. "You were incredibly wrong about Michael. Where is he?" I'd asked him a dozen times already, and each time he hedged. My father would have been impressed with his ability to deflect questions with more questions, like arrows fired against an impenetrable shield, bouncing lazily off the surface.

CHAPTER TWENTY-SIX

Michael

I made it to the wood line, but I could smell Kushiel closing in and heard the mighty beating of his wings. The trees sheltered me from the wind, and the farther I ran into the forest, the more cover I had. I stopped, willing the fire to burst from my fingertips, easing my hands up against the bark of an enormous pine.

I had to relight it seven times, but it finally worked. My bonds sizzled as they unraveled, falling to my feet. The sound of a whip cracking came surging from behind. He'd caught up with me.

Keeping my back to him, the forest behind me, I dared him to come closer. He wouldn't win this battle. There was too much at stake. I had to get back to her.

"You and a human?" he asked.

"I love her. I won't apologize for it."

His head tipped to the side. "It must be worth it."

"It's worth everything. She is worth everything."

Kushiel was unusual. Maybe it was from the position he held, to be a punisher of angels, of his own kind. Maybe it was how he was created to be. His eyes were bigger than they should be, sharper somehow, like those of a bird of prey. They crackled with the fire that lived within him.

"I'll make you a deal, Keeper." My shoulders pushed back, hope once again filling me with strength I didn't think would renew in this forsaken place. "We'll race through the forest. If you win, I won't kill you. I'll fly you to Earth myself."

"Then you would be punished."

He grinned. "Let them try."

"On foot," I said. "I'll agree if you race on foot."

The grin fell from his face as he attached the whip to his belt. "Very well. I do love a challenge. So let it be." With those words, he sprinted into the trees beyond me. I pushed against the ground, taking off after him. I had to be faster… stronger. I had to get to her.

Gabriel would let her die. He would let her drown in the power of Malchazze. I still couldn't believe he'd turned his back on me or her. Pumping my arms, I was a blur through the forest. Kushiel had a head start, but I was fit and nimble compared to his hulking size.

The tree trunks were a maze, one I had to navigate faster than the speed of sound or light. When they thinned again, I didn't let up. I pushed forward until I felt him behind me. Kushiel panted, laughing with his head tilted toward the roiling clouds above. "I concede!"

"I'm not sure if you truly wanted to win, or if you just wanted to pick a fight with your own kind."

He smiled. "I'll never tell." Bracing his hands on his hips, his wings snapped from his back, flexing to and fro. "Anyway, a deal is a deal. I'll take you to Earth."

"To the ground," I clarified.

He chuckled. "I would have loved seeing you cry, Michael. As it turns out, you're smarter than the other archs. I will see you safely to the ground."

I knew what it meant for him. "Why are you doing this?"

Kushiel never answered; he just lifted me from the ground and raised us both into the sky. Within moments, we were plummeting toward the ground. I'd forgotten the feeling of freedom and was grateful for a momentary taste.

It was over as quickly as it began. He landed in a field of wheat, our feet crushing the crop around us. "Where are we?" I asked.

"Earth," he answered with an enigmatic smile.

"Where on Earth?"

"Not my problem, archangel. Figure it out. *If* she's worth it."

I narrowed my eyes at him. Of all the angels, I wouldn't have expected it. "You loved someone."

His smile fell away. "I did. And I'm still being punished for it."

It was clear then that we weren't allowed second chances. I was meant to stay in Purgatory for an eternity, just as he was meant to punish his own when they stepped out of line. Fairness flew out the window as swiftly as a crow.

"Thank you," I said.

He inclined his head and sprang up into the air, spiraling toward the heavens. I wondered what would happen to him now. The thought faded as I realized I was in the middle of nowhere. Making a trail through the wheat, I found my way to a paved, one-lane road. It seemed like the best option, so I followed it until the sun set in an inferno in front of me.

I couldn't feel Gabriel. I couldn't feel my crows or her. There was nothing. I was alone.

Somehow, I had to find my way back to Purgatory.

Carmen

Gabriel was angry. He brooded day and night, training every hour of that time as if his archangel-ness was going to somehow increase. Dressed in the black chain mail, I watched him swing his sword in great arcs.

"Let me fight you, or spar with you, or whatever it's called," I said, pushing myself up off the wooden chair.

With a chuckle, Gabriel dismissed me with a firm, "No."

"Yes." I jogged down the hall to the room lined with row after row of gleaming metal swords and daggers, testing the weight of those I could reach. The broadswords were too heavy, but the thinner ones were in the Goldilocks zone: they were just right. I ran back to the training room, to the brooding archangel.

"I'm ready," I challenged.

"No, you aren't, and I'm not sparring with you."

"Yes, you are. Stop being such a misogynist."

"I don't want to hurt you," he explained, easing the tip of his sword to the ground and leaning over it.

"Yes, you do. I piss you off. I'm not asking you to cut a limb off, but let me try to help."

This was stupid. He probably thought I'd lost my mind. Maybe I had. A girl helping an archangel? What could I possibly do to make him better? Raising the sword over my head, I brought it down slowly, wincing when the metal slammed into his blade. I never even saw him move his arms to protect himself.

Fire blazed in his eyes. "Is that all you've got?"

Oh, hell no. I brought the sword up again, and this time, there was no wincing; just the glorious sound of surprise when Gabriel defended himself with metal and a grunt I knew he didn't mean to let out.

I grinned in victory, right up until he raised his sword at me. Then, I nearly shit myself.

"Uh…"

He smirked. "You said you wanted to spar."

Sparring, to Gabriel, meant pushing my body to its limits. My muscles were puddles of gelatinous goo when he finally stopped attacking me.

"I wasn't attacking you," he said, responding to my inner thoughts. "I was training you."

"For what? Armageddon?"

"What if something happens and I'm called away, maybe given a new assignment? I'm unassigned right now, and it's been the longest time between assignments I can recall. If I'm called away, you'll be unprotected."

"The crows will protect me."

"I'm not sure I'd place my faith in them being able to beat Lucifer. He's the oldest evil in the world. He has tricks up his sleeve even *I* can't comprehend, and I've seen a lot of them over the millennia."

I let that sink in. Gabriel might have to leave. He hadn't been here long, just a couple of days, but if he left, I'd have to soften the veil and weaken the shield that so far, had held against Lucifer. If Gabriel was right and Lucifer was testing it and me for weaknesses, he would find one soon enough.

Gabriel was quiet. I knew he heard my thoughts, so I sent another to him.

Strengthen me again.

"I shouldn't. I won't always be here to bolster you."

"But you're here now, and I agree with you. I need to train."

Gabriel's sword gently slid between his wings, adhering magically.

"Magic has nothing to do with it."

Gabriel was about the same size as Michael, built the same. His tattoos flowed gently. When he looked up, his eyes softened to a caramel color. "I'm not him."

"I know. You look so much alike, and while there are things you share, like the tattoo thing, you aren't him." Gabriel's chin lifted a tick. "You're glad not to be him."

"I am."

"Pride isn't a sin anymore?" I smiled.

His eyes burned, scorching the caramel and charring it. "I'm not proud. I only do what I must because that's what I was created for. Nothing more, nothing less." He looked away, effectively dismissing me.

It was the saddest thing I'd ever heard.

His eyes snapped to mine again. "Why would you feel sadness for an archangel?" he scoffed.

"I don't feel sadness for an archangel. I'm sad for you, that you think you're only valuable for one reason, when there are so many things that make you amazing." When he opened his mouth to protest, I held my hand up. "You aren't Michael, and I'm not in love with you, but you're worth so much more than you give yourself credit for. As a friend, I think you should hear that once in a while."

"We're friends?" he asked quietly.

"Duh. Now make me superhero strong so I can kick some devil ass."

He chuckled lightly. "You're the strangest human I've ever met."

"Because I'm the first you've taken the time to get to know," I said, sticking my tongue out at him.

"Come on," I instructed, waving to him. "Make me strong again. I'll warm up my ass-kicking skills on you."

His brows raised. "I'll make you strong, but only because I don't want to hurt you, human." When his thumb brushed my forehead, it was like a line of frost had been drawn. I wasn't burning from flame, but from ice. I was turning to stone. Pure strength, better than adrenaline, coursed through my body and I reveled in the feel of it. Soon, the soreness was gone. The fatigue vanished.

Literally bouncing on my toes, I told him, "I need you to bottle that just for me. This is like a thousand energy drinks, only it won't explode your heart."

CHAPTER

TWENTY-SEVEN

We fought, blade against blade, until Gabriel was breaking out in a sweat, his body coated in a beaded sheen. The crows watched from the windows, each bird's eye focusing on the way the blades sliced through the air before they found their mark. "I gave you too much strength," he grunted, shoving me away from him.

I just grinned. "I love it. I'm not sure there's such a thing as too much."

"Every human loves power. It's your nature."

"It's not yours? You don't love what you do? You're an angelic warrior with pretty wings, for crying out loud."

"My wings are 'pretty'? That's the word you'd use to describe them?"

"Yes. What's wrong with pretty?"

He shook his head slowly. "Nothing. I've just never heard them called pretty before."

"Never?"

"No. Never."

"Hmm. They are, you know," I said with a shrug.

He just smiled, his cheeks flushing. "I see it now."

"See what?" I asked, catching my breath.

"I see why he's so taken with you."

Uh. How to respond? Gabriel was definitely a friend, but he would never be more.

"I know that," he hissed, charging at me with a look of fierce determination on his face. I didn't mean to embarrass him. As I raised my sword to block his blow, the block beneath my feet shifted to the side. Actually, the whole castle did. Dust from the grout above us flurried onto our heads.

"What the hell was that?" I asked breathlessly. Another jolt and the world lurched again. Screams erupted outside. The crows took to the sky, cawing loudly.

Flinging the large wooden door open, I ran outside. The Earth shook again. No, not Earth. Purgatory. Purgatory was being attacked. The veil shimmered with each jolt. Dark flashes filtered across the sky, like macabre northern lights.

"It's him," Gabriel said, sword at the ready, standing by my side.

"I'm not ready!" I yelled over the commotion.

"Did you really think he would wait until you were?"

I wanted to run, scream, or cry. Maybe all three.

"You should go inside," Gabriel said softly, turning me to look at him. "This is my assignment."

"What is? Battling the devil?"

"No," he said, smiling slightly. "Defending the Keeper of Crows."

My mind flashed to Michael, but I remembered that I'd taken the position from him when I threw him from this gray place.

The ground jolted again. "Get Lucifer's sword and cloak it! Then relax the veil and let him fall into this place. He'll expect you to strengthen the barrier. He won't expect you to let him in."

Everything in me wanted to make the veil stronger than titanium, to keep Lucifer away from this place and away from Gabriel, the sword, and the souls below.

"Go, Carmen," Gabriel said sternly. "If he gets the sword, any soul he touches with it will be sent to Hell whether they belong there or not."

"And you? What happens if he hurts you with it?"

Gabriel shook his head. "Don't worry about me."

"Will it kill you? Or will it send you to Hell?"

"What's the difference?" he asked pointedly. And he was right. There wasn't one.

I ran. I had to hide the sword.

My feet stopped inside the stone walls, arms raised to cover my head every time the castle shook above my head. A single crow flew alongside me. The sword was wrapped in the fabric I'd wound it in while practicing, but it still needed to be contained. The veil had to be solidified. I needed to make it much stronger than what I'd been able to make it so far, because it was about to fail entirely.

Focusing on solidifying the fabric was easy. What was hard was ignoring the screams of the souls outside. I told the veil to let Lucifer in, and then Gabriel roared as a bright flash of light heralded the arrival of Satan himself.

Focus, I told myself.

The clashing of Gabriel's sword rang out, metal on metal, and the shrieking intensified all over Purgatory. I moved to the balcony. Wisps of souls flew frantically through the air. I sent the crows to care for them and the birds obeyed, swooping to collect them.

Demons poured in through the torn fabric. No chance of escape for souls, they ran through the streets and hid in their homes. When the demons found them there, they tried to get away…but there was nowhere for them to go.

Below me, Lucifer, clad in white chain mail, collided with Gabriel, his pearly teeth bared menacingly. Gabriel shoved him away and regained his footing, but Lucifer was stronger. I could see it, feel it. He wouldn't be stopped. He wanted Purgatory for himself.

The devil's eyes snapped to mine and he smiled lazily.

Gabriel looked at me over his shoulder and shouted, "No!"

The half second it took for him to worry about me gave Lucifer exactly what he wanted: a moment of weakness. Gabriel paid for it as Lucifer drove a sword into Gabriel's side with a fierce grunt. "She's next," the devil hissed into his former friend's ear.

I knew he was coming for me. Gabriel was dying. Could he die? The veil was torn. Demons. Killing. Torture. The souls screamed.

Calling the crows, I told them to dispatch the demons. "Send them back to Hell!" I commanded.

Cawing in unison, they dove, shooting deadly feathers at those breaching the barrier, the demons who chased the souls, and the ones who dispatched them. I called to the

Lessons to end the demons as well. *Come into the city and stop them.*

The crows and Lessons weren't the only things that obeyed me. With everything in me, I called to the veil. *Conceal me.*

It stretched toward me from above, the fabric wrapping around my body until I couldn't tell where it ended and I began. My vision of Purgatory was darkened, but clear through the swirling tempest. Lucifer flew to the balcony, searching for me. I released the sword from the fabric that bound it and clutched the handle in my palm, squeezing tight. The sword hummed, calling its master, but Lucifer couldn't hear it, he couldn't feel it, and he couldn't see me.

"Where are you, Carmen?" he shouted into the castle. "We can come to a deal, you and me."

The sounds of torment below didn't bother him in the slightest, while it made my stomach sour. He made me sick, and I wasn't in the mood for bargaining. I just hoped Gabriel could hold on a little longer.

When he began walking, I asked the fabric to stretch and move with me. When I was right at his heel, I shoved the sword of Lucifer into its master's back, impaling him. His loud gasp filled the air, despite the cacophony of screams around us. I asked the fabric to fall away and it retracted.

"That was unexpected." He coughed, eyes wide as he turned around to face me. The devil could bleed. He wiped a string of blood from his mouth.

But he would see no mercy from me. "You should have been more creative. Giving my father the only sword that could kill an angel wasn't your brightest move."

"He never would have betrayed me."

"He was weak!" I screamed.

The darkness faded from his eyes, leaving them crystalline blue as he fell to his side, his feet scooting against the stone one last time as his muscles gave a jerk.

It felt like the darkness he lost had found its way to me, that it seeped into my tissue and filled my lungs. Calling the crows again, I ordered them to carry him away. The demons in Purgatory stilled as their master's life faded into nothing, as he became nothing...nothing but a puddle of tar.

I sealed the fissure they'd made, and with it, entombed the demons that dared to attack this place. The crows dispatched them all with deadly accuracy. The only remnants of them were the oil slicks where they once stood.

And emptiness.

Everything was empty. So many souls were killed.

And Gabriel... Where was he?

Crows descended and carried me to where he lay beneath the balcony, wings outstretched, wincing in pain. He wasn't dead.

"Are you okay?" I cried, my voice hitting an octave I didn't know existed.

"You're asking me if *I'm* okay? Are *you* okay?"

"I'm fine! You're bleeding. Oh, God. What do I do?" I searched for something to hold to his side, where blood was bubbling like a spring. He coughed violently, making the blood gush like a geyser.

"You have to leave this place to heal, don't you?"

He nodded, again wincing, a sheen of sweat on his brow and upper lip. "I can have them take you," I offered, ticking my head to the crows. *If it were possible, I'd take him myself.*

"I know you would. Let them carry me."

Calling them by the thousands, I helped Gabriel to his feet.

"Lucifer?" he asked haltingly. His eyes were glassy, feverish.

"Dead."

"How?" His mouth gaped open, more blood webbing at the corners.

I leaned my forehead against his as the crows swirled around him, giving him the memory. His eyes widened as he took in the scene. "You used his sword against him? But that doesn't make sense... an angel can't die from his own sword."

"You saw it, through my eyes. He was dead, lifeless. That should get me a bargain with Heaven. You tell them that!" The crows I called lifted him into the sky and I relaxed the veil just enough to let them through.

His blood dripped from the sky above me until he crossed the barrier and disappeared, nothing but feathers fluttering angrily in the air.

Lessons and the remaining crows continued hunting down the demons that were still trapped. I walked away from the castle, energy and power still coursing through me. I'd never hunted before, but there was a first time for everything.

When only tar puddles remained, the Lessons stilled and waited for further instruction. I asked them to line up, dispatching each with the sword of Lucifer. The demons had used Purgatory as a dumping ground for long enough, and while they'd helped me send the ones who created them back to Hell, I was done with those assholes.

The ones who attacked the safe house Michael and I stayed at seemed cognizant, aware of who we were and what they were doing. I realized now that was because my father made them that way. The Lessons were blank, mindless soldiers used as pawns. But beneath it all, they were people. They were bad people, but did they deserve to be used like puppets? No. If they deserved to burn, it was best to get on with it.

The sword hummed in my hand as I shoved it into the heart of each Lesson. When I came to Dimitri, it emitted a high-pitched howl, as if sensing my connection to him and the fact that I enjoyed ending him for good. He was hollow, a void. He'd become his own worst nightmare, a puppet for my father. Something easily discarded. Trash.

He would never hurt another person or soul, living or in the in-between. When his soul flew from his body, I watched as a crow swallowed it whole and dove into the concrete beside me, the stone rippling like water.

I didn't linger on him. He wasn't worth it. I kept killing them until it was second-nature; until their gray skin was cut cleanly and the birds knew the routine well.

The Lessons had no orders but mine, which meant they never fought back because I wouldn't allow it.

When there were no more Lessons, I called a single crow to me. Number two hundred thirty-five. "Fly to Gabriel."

Was he healed? Was he dead? Where was Michael? The questions flitted through my mind. Did Gabriel hear me when I told him Heaven owed me a bargain? I had killed the one their warriors couldn't, and now I wanted Michael. I wanted out of here and I wanted to be with him, without consequences.

———

Having returned from Heaven, Gabriel waltzed down the invisible steps an hour later, stepping onto my balcony. "How did they heal you so fast?" I asked him.

"It wasn't fast. Time works differently in Heaven. It passes differently on Earth, too."

"Did you tell them?"

"The host of Heaven celebrates your victory."

Heaven could celebrate all they wanted. I wasn't happy.

"Did you tell them that I want something in return for having killed him?"

"Heaven rarely strikes bargains, Carmen," he said softly, his toes stepping up to mine.

"The fact that Lucifer is gone should force an exception."

"What do you want?"

"You know what I want, Gabriel." I held his stare until he looked above, communicating with someone or something.

"There is a condition," he replied, his eyes darkening in anger. Gabriel didn't like it any better than I did.

"Name it."

"You have to serve here for two thousand years, and then return to Earth to live out the rest of your natural life. Then, and only then, can you be together. If you and Michael have contact before you're released, Michael's soul will be forfeit."

I inhaled sharply. "Two thousand years? My body won't be alive on Earth by then. I don't want to be a skinwalker like my father."

He shook his head. "Remember – time moves differently, Carmen. Your body will be alive and waiting for you."

"Serve here, live my life back home, and then I can be with him?"

"That's the deal."

I stared at Gabriel. "How long can I be with him? Is there some fine print you aren't reading to me?"

He smiled sadly. "Nothing is being hidden. If you serve here and then live your life on Earth, you and Michael can be together for the rest of eternity."

"In Heaven?"

"Wherever you both decide. Heaven. Earth. Purgatory."

"Fuck that. I want out of this place, and when I get out, I'm *not* coming back."

He smiled. "I understand."

"Where is he?"

"He's on Earth at the moment."

"You found him?" I asked, tears welling in my eyes. What I wouldn't give to see him, to hear his voice.

"I did. Somehow, he managed to escape Heaven." When he saw my look of confusion, he added, "With no wings, he came to Earth and was searching for a way to get to you. He was coming for you."

Tears flooded my eyes.

"Can I negotiate one more thing?" I asked.

Gabriel inclined his head. "You can ask, although I can't guarantee that your request will be granted."

"I want to see him. Just for a few minutes. If they let me see him, I'll agree. I'll do it."

Gabriel swallowed thickly. "Are you sure, Carmen? You could go home now and not agree to any of it. Is he worth this?"

"He's worth everything!" I cried. "Ask them. Please."

He looked above, relaying my request. When his mouth pursed into a straight line, I knew they weren't going to let me see him. Anger, red-hot and fiery, rushed through my body.

"I'll tear the veil. I'll rip it to fucking shreds! I just want to see him for a few minutes! Just for a few minutes, and then I'll take the deal. I'll manage this place and then live my life on Earth. I promise, I'll do as they ask. I just want to see him."

"Heaven doesn't appreciate threats, Carmen," he said with a smile. "But they have certainly responded. I'll be back soon."

"With him?" I shrieked as he ascended the steps again. Gabriel turned and winked as he disappeared.

I wrung my hands, picturing Gabriel's neck between them. Was he going to get Michael? I just wanted to see him, touch him one last time, before I couldn't. Before time and distance kept us apart. Archangels were fast. Gabriel was back in seconds, and Michael jogged down those steps, easing around Gabriel. When he saw me, he ran. So did I, and we collided, his arms wrapping around me and mine around him, touching, feeling, memorizing. My tears wet his cheeks as he kissed me.

"My God. You're okay. You…" He felt all of me, hands searching for damage. "You fought Lucifer?" his voice broke on the name.

"I'm going to miss you so much!" I cried, kissing his neck, his mouth, and his cheeks. His stubble raked beneath my fingernails.

Gabriel cleared his throat, looking anywhere but at the pair of us.

"I love you," he said breathily.

"I love you," I cried.

"It's time," interrupted Gabriel. "I'm sorry."

I held him tightly. "No! Please." *Please don't leave me. Don't take him away. Don't…*

"I'm sorry," Gabriel said, and meant it. It was written on his normally steely features.

"Michael? Wait for me," I pleaded, kissing him one last time.

He ended the kiss and pulled away, his cheeks glistening with my tears and his; a mixture of excruciating sadness and hope. "I will wait for you. No matter what."

"No matter what." I kissed him again tenderly.

"We have to go," Gabriel instructed as he walked up one of the steps.

"No," I whimpered as Michael pulled away from me and took his friend's hand.

"It won't be long," Michael comforted me. "Be strong, Carmen. It's what you're best at."

His eyes roiled, every color of the rainbow bursting through his irises as he left me in Purgatory and ascended to I didn't know where. My heart splintered, its fragments bursting violently apart.

Gabriel returned, descending the steps alone, and folded me in his arms. I sobbed on his chest until he, too, pulled away. "I've been assigned somewhere else. Remember, you just have to get through this; get through your time here. Make Purgatory what it was meant to be. Don't let the darkness seep in. Don't lose yourself to this place, Carmen. Remember who you are and why you're doing this. In the darkness, remember the light."

"All I see is gray," I blubbered, giving Pamela a run for her money.

"When you leave this place, nothing will make sense. Just remember him. Remember Michael. He'll be waiting for you on the other side."

"Will I see you again?"

He shook his head. "Not until the time of your bargain is up."

That made me cry harder. With Michael I had love, and with Gabriel, friendship. Now I was losing both and would have nothing.

"You'll always have my friendship," Gabriel answered my thoughts. "I've learned so much from you, Carmen. Love isn't contingent upon time or distance; it exists because it has to. Just remember that love – the love of a friend, the love of your soul mate. No matter what anyone says, remember…"

I handed the sword of Lucifer to him. "I will make sure it is kept safe." He accepted the blade, and with an inclination of his head, he was gone.

I was alone, save for the crows and souls below.

Michael

Leaving her was the hardest thing I'd ever done. I wanted to kill everyone and everything that stood between me and her, starting with Gabriel. When he came for me, I was surprised, but the look on his face wasn't angry. It was filled with pity. He understood...finally.

Her touch, the taste of her. I would hold onto the handful of memories I had until she came to me. Until then, I would have to work.

I would bide my time on Earth, where it seemed to pass slowest. Unwelcome in Heaven, unable to return to Purgatory.

I hoped Carmen could somehow feel my love for her through the realms, through time and space. She was strong. She could do this. And so could I. Forever was waiting for both of us.

Carmen

Purgatory somehow looked brighter. The longer I spent here, the more I was able to clean it up. The Meat Market? Obliterated. The outskirts? No longer needed. Destroyed. The wall? Not necessary. It was the last to go. Most of the souls who survived the invasion were now rested. Many were gone, but new ones arrived each day. An ebb and flow had been established, peaceful and teeming with purpose.

The crows couriered them back and forth across the boundary. Other than to stroke their silken feathers and remember him, I didn't even have to tell them what to do. It was innate. They were made for this.

I walked through the city, waving at the souls who greeted me. I doubted most knew they were even in Purgatory now. They went about daily life as they would have on Earth, with the exceptions of the manna provided and the cleansing every day.

Nothing threatened them now. They could rest.

I could rest.

So I did.

Perhaps that was *my* lesson: Patience.

PART
THREE

CHAPTER

TWENTY-EIGHT

Beeping, whooshing, a song whistled sweetly, expertly. My eyes fluttered open and I stared at the speckled drop ceiling above me, the same one I'd hovered above when this all began. Something was gagging me. The beeps from the machines beside me became frantic. A nurse rushed in. "No wonder the machines are chirping! Look at you. You're awake!"

She was a sweet, middle-aged woman with skin the color of dark chocolate. It looked as soft as her hair, pinned in waves along her scalp. "I didn't expect you to wake up today. I'll get the doctor."

My chest hurt. Something was... I was choking. I gagged.

"Easy, honey. There's a tube down your throat."

I gagged again. My eyes watered as I fought against the intrusion. "It's okay. It had to breathe for you for a while. I'll check with the doctor and see if he wants to remove the tube, but for now…" She bent over and scanned a syringe with her machine, waiting until it beeped. Staring at the computer, she smiled. "This should make you relax. You'll feel better soon. You're very lucky to have survived such a crash." She patted my hand. "Be right back."

The medicine was fast. It relaxed my muscles and I stopped struggling against the tube, relaxing the muscles in my throat. The window blinds were pulled, but I could see the sunshine peeking in between every vertical piece of plastic. Two chairs next to my bed sat empty.

My muscles were sore. Everything hurt. I tried to reposition myself, to find a comfortable way to lay, but couldn't move. The nurse strolled back into the room with a smile.

"Doctor Bragg is on his way. He's going to evaluate you and see if we might be able to get rid of that tube."

Doctor Bragg? He was the same doctor who helped me after the car wreck.

I nodded, tears welling in my eyes, blurring her for a moment.

"We called your father, but he isn't here yet. I'm sure he'll come as soon as he can. Is there anyone else I can call for you?"

What the hell was happening? This was enough deja-fucking-vu.

She waited, eyebrows raised until I shook my head no.

The clock on the wall opposite my bed read three forty-five. *The same time I woke from being in the… wreck. But that was so long ago… I'd spent two thousand years in Purgatory. He warned me that time worked differently, but this was time reversed altogether. That wasn't possible. This didn't make sense at all.*

The doctor, a middle-aged man wearing royal blue scrubs, a stethoscope, and a frown stepped into the room. He pumped the hand sanitizer and rubbed it in, staring at me as if I were a waste of his time. I'd had two rounds of his shitty bedside manner.

He was none too gentle about poking and prodding me. "We can remove your tube, but you aren't well enough to leave the unit. You'll be here for a while, and you have to take it easy. Do you understand?"

I nodded.

He typed a few things into the rolling computer and then motioned for the nurse to help him. As the intubation was removed, I gagged on plastic, confusion, and spit.

"Try to speak," he instructed coldly.

I opened my mouth and rasped, "Where… where is he?" The medicine was working too well for me to keep my thoughts straight.

"Where is who? Your father? Probably in the cafeteria or grabbing a shower," the nurse answered. "He's been by your side since the accident."

"What accident?" I asked, wincing when I tried to push myself up. My foot was in a sling. I cursed Dimitri again for putting me in this place, but smiled as I remembered where I sent him.

"A motor vehicle accident," the doctor answered in a bored tone. "Do you recall the night of the crash?"

"I'm not here because of a crash. Not this time."

The doctor's bushy eyebrows furrowed. "Why do you think you're here?"

"I'm here because I was beaten half to death, asshole. You need to grow some compassion before you talk to any more patients today."

He scowled at me as the nurse turned away, stifling a laugh.

My mind felt fuzzy. "Where is Michael? Where is the Keeper of Crows?"

"What did you give her?" the doctor asked the nurse. She rattled off some long, stupid medicinal name and he huffed.

"Let it wear off, but I think we may need an MRI if she keeps talking nonsense."

"I'll show you nonsense, asshole," I muttered. Then I promptly fell asleep.

———

When I woke, I was still in the hospital bed, in the same cookie cutter room that was beside Pamela's.

When the nurse came back in, she asked me question after question.

What was my name? *Carmen Kennedy.*

What date was it? *Who the fuck knew?*

What type of car did I crash? *Why are you asking me about a car? Dimitri put me here!*

Who was Dimitri?

When my father strolled into the room, steaming coffee in hand, I screamed, trying to sit up in the bed. It was him! He wasn't gray and he wasn't alive. He was dead. How was he here? Was he going to kill me?

"He's going to kill me!" I shrieked, trying to get away from him, clutching the thread-bare sheets beneath me for leverage.

The nurse told Father it would be best if he left for a few minutes.

"Try forever! I don't know how you're even alive!"

"What was that all about?" the nurse asked, wide-eyed.

"He's...the fucking antichrist, and he's going to kill me. He came back to kill me! I had the crows end him. Their feathers impaled his heart, but evil doesn't stay fucking dead!" I roared so he could hear me.

"Calm down," she tried to soothe.

Another nurse came into the room. A woman. Then another. A man.

They approached either side of my bed with their hands up. "Don't touch me! Don't touch me!" I screamed, thrashing wildly until my leg screamed in pain. I cried, trying to get them to leave me alone.

"Keep away from me. I'll kill you! I'll kill you all!"

I called for the crows. Did I lose the power over them when I woke up? Where the hell were they? I needed them.

A nurse pushed a syringe into the IV port as two others held my arms still. Soon, my body felt warm. My veins. My head. Warm.

"That's it. Relax."

"Don't let him kill me..."

"I won't, sweetheart. Get some rest. I'll talk with the doctor."

"Don't... let..."

Her footsteps on the tile echoed through my mind.

CHAPTER

TWENTY-NINE

When I woke, my hands were in soft restraints. So was my unbroken leg. I waited for the nurse. The remote at my side had a red button that was supposed to summon them, but after several clicks they still weren't coming.

A male nurse with dark blue scrubs finally stepped in, pumping the hand sanitizer dispenser once and rubbing the teal goop into his hands before approaching. "How are you feeling?"

"Like absolute shit. Now, why am I tied down?"

"We need to assess you. While you were sedated, an MRI was performed."

"I didn't hit my head, dickhole."

"You're belligerent," he deadpanned, pecking the keys on the computer's keyboard one at a time. He sighed and turned to face me, crossing his arms.

"What is your name?"

"I've already told you my name."

"Humor me," he said.

"Carmen Kennedy."

"What year is it?"

"Does it really matter? Why do you keep repeating the same questions over and over?"

"Who is your father?"

"Warren Kennedy."

"Is he the antichrist?" The nurse narrowed his eyes in challenge.

"YES!"

He smirked as he pecked the keyboard again, dismissing me.

"Do you remember the car accident?"

"I'm not in here because of a fucking wreck! I'm in here because Dimitri beat me senseless. He almost killed me, and when I was put in this hell hole, I floated—my soul floated above my body. Then these men with lightning leashes captured me and pulled me through the veil into Purgatory and everything was gray, and they were trying to sell me into… sex slavery, and then I learned that my father is the antichrist. He was setting up a kingdom, and there were Lessons there." I jerked my arms, trying to free myself. "Some had no eyes, some had their ears filled with tar, and others had skin over their mouths. Demons put them there. Demons! Because my father was one of them. Lucifer gave him his sword, but in the end…" I smiled. "I killed him. I killed the devil."

The doctor on duty, a petite woman with a hairstyle from 1990, stepped into the room. "Did you hear all that?" the male nurse asked her.

"I did." She stepped toward me. "Your MRI showed no trauma. At this point, I think it's best that we ask our on-staff psychiatric team to evaluate you."

"Psychiatric team? I'm not crazy!" I thrashed against the bed. "Untie me. Please, doctor. I'll tell you all about it. Everything you want to know. Oprah would want to interview me for this. She would love the story. Trust me when I say that I know I'm sane."

"I know, dear. But you need the best care possible to recover from this." Her eyes flicked to the nurse and then to the screen. "I've given the okay for them to move you to a new unit."

"I'm not crazy," my scratchy voice pleaded.

"I know—"

"You *don't* know!" I kicked and flailed. "Because you won't listen."

"Call psych and ask the on-duty if they want us to tranquilize her before we send her up."

The nurse nodded. "Will do."

"I don't need tranquilizers. I'm not an animal. What is *wrong* with you people?" I shouted. Then the tears began to flow. When they started, gut-wrenching sobs wracked my body. My tired body. I was so tired.

Tired of yelling. Tired of fighting. Tired of hurting. My leg hurt so badly. My head throbbed.

"Just let me out of here," I sobbed dejectedly.

The doctor turned to leave, but looked over her shoulder. "I'm afraid we can't until you're stable."

"I *am* stable. Send me home."

"With the man you believe is the antichrist?"

Fuck my life. I had no home now. Gabriel told me it would be this way. That things would be different, that time would be strange. It sure as hell was. He was right. *Where was he?*

"Gabriel?" I screamed at the top of my lungs. "Gabriel? Michael? Where are you? Are you close? Can you hear me?"

The nurse stepped back into the room. "You can't yell like that," he admonished.

"I sure as hell can! GABRIEL!"

Another nurse jogged to the doorway. "Psych said to sedate her."

"Fuck, no! No! Gabriel! GABRIEL! Help me!" The male nurse and two more came into the room, but it would take more than that to hold me down. I fought them, and then two more showed up. My arm was held still, their bodies weighing me down, weighing my body down, and then the medicine was pushed into my arm. Tranquilizer. Sedation.

Quiet.

Peace.

"Gabri—"

The nurse shook his head as he climbed off me and turned to his co-workers. "Is it a full moon? The crazies are in full effect."

They chuckled as they left me. In my mind, I called for Michael. Called for Gabriel. Called for my crows to pluck the nurses' eyes out.

I'd... kill them... all.

━━━━━━

I woke in another room, my arms and uninjured leg still restrained. I was in the psych ward with doors that locked and only the smallest of windows through which the staff spied on their patients. I hated them all. Everyone who worked here.

The doctors were all a joke. My father had probably hired them to treat me like I'd lost my mind. How was he alive? I saw his body. I saw the feathers buried in his chest. I saw his soul fly, and then I sent a crow to gobble it up and spit it into Hell. I *saw* it.

"I saw it!" I screamed. "Gabriel!"

For days I screamed for Gabriel, Michael, Malchazze…anyone who would tell them I was right, that I wasn't crazy. No one came.

Eventually, my body healed and they couldn't keep me in the ward anymore, so my father paid for me to be transferred to a mental health facility. I was bundled up in an ambulance and taken there against my will.

Obviously, screaming wasn't working. I was never going to get out of there if I didn't shut my mouth, so that was what I decided to do. While the ambulance rocked over bumps and pot holes, I decided to keep quiet, to observe and figure a way out of this situation. Freedom. Tasting freedom would be worth the lying it would take to get out, and then I just had to bide my time. I had to live out my natural life—I couldn't end it prematurely—and then I could be with him, and him with me. He would love me forever and I would love him.

I couldn't wait to see him, so I kept quiet. The gravel under the tires stopped crunching when the brakes squealed and the vehicle came to a stop. The medics slammed their doors and opened the rear of the car, blinding me with the evening sunlight. The mental hospital looked more like an old brick boarding house. A painted-white, iron cross stood sentry over the grounds. I knew I'd been sent there for a reason. It was a sign that Michael was watching over me. Maybe I'd see him, perhaps catch a glimpse somehow. We couldn't talk, but could I see him? Just once?

I wanted my crows to circle the cross, to give him a sign that I knew he'd sent me here for a reason, but they didn't respond. They must be busy, or maybe they were stuck in Purgatory. Did I make the veil available for them, or were they trapped?

They eased my gurney to the ground and then unfolded a wheelchair. My leg was in a white cast and the hospital gown barely covered me, having come undone in the back. The medic was overweight by a hundred or so pounds, but his smile and eyes were kind. Wes was his name, according to his badge.

"We have to take the bed back, but the doc thought you'd be more comfortable lying down for the ride. It probably kept your foot from swelling in that cast. It'll sweat though," he chatted merrily.

Fuck casts and sweat, I thought. Where was Gabriel? I wasn't forbidden from seeing *him*. Where in the world was he? Was he on assignment in some remote part of the realm? Fighting evil? Flying around in Heaven? Why couldn't he come visit me?

The sound of popping gravel caught my attention as they helped me into the wheelchair and adjusted the footplates, easing my foot and cast onto them. I looked behind me as they wheeled me onto the concrete ramp and pushed me around the turn toward the front porch. From the rafters on the porch's cover flew a dove. Its gray feathers told me Gabriel was close. I searched for him, finding only my father's face. The silence ended in that moment.

"Wes, get me away from him! He's going to kill me!" I screamed, taking hold of the wheels and pushing them forward and up the concrete.

Father put his hands out beseechingly. I moved my eyes from the door, to him, and then back to the door. "I'm not going to hurt you, Carmen," he pleaded.

He had the audacity to act hurt. Fuck that. He wasn't hurt. He was the one who caused pain. "Get away!" my voice shrilled.

He stopped walking and stood back, hands on his hips as Wes and his friend wheeled me inside the glass double-doors that opened with the automatic button I pushed.

"Let's get her inside and then-" Wes told my father.

"Don't help him! He's evil!"

Wes's eyes went wide. "Okay."

Good thing he was smart enough to be afraid of Malchazze. If he could raise himself from the dead… Wait. Was he really alive, or was this just his skin? The one my father possessed? "Was he really out there?" I whispered.

"Yes," Wes answered, leaning down to me. "I saw him."

He was kind. Wes was kind and nice to me, so I didn't claw his face. The lady behind the glass window in the lobby? She was a horrible bitch. She nagged poor Wes to death as they tried to explain that I was being transferred. She had no record of such a transfer, blah, blah, blah. But when the bitch checked her fax machine…boom. There it was. Hallelujah. We'd just witnessed a miracle.

A male orderly appeared through a security door. "I'll take her to her room and get her settled," he said with a smile.

I looked up at Wes and a tear fell from my eye. "I'm not crazy."

He shook his head. "I know you're not. You'll be okay. These nice folks will help you." I couldn't place his accent, but it was southern and soothing. I nodded, wiping my nose on the back of my hand. I'd morphed into Pamela, but I wasn't even in Purgatory anymore. I was on Earth. I woke up.

I came back.

My soul found my body and time was erased, and this… "Wes?" I yelled as he pushed the door open to leave.

"Yeah?"

"Thank you."

He smiled slightly, his cheeks glowing red. "You're welcome, ma'am."

That afternoon, when the steel door slammed behind me, I made a decision. I would fake the hell out of this until they let me go. I would turn to steel—just like the door that held me in. And then I'd waltz out of this place and never, ever look back.

CHAPTER

THIRTY

Doctor Stein was more clinical than Doc Coleman. The diplomas and certificates on the walls in her tidy, pristine office showed that she was a psychiatrist. There were no pelvis-shaped inkblots anywhere in this place. The halls were empty, washed in white, like everything else—even the clothing they provided.

She had a permanent crease in the center of her forehead despite the tight, ebony ponytail that pulled her hair away from her face. She wasn't friendly; she didn't bullshit and didn't care or pretend to care. The dark frames of her glasses overwhelmed her delicately featured face, but somehow it worked for her. There were no clocks on any of the four walls, and she kept the blinds drawn in her darkly painted office, a comforting shade of brown-gray.

She kept the blinds closed for me. I had issues with windows, they said. They were wrong. My issues weren't with the windows; my issues were with the doves that perched on the sill, cooing happily. Gabriel sent them. Their feathers matched his. He must be the Keeper of Doves. It made complete sense. But Gabriel had yet to show his face. It had been over two weeks and he hadn't visited me on Earth, or in this place. Pissed off didn't even begin to describe how I felt about that. I knew Michael couldn't come, but Gabriel was my friend. He should at least check in on me.

She stared at me with her arms crossed over her chest, waiting. This was her way. She didn't push. She asked a question and even if it took the entire session for me to answer, she waited patiently for it. For some reason, the comfort of knowing I had all the time in the world to answer, or the freedom to tell her to go to hell for asking made me more loose-lipped than I'd imagined was possible.

"Your father came to see you today."

I shifted in my seat. He had come to see me. Sure. That's what he wanted them to believe. I knew the truth. He was either trying to kill me – Malchazze returned – or he was just a stranger's skin that my father occupied for a time. Either option was bad. I didn't want anything to do with him. Why couldn't they understand that?

"Do you want to harm him?"

"No."

"Did you think of harming him or killing him at all?" Her lips pursed, sharp, dark eyes waiting for an answer.

"He's not my father."

"He is your biological father," she corrected.

"But he isn't the one who raised me. I have no feelings about him whatsoever. He's a stranger to me."

She jotted a note. "There are pictures, family portraits of you, him, and your mother. He isn't a stranger."

"Yes, he is."

"You still hold to your story? That you killed his soul in Purgatory and sent it to Hell?"

I smiled. I had done that. Even the medicine, the dosages they kept increasing, couldn't squash the memory of Malchazze, of those feathers embedded in his chest, the look of shocked surprise on his lips, in his eyes.

"You believe," she flipped to another page, another scribbled note, "that he only used a body to travel around on Earth—the same body of the man you call a stranger now."

"Yes. That's one possibility. The other is that he found a way to come back and he's biding his time. He'll kill me if that's the case."

"Both scenarios sound far-fetched. You know what I think?"

"I'm sure you're going to tell me, Doctor Stein."

"I think you know that all this was a dream. You were in a coma, Carmen. A drug-induced coma. For weeks, you lay in a hospital bed. This was nothing more than a dream, a hallucination. If you can admit that to yourself, you'll be better off."

"Sometimes it feels like it was a dream," I told her. "Sometimes, this room feels like I'm trapped in a dream. The line between what's real and what's imaginary is very blurry for me." She took the bait I offered. I was going to get the hell out of here, but my recovery had to be gradual or it would seem contrived.

She nodded, a slight smile on her face. "Your admission of that alone is progress, Carmen. We're done for the day, but I want you to do me a favor. Write it all down. Everything you remember about your dream, about Purgatory. Bring it with you tomorrow."

It would take a year to detail it all, but I could write something by then.

———

My room was white. The walls bled purity onto the floor. Even the bedclothes were sterile, devoid of everything. The white made me appreciate the tumultuous gray of Purgatory. At least the gray was alive, whereas the white was empty and dead. As long a time as I spent in the gray realm alone, I was far lonelier on Earth. Because *he* wasn't here, and I wasn't allowed to see him. It was part of the bargain struck. I survived two thousand years of servitude in Purgatory, but only days on Earth had passed during that time. Days where my shattered body healed. Days where Gabriel gave my biological father a new memory and by extension, a new future for me. At least I thought he did. The jury was still out on that one. Every time I saw my father's face, my skin crawled to get away from him. Fight or flight reflexes kicked in, and I wanted to run away or stab him in the throat. Either would have sufficed.

But if it was just the man whose skin my father wore, how could I kill him? He was innocent. I had to figure out a way to tell…

The orderly peeked into my room through the small window. I had been given a pencil and paper, so they would watch me closely. Sharp objects weren't given without supervision, and believe me, I would yield it as a weapon—a weapon in the battle for my own emancipation.

In my scrawling handwriting, I wrote what I knew:

My father was the antichrist.

I was dragged to Purgatory from the hospital after someone beat me almost to death.

The Keeper of Crows saved me.

And then we saved each other.

I slew my father and then the devil himself.

Purgatory's balance has been restored, but my faith has been shattered.

I'm forbidden to see him until death claims me.

I long for death, but suicide forfeits the agreement. I have to wait for it, and they will make me wait for a very long time.

I love him.

He loves me.

Even through the distance between us, I feel him.

One day, we'll be together. I will feel his fingers on my skin, his breath on my neck, his lips on mine, and it will all have been worth it.

When I woke, everyone thought I was crazy. They still do.

But I know something they don't.

I'm not crazy at all.

When I was finished and satisfied, I waved the orderly into my room and surrendered the pencil to him. "Thank you, Ms. Kennedy." He smiled. I knew my fractured reality had actually happened, because if it hadn't, I'd be trying to lure him into bed. I'd flash a smile and ask him to help me. But the thought of any man touching me—any man but Michael—made me sick. My stomach churned at the thought.

The next day, I gave Doctor Stein the paper. She read each sentence slowly and then re-read them, glancing up at me. "Near-death experiences are common. Across every culture in this world, even ones the modern world hasn't touched. Did you know that?"

"I did."

"I have a patient now who tells a very similar account of her brush with death."

"A man or woman?" I asked.

"The patient is a woman. You see, Carmen, the mind is very complex. Even when a person's body shuts down, their mind still functions on all cylinders. Unless there is trauma to the brain itself, it works. Your neurons fire. Your imagination can run wild. Through every culture, in every walk of life, there are stories of people emerging from light or from a place like you've described. It's one universal thread that ties us together, but it isn't a real one. It's a testament to the power of our minds to escape from trauma."

"Or else it actually occurs," I countered. "That would be the alternative, right?"

She cleared her throat. "I suppose, but remember Occam 's razor. The simplest explanation is usually the right one."

Was it simpler to think that my brain created a world that other people had also dreamed about? Or was it simpler to believe that world actually existed? I thought the latter made more sense.

What were the chances…? "Doctor Stein, is her name Pamela, by any chance?"

Doctor Stein stilled. "I can't discuss my patient or her experiences with you any further. I don't feel that it would do any good, and I won't violate her privacy as I wouldn't violate yours. Now, let's talk about what you wrote here."

I flashed a victorious Cheshire cat grin. "Does she mention the Keeper as well? Has she mentioned me?"

Doctor Stein shook her head. "You aren't listening today, Carmen. Unless you're willing to focus and work to get better, you're wasting my time. I refuse to go over this with you again. There is no Keeper of Crows." Unable to hide that she was flustered, Stein hit a button on her phone and called for the orderlies to remove me from her office.

"We made a lot of progress today, Doctor. Thank you." I smiled as I was wrenched from the room by two large males who obviously worked out. Those bastards were strong.

I clawed toward her, trying to wriggle my arms out of their steely grips. "I know you know he's real! He *is* real! It was *all* real! It happened! I'm not CRAZY! I AM NOT CRAZY!" I screamed, kicking out at her desk. Her face was one of shocked horror and I loved it.

The orderlies threw me in my room and locked the door. Alone, I paced until I couldn't stand walking on the same twelve tiles anymore. I spent the rest of the afternoon staring at the ceiling with a smile on my face. Pam didn't forget me, after all.

CHAPTER THIRTY-ONE

"We're going to try Lithium." Those words bounced around in my mind several times each day. Every time the nausea started, I made one of my frequent trips to the bathroom where I wasn't sure which was more urgent: the vomit rising from my stomach, or the diarrhea I could barely control. Adding to the fun, the medicine made my legs swell and my tongue feel dry as the desert.

Doctor Stein was adamant that my experiences weren't real; so much so, that I began to believe her. Maybe her other patient really wasn't named Pamela. Maybe I imagined everything. After all, I'd only been in the hospital a short time. That information was in black and white. I saw the medical charts.

After telling Stein that I'd only believe her if she showed me proof, she called the hospital, obtained my signature for the medical release, and they faxed bills and records of my stay to her office. She personally delivered the file to my room and I spent hours combing through dates and treatments, diagnoses and nurse's notes. Also in the file was a motor vehicle accident report. It said I lost control on the highway, flipping my car. The ambulance had taken me from the scene of the crash to the hospital.

The hospital report said that I was in intensive care for twenty-eight days, transferred to a room on the psychiatric floor for another week, and then released into the care of the mental institution in which I now sat.

In the end, it documented my entire journey. The truth was in black and white ink. The next day during our session, she produced my mother's death certificate. The cause of death did not read suicide, overdose, or anything about pills or alcoholism. There were no notes about anti-depressants, or that my mom was on any medication at all. It said she'd had an aortic aneurysm and the main wall of her aorta had weakened, thinned, and then collapsed. Doctor Stein stared at me from across her desk and gently pushed a small pile of paper toward me. The papers were Google search results regarding the condition. I took comfort in the fact that she would have died instantly; she didn't suffer. But did Father use his connections to alter the records?

When I voiced that concern, Stein was ready for it. "Occam's Razor."

The simplest answer was probably the correct one.

"So, she died from a heart issue?" I asked tentatively. My head was filled with fog. "Could that really be true?"

"You tell me," she answered gently, smiling.

I brought my file with me to that session. "This says I was in a car accident; that I met friends at The Castle and wrecked on the way home. No alcohol or drugs were found in my system. Did I go to rehab at all?"

Stein shook her head. "It never happened. There isn't even a facility named Sunny Bridge in the state of California. There is one in Rhode Island, but it's a nursing home." She sat back in her seat. "Carmen, you never went to rehab, and there isn't a Doctor by the name of Verlund Coleman in the United States. Never has been. I checked. Twice."

Doc wasn't real and Sunny Bridge didn't exist. I felt like I'd been sucked into a rerun of *Buffy the Vampire Slayer*. "There is no Pamela?"

She shook her head, pursing her lips. "There is no Pamela," she whispered gently. "You keep saying I reacted when you mentioned that name, but Carmen, I didn't. I have no patient named Pamela. The last time I saw a patient named Pamela was six years ago, and she was treated for schizophrenia. She had no near-death experience to speak of."

I clutched my temples, pushing them and my head to get things straight. Weren't they straight already? Nothing made sense, so no. They weren't.

I was Carmen Elaine Kennedy.

My father was running for President.

My mother was dead. She killed herself.

I was in Purgatory.

It was real.

I killed the devil.

It happened.

He was real.

Michael, the Keeper of Crows, was real.

"I know this is a lot to take in, Carmen, but you need to look, really look, at what's in front of you. I can help you if you want to let me, but if you keep refusing, you'll be in this hospital for a very long time." She let out a sigh. "Do you want me to go over it with you again?"

I nodded numbly.

That was all I could feel: numbness. She showed me the accident report and medical records again, gently noting the facts and dates. She combed over every detail of Mom's death certificate.

"Carmen, there isn't a single fact here to support the story you've given me. And if you'll listen, I think you'll come to the same conclusion I have. You were in a very bad accident. Your body, its bones, your brain itself, was broken. You were broken. The hospital had to induce a coma to allow you to heal. The medication you were on was powerful, and what you experienced was an intense response to that medicine. It's like when you fall asleep and your muscles begin to spasm—as everyone's do—and your mind creates a scene where you're kicking a soccer ball, for instance. Your mind makes your foot jerk forward and it wakes you."

I nodded. I'd experienced that before. Mine was a dream about a shark shredding my leg into pieces and I'd woken with a Charlie horse. But still. Same thing.

"While in the coma," she continued, "your mind created an entire world to cope with what you were experiencing. The mind is a terrible, powerful thing. We don't understand why it does this, but perhaps it's a shield to keep you from feeling pain or remembering the trauma before you're able to cope with it. Whatever the reason, it does happen in cases like yours."

"But you said near-death experiences were universal."

"They are, because people with trauma respond in much the same way. The brain functions in the same way regardless of creed, color, zip code, or religious affiliation. That's why the experiences are similar across the board; not because those places exist. It's why people see different things. Some see a bright light, some feel happiness, and some feel despair and toil in the darkness. Everyone's emotions are different. Their life experiences differ. You are different from everyone else who's had such an experience, and so yours is unique to you. Theirs is unique to them. Do you understand what I'm saying? I don't doubt you remember the dream you had and that it seemed very real to you, but it *wasn't* real. When you accept that fact, we can make progress and strides in the right direction."

I wanted to.

I wanted to get better.

I wanted to leave this place.

"I'll try," I muttered, my voice like gravel.

She smiled slightly. "That's all I ask."

CHAPTER
THIRTY-TWO

Another month. Another session with Doctor Stein. She sat across her desk with a pensive look, creasing the deep wrinkle between her brows. "Over a month ago, you wrote this. Do you remember doing it?"

She pushed a piece of plain, white paper toward me, sliced with teal lines and slashed down the side with a red one. It had seen happier days. Crinkled and bent, it hadn't been taken care of. I eased the paper closer and looked at the handwriting. My handwriting.

"Tell me what you remember now," she instructed. "Which of these things do you recall from your dream? In fact," she added, holding out a pen. "Cross through everything you don't remember."

My father was the antichrist.

I was dragged to Purgatory from the hospital ~~after someone beat me almost to death.~~

The Keeper of Crows saved me.

~~And then we saved each other.~~

I slew my father ~~and then the devil himself.~~

Purgatory's balance has been restored~~, but my faith has been shattered.~~

~~I'm forbidden to see him until death claims me.~~

~~I long for death, but suicide forfeits the agreement. I have to wait for it, and they will make me wait for a very long time.~~

~~I love him.~~

~~He loves me.~~

~~Even through the distance between us, I feel him.~~

~~One day, we'll be together. I will feel his fingers on my skin, his breath on my neck, his lips on mine, and it will all have been worth it.~~

~~When I woke, everyone thought I was crazy. They still do.~~

~~But I know something they don't.~~

~~I'm not crazy at all.~~

"I'm sorry. I still remember some of it. It's all fuzzy, sort of foggy, and I know it wasn't real, but some of the memories of the dream linger. Mostly about my father."

She smiled and nodded, accepting the pen from me.

"Good. You're doing very well, Carmen. The medicine is working. I can't tell you how proud I am of your progress."

CHAPTER

THIRTY-THREE

Two months and several intense sessions later, Doctor Stein smiled from the doorway of my room. I knew from the look on her face she was ready to give me the news I'd been waiting to hear.

"You've made great strides, and I believe you can continue your care on an outpatient basis. Your father has agreed. He ended his run for the Presidency and has resigned his position."

My father wasn't running for president? Would the paparazzi finally leave us alone?

Could life really go back to being normal?

I hoped so. My head tingled. I sipped from the plastic cup of water and thanked the doctor. Would my bed at home feel soft? The mattress under my legs was squeaky and lumpy and hella uncomfortable. I'd done well so far. I could do this.

Mom wouldn't be there. I couldn't remember Father when he wasn't something important—CEO, Presidential candidate, Community Preparation Specialist. Would there be an awkwardness between us? Would I be welcomed home? I'd no doubt humiliated him. Telling the world he had to drop out of the race because his daughter was mentally ill must have crushed him. Father hated to lose, and I made him forfeit everything in a very public way.

"When can I go home?" I asked, faking a smile.

"You can leave here tomorrow."

"Will I see you before then?"

"I'll see you tomorrow at discharge." She smiled genuinely.

The next morning I dressed in a fresh pair of scrubs and sat on the mattress, calmly sipping water after the good doctor left me with a small wave of her hand. An orderly brought my morning doses of psychotropic meds and I swallowed them down quickly, opening my mouth wide so she could see I'd swallowed them. She nodded and told me she would be back as soon as she finished the morning round. Doctor Stein had just begun to fill out my discharge papers.

My mind was still a jumble, but she promised to help me through everything. The last of the dream I had while comatose was still fresh in my mind.

Gabriel telling me to be strong, that two thousand years in Purgatory would pass quickly, that my sentence would be over before I knew it, and that after I served those years, my soul would return to Earth, to my body, and I just had to live out my natural life. Then, *he* would be there. Keeper was waiting for me. Gabriel would watch over me, and I would soon be with the one I loved.

While the delusion was a nice one, I knew it wasn't true. The medicine showed me that the tether I thought I felt between his heart and mine was all imagined. It wasn't real. He wasn't real. But I had felt it...

"Ready, Ms. Kennedy?" the orderly asked as she smiled brightly.

"I've never been more ready." It wasn't a lie, but I was afraid. Part of me still needed to be convinced that it was a dream. Part of me still felt him.

I flipped through mental images of the hospital records, reminding myself of the facts.

Facts that were documented.

Facts that were real.

He wasn't real. Keeper wasn't real.

"I'm very happy for you, dear," the orderly said with a smile.

"Thank you," I whispered, listening to the door lock behind me, wishing I'd taken my cup of water with me. My mouth became more barren with each step. The hallway was empty except for the janitor, who was using a large machine to polish the already shiny white tile. He nodded in my direction and I returned the gesture.

Doctor Stein was waiting for me near the front office. She glanced up from the papers she was signing and smiled. "Ready to go home?"

"Yeah."

"Your father is waiting. He's sitting in the chairs on the back wall, just on the other side of that window." She pointed the end of her pen toward the rows of chairs in the front entrance. I knew she was testing my reaction. I saw my father slouched forward, elbows on his knees, looking older than I'd ever seen him. I didn't bother to tell her that man wasn't the one who raised me or try to bring up Malchazze again. She'd promised the questions about the dream might linger for some time, and that we would work through them together three times each week.

However, I knew that if I started up now, she might tell the orderly to turn right around and take me back to my room. *Think about water*, I thought, my mouth feeling like cotton. Looking at my father almost made me throw a fit to get put back in. His eyes found mine and the same fear I felt was reflected in them.

My body was fine. My broken leg had healed and the cast was off. My muscles weren't sore. The bruises had faded from my body. My hair was short again, spiked, and there was a raised scar on my scalp from the stitches and staples I'd had removed weeks ago. I wondered if my physical appearance scared him worse than my mental state.

I doubted it.

Doctor Stein led me out of the secured door and into the waiting area. Father stood, his smile wobbling as tears filled his eyes. Whoever this man was, he wasn't Malchazze.

"I'm so proud of you," he whispered as he hugged my neck. I patted his back awkwardly, watching Stein take us in, a concerned look furrowing her brow, deepening her wrinkle. He pulled back, grabbed my elbow, and said, "Let's go home."

Again, I gave a fake smile. We stepped through the double-doors and into the sun, where Father led me to his white Range Rover. The drive home was quiet. I reveled in the feeling of the warmth left by the sun on the tan leather seats and stared at the passing cars, houses, buildings, life. All around us was life. Everything was normal.

It teemed all around us.

"I stocked the refrigerator with all your favorites. I can make us something for lunch when we get home," he offered. "And I dismissed the staff. I thought it might be less overwhelming if it was just you and me for a time."

"Okay." I was hungry and tired. No, tired was too small a word. I was exhausted to the bone, and not from physical exertion. Tonight... I would sleep in my bed tonight.

Would I stay at my house?

I would for a while. I had two days until my first outpatient appointment with Doctor Stein.

She actually let me go.

I wasn't ready.

My breaths became erratic.

Pinching my eyes closed, I chanted in my head, *I imagined him. I imagined him.*

The Keeper of Crows. What color was his hair? What color were his eyes?

CHAPTER THIRTY THREE
AND A HALF

Doctor Cynthia Stein watched as the white Range Rover backed out of its space and drove out of the parking lot. She let the sun warm her skin through the glass doors. She'd been cold since Carmen named her other patient; the woman who had been plagued with nightmares so vivid, she believed they were real. Perhaps they were, because she had specifically mentioned someone by name: The Keeper of Crows.

But that was merely a coincidence, she scoffed to herself. It wasn't possible that he actually existed. Novelists came up with similar ideas, each writing books about the same topic but in their own words, in their own way. Filmmakers, songwriters…the creativity of the world often overlapped. *This is no different*, she told herself.

The mind was a powerful thing, and just because it was unique to the individual, didn't mean that all thought was unique.

The two women experienced something similar. That was all. Their brains had to cope somehow. Maybe it was something they heard. They were admitted to the same hospital at the same time, and they were in the Intensive Care Unit one room away from each another, according to their records. Maybe it was a song played softly through the speakers, a song whistled or sung by a nurse they shared and both heard. It had to be something rooted in reality that their imaginations ran wild with.

In the afternoon sun, doves cooed loudly from the eaves of the front porch and flew away, following the Rover down the long, gravel driveway.

She snapped out of her daze and turned to swipe her security card by the door, movement in her periphery making her turn her head. In the center of the glossy white tile of the lobby, fluttering in the wind made by the ceiling's air conditioning vent, was a single, black, downy feather.

THE KEEPER OF CROWS PLAYLIST

The A Team—Ed Sheeran
Royals—Lorde
Castle—Halsey
Hold Me Down—Halsey
Human—Christina Perri
Control—Halsey
Jar of Hearts—Christina Perri
Breath of Life—Florence + The Machine
Gasoline—Halsey
Close—Nick Jonas (feat. Tove Lo)
Let's Hurt Tonight—OneRepublic
Lights Down Low—Gnash
Kingdom Come—Demi Lovato (feat. Iggy Azalea)
Rise—Katy Perry
Every Little Thing—Carly Pearce
She Talks to Angels—The Black Crowes

ACKNOWLEDGMENTS

Keeper of Crows is a book that has significant meaning to me. I started it, wrote 30,000 words and got stuck on the plot, so I put it away. A very important person in my life passed away after that and I had trouble concentrating on much of anything. My grandmother was more than just that. She was one of my best friends and every time I think of her, my heart hurts because I know I can't pick up the phone and call her. I can't take my kids to go see her. She's gone…and until I am, I can't see her. But I can feel her. And she kicked me in the butt to finish this book.

So, I need to thank her. For all the lessons she taught me, for just being there and for being such a strong presence in my life and in the lives of my children. When her heart broke, so did mine. Mine hasn't healed yet. It may never.

I needed help. After writing and writing, the plot wasn't coming together how I wanted it to, how I knew it could. So, I talked to my hubby about hiring a content editor. He's amazing (always) and very supportive. In short, he said to go for it. I think he knew I needed it. I was falling apart in more ways than one.

Angela Marshall Smith, who is named for the angels, helped me with the plot of Keeper of Crows. She's an amazing content editor and brought a level of depth to the book that I couldn't unearth myself. For that, I'm forever grateful. I'm also grateful to have found a friend.

Regina Wamba designed the cover of Keeper of Crows as a pre-made and posted it in her group. For weeks, I stared at it. I visited her site just to look at it and finally decided to message her to see if it was still available. It was and I considered that a sign. As ever, she was wonderful to work with.

Stacy Sanford is an amazing editor to work with. She tirelessly devotes her time to perfecting a project and I'm blessed to have found her. I'm so glad we clicked.

Marisa Shor and Allyson Gottlieb formatted the paperback version of the book and it's stunning. I created the e-book version just so that I could update the content whenever I need to. It's not as pretty, but it works.

The map in the front of the book was drawn by Sydney Provencher. She took a scrawled, sad drawing from an author who is in no way an artist, and brought Purgatory to life. I can't thank her enough for the long hours she spent perfecting the details on this beautiful map. It's truly a work of art.

I need to thank my betas: Ashley Cestra, Cristie Alleman, Rachael Geraci and Kelly Martin. They were willing to give me honest and valuable feedback and I can't thank them enough.

My mom always reads my books and I love her so much. She and Dad are two of my biggest supporters. The others are my husband and children. I couldn't do this without their love, patience and understanding that Mommy cannot hear you when she's writing unless you get her attention first. LOL!

And, most of all, I thank God for his blessings in my life. I'd be nothing without Him.

ABOUT THE AUTHOR

Award-winning author Casey L. Bond lives in Milton, West Virginia with her husband and their two beautiful daughters. When she's not busy being a domestic goddess and chasing her baby girls, she loves to write romance in all its glorious forms.

45620657R00163

Made in the USA
Middletown, DE
09 July 2017